W9-BVJ-242

Keep Your Mouth Shut and Wear Beige

Center Point
Large Print

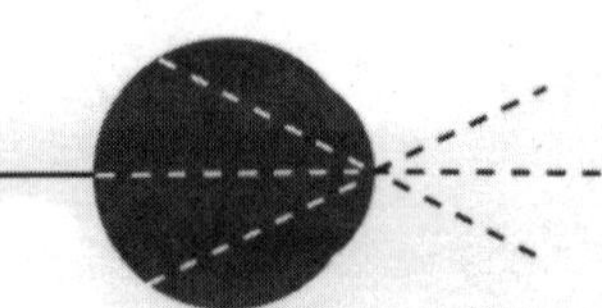

This Large Print Book carries the
Seal of Approval of N.A.V.H.

Keep Your Mouth Shut and Wear Beige

Kathleen Gilles Seidel

CENTER POINT PUBLISHING
THORNDIKE, MAINE

This Center Point Large Print edition
is published in the year 2008 by arrangement with
St. Martin's Press.

The text of this Large Print edition is unabridged. In other
aspects, this book may vary from the original edition.
Printed in the United States of America.
Set in 16-point Times New Roman type.

ISBN: 978-1-60285-264-8

Library of Congress Cataloging-in-Publication Data

Seidel, Kathleen Gilles.
Keep your mouth shut and wear beige / Kathleen Gilles Seidel.--Center Point large print ed.
p. cm.
ISBN: 978-1-60285-264-8 (lib. bdg. : alk. paper)
1. Divorced mothers--Fiction. 2. Weddings--Planning--Fiction. 3. Parents-in-law--Fiction.
4. Large type books. I. Title.

PS3569.E5136K44 2008b
813'.54--dc22

2008015277

If my bridge club played more and talked less, our card play would be much better and my life would be much worse. With gratitude and affection, I dedicate this book to:

Marcia Dodge
Mary Gore
Jeannie Lewis
Edie Mansa
Caroline Roberts
Anne Smoler
Sue Whittier

One

I was going to be happy about this. I'd made a decision; it was the right decision. I wasn't going to throw myself off a bridge with a lot of boo-hoo regrets.

My name is Darcy Van Aiken, and I'd moved from a spacious, stately Victorian-era house in the Forest Hills neighborhood of Washington, D.C., to this much smaller house in the Virginia suburbs. My ex-husband hadn't wanted me to move. He kept telling me that I didn't need to sell what had been our family home, that I could afford to stay there.

On paper, I could afford to keep the old house. But being able to afford something on paper is different from actually being able to. Oh, gosh, you think, who needs a lawn service, when the front yard is so small and the backyard is planted with ground cover, but then when you have to spend the whole summer planning your week around getting out the mower, suddenly you start missing that lawn service. And the ground cover does fine for a while, but by September it starts to look a little ratty, and come June the following year the weeds come up with "ding, dong, the witch is dead" exuberance. Either I needed to enlist myself in a Gettysburg-size battle with poison ivy and Virginia creeper or I could move.

So I moved. Who wouldn't?

If I'd stayed in the old house, I would have been chained to my job. What if my dad got sick and I wanted to take a month off work? What if I wanted to take some classes so that I could get a different job? What about travel and symphony tickets? What if I had to choose between them and a new roof? I didn't want my life to become small because I was clinging to a big house.

So I moved . . . even though I always fall asleep at the symphony.

If Zack, my younger son, had wanted to stay in Forest Hills through the rest of high school, I would have. But he didn't have such great memories of that house, and if we moved, he would get a parking place in the school lot, whereas if we stayed in Forest Hills, he would have to go on taking the city bus.

If a parking sticker isn't a reason for moving, I don't know what is.

Then there was the fact that Mike, my ex-husband, still walked into the Forest Hills house without knocking. His tools were in the garage workshop. His grandparents' unsorted memorabilia was boxed up in the basement. He nagged me about having the gutters cleaned and the windows recaulked. The Forest Hills house still felt like home to him.

That, which could have been fixed through goodwill and improved communication skills, would not have been a good reason for moving and so played no role in my decision whatsoever.

Or so I kept telling myself.

Mike and I had been divorced for one year and separated for two years before that.

He was the one who had left. I suppose there's never a great time to surprise your wife with the news that you're moving out, but his timing was particularly bad. We had just returned from taking our older son, Jeremy, to California for his freshman year of college.

"I made dinner reservations for tomorrow night." Mike stopped me as I was carrying a basket of laundry to the basement. "There're some things we need to talk about."

I didn't like the sound of that. Spending twenty-four hours with "some things we need to talk about" hanging over my head? That made me feel like a kid waiting to get lectured about falling grades or smoking behind the school Dumpster. Although I'd turned out fine, I hadn't exactly been Miss Perfect during my high-school years, and I still have moments of expecting that the entire world is going to starting lecturing me about some failing or another.

"Why wait until tomorrow? Why can't we talk about it now?"

"Tomorrow will be fine."

"Not for me. I have the night shift this week." I'm a nurse in the intensive-care unit. If we went out to dinner, we would have to eat very early, and I wouldn't be able to drink.

"Oh." Apparently he hadn't checked my schedule, which was, as always, stuck on the refrigerator. He took a breath. "Okay, Darcy, I need you to understand that this is just temporary."

I set the laundry down. "That sounds bad."

"No, I think it may be a very positive step for both of us."

That was strange. Our marriage could, I'd be the first to admit, use some positive steps, but it sounded as if he was saying that this time we were both taking a step. He'd always maintained that I, and I alone, was the one who needed to pick up the pace.

We'd met when he was a stressed-out graduate student in economics and I was in nursing school. I have a very good memory, and my dad's a doctor and my mom was the nurse in his office so I was pretty much born knowing the names of all the bones in the foot. Nursing school was easy for me, and as a result, I was a whole lot more fun than Mike's fellow stressed-out graduate students. A tomboy as a kid, I love the outdoors, and I'm willing to try any physical activity, even the ones I am really bad at. Mike fell in love with me for who I was and then immediately set about to change me.

It drove him crazy that I could not close the doors to the kitchen cabinets. I could not, he quickly discovered, be relied on to get the car inspected. There were no systems in our family, and whenever he would set one up—our two boys needing to do specific chores for specific percentages of their allowances—I was incapable of enforcing it. Nor was there any order in our house. He could never find anything. His athletic socks were sometimes in the drawer with his dress socks, and sometimes they were with his briefs and undershirts, depending on whether or not I had been thinking of myself as sorting socks or washing whites. There were still *Sesame Street* tapes in the kitchen drawer and broken crayons in a bowl on the bookshelf long after the boys had topped six feet in height.

I never sat still to watch television or listen to music; I was always jumping up and doing six things at once. At work I was crisp and decisive, but at home I never labeled anything. I did everything at the last minute. I was, again according to him, chaotic and unreliable.

The "unreliable" had stung. I wasn't unreliable about important things, not about anything to do with the boys' health or safety. I was meticulous at work. I had never harmed a patient, and my ability to do six things at once had probably saved dozens and dozens of them.

I never defended myself against Mike's accusations. All the specifics in his list of charges were so accurate—I could buy a huge Costco multipack of batteries one day, and the next day not be able to find a single one—that I felt as guilty as I had when caught smoking behind the high-school Dumpster. When Mike attacked me, I could never remember anything I had done right—the heart-rate monitors that suddenly reestablished themselves into a regular rhythm; the IV line that no one could get in but me; my own boys slipping their hands into mine and rubbing their cheeks against my arm. I could only think about everything that was wrong with me.

So I would never stand up for myself, and I do not respect people who won't stand up for themselves.

"What are you talking about?" I asked on that August evening. "What kind of step?"

"It would seem to me," he answered, "that without the petty irritants of day-to-day life, we could focus better on our core issues."

Petty irritants? Core issues? What was he talking about?

Then I got it. "You're moving out." I couldn't believe it. One minute I had been on my way to the basement with a load of laundry, and now I was hearing this. "You've found someplace else to live."

"As I said, it's a temporary measure to give us time. We need to get some clarity on our situation."

If he'd chosen any other time, I probably would have reacted in my normal, pathetic way. I would have felt rejected and humiliated; I would have begged; I would have promised to change, saying all the millions of things I had said a million times before.

But today I was pissed off. Last week—while he had been finding an apartment and signing a lease—I'd been getting Jeremy ready for college, and Mike, the organized one, the list maker, hadn't helped one bit. Okay, I could understand his not getting interested in the extra-long twin sheets and the shower tote, but the new laptop, the credit- or debit-card issue? Mike could at least have helped with the research on that, couldn't he? At a minimum, he could have spent more time with Jeremy. Jeremy normally prided himself on being sensible and focused, but he'd dithered his way through this preparation. One day he'd say that we should buy all the sheets and towels in California, and then the next day he'd say no, it would be better to get them here.

His behavior had made no sense . . . unless—I suddenly thought—it did.

"You didn't tell Jeremy before you told me," I demanded of Mike. "You couldn't have done that. No one would do that."

"Well, it might seem like a mistake, but . . ."

"Might seem like a mistake?" I shrieked. "*Might?* Have you lost your mind?"

Mike hates to be wrong, and, had I been more rational, I would have known that his saying that something "might have been a mistake" was as far as he was going to go. But I was not rational.

"No wonder he was such a wreck," I snapped. "What kind of thing is that to ask of a kid, to keep a secret like that? What were you thinking?"

"Admittedly I didn't expect him to react so strongly." Mike was trying to stay calm. That gave him more power. "Because this is—"

"Yes, I know," I chimed in sarcastically, " 'only temporary.' "

He ignored me. "I didn't think it was fair to tell him over the phone, but if he knew and could see that we were still functioning as a family, then—"

"We were still functioning as a family because you and he were the only ones who knew that we weren't."

"You're overreacting. We are still a family. This is

just so that you and I can get ourselves back on track. It has nothing to do with the boys."

"You told Jeremy before you told me!" That's what I focused on that first night—not the message itself, but how he had told it. That was an issue I could understand and be outraged about. I knew how I felt about that. Mike had been wrong to tell Jeremy before he told me. Very, very wrong.

Everything else, the fact that my husband was moving out . . . well, that was too much to think about, too much to endure.

The basket of laundry I'd been carrying sat on the kitchen floor for four days. Occasionally I gave it a shove with my foot to get it out of the way, but I refused to pick it up and take it to the basement.

We did go together to see a therapist. Mike had asked that the therapist be a man. He probably thought a man would sympathize with how impossible it was to live with me. But the therapist had instead wanted to talk about Mike's resentment and Mike's determination that I, and I alone, needed to change. The therapist—traitor to his gender—seemed to be implying that Mike's attitude was a bigger problem in our marriage than the disorganized state of our kitchen drawers.

This was not what Mike wanted to hear. He started finding himself with last-minute commitments that conflicted with the therapy sessions . . . although "last minute" had always been my specialty, not his. But he always urged me to keep the appointment anyway since I, and I alone, was the problem.

"I work with couples," the therapist said, "and Mike is not here."

So he turned me over to one of his associates, a nice, middle-aged-mom type who helped me see what changes I wanted to make for myself.

She helped me understand why I, who stand up to insecure interns and pompous doctors every day of my working life, wilted in the face of Mike's criticism. I had been rebellious as a kid. Tired of being known around Grand Rapids as "Dr. Bowersett's little girl," sick of being compared to my perfect older brother, I had hung out with the vo-tech kids, refused to take any AP courses, and then nailed a 1500 on my SATs. Rather than be angry, my parents were anxious and disappointed, and I had never known how to explain myself.

So while Mike and I were separated, I did change. I started getting places on time; I kept track of tickets and appointment times. But I didn't change to please Mike. I found I didn't want him back. When you live with a critical person, you're always hearing his voice in your head. You're always trying to anticipate that voice, trying to figure out what to do to avoid being criticized. But when I wasn't living with Mike, I stopped hearing that voice. I felt light and free.

I also couldn't forgive him for what he had done to Zack, the son whom he didn't tell. Mike might have believed that this separation was only about the two of us, but Zack didn't see it that way.

Our boys were very different. Jeremy, the older by four years, had been easy to raise. He was his father's son, intense and competitive, driven to push himself. He did well in school, he did well in sports, ultimately captaining his high school's crew team during his senior year. Like a lot of firstborn children, he could be rigid, and he kept out of trouble because he didn't like to take risks. He was deliberate, methodical, excessively prepared at all times, and it was no huge surprise that he had viewed college as a launching pad for medical school.

Zack, on the other hand, couldn't seem to do anything right. At the age of four he could lose his lunch box during the very well supervised walk from the preschool's front door to his little storage cubby. Once he started elementary school, I contemplated getting a pair of handcuffs to padlock him to his homework, despairing of any other way of getting his assignments to his teachers.

Both Mike and Jeremy were athletic. They had played catch, shot baskets, taken their clubs to the driving range. They had gone to Maryland football and Georgetown basketball games together, watched the World Series on TV together. When Jeremy had been in high school, Mike, an only child, probably felt that he had not only a son but also a brother.

But Zack hated organized sports. He was agile enough, but skateboarding, not baseball, had been his thing. His fine-motor skills were excellent—give him a set of LEGOs and he could build a working model of the Louvre—but he didn't have the physical urge to move that the rest of us had.

As early as middle school he'd let his hair grow and gotten involved in the theater. Because he'd worked backstage, it had been hard for us to appreciate his contributions as easily as we could Jeremy's athletic performances. I'd always baked tons of cookies to send to the theater with him, and he knew that I cared about his activities even if I didn't understand what he was doing. He wasn't so sure about Mike.

Then Mike moved out right after Jeremy went to college. Zack couldn't help thinking that he hadn't been worth staying home for.

"I guess Dad's lost his little playmate," he'd said bitterly.

I would never, not ever, forgive Mike for that.

Mike didn't understand how angry I was during our separation. Once I started writing "paid" on the bottom of bills after I paid them, he was pleased. He thought his "break some eggs to make an omelet" strategy had succeeded. Just when he thought that he would be able to live with me again, just when he thought that the omelet was setting and browning nicely, I filed for divorce, and he found himself with neither eggs nor omelet, but the cardboard carton in which some eggs had accidentally broken, the shards of the shattered white shells glued to the cardboard by crusting albumin.

• • •

Three important things had happened during the year following the divorce decree. Zack and I decided to move, Mike got a lady friend, and Jeremy, about to begin his senior year in college, resolved to propose to his girlfriend, fellow pre-med Cami Zander-Brown.

Last spring Jeremy and Cami had decided to take an apartment together, and since then he had been deliberating about whether or not to propose. Getting married right out of college wasn't what kids his age were doing, but he and Cami had already decided that they wanted to be at the same medical school, even if that meant going to a less prestigious school or taking a year off and applying again. That was, he told me, a code for talking about what kind of commitment they wanted to make to each other.

Mike had thought that they were too young and that we—i.e., me—should tell them to go on living together and weather at least a year of medical school. But I'm a "throw your heart over the fence" kind of person. The best way for Cami and Jeremy to survive medical school and then their internships and residencies as a couple was to believe that they could.

All three of these new elements were coming together on my first day in my new house. Jeremy, whose "make yourself look great on your med-school applications" summer job was in California, had come home to sort through his stuff and help with the move. He was also picking up my late mother's engagement ring, which had been left to him as the eldest grandchild. Mike's name was still on our safe deposit box, so Mike was going to go with him to get the ring after they had lunch with Claudia Postlewaite, the lady friend. Zack had already met her a few times; Jeremy and I never had.

Even though I still had a lot of unpacking to do, I spent a couple of hours of that first day in the kitchen. I poached a salmon fillet for our dinner. I made a dill sauce and reduced apple juice for a grainy mustard sauce. I roasted some red peppers for a cold soup that wouldn't be ready until tomorrow. I made my grandmother's ginger cookies for Jeremy to take back to California.

I was outside, looking for a good spot to plant herbs, when I saw Mike's very new, very impractical car coming around the curve of my hilly, wooded street. The house was partly screened from the street by a big oak tree, which the driveway looped around. Mike maneuvered the loop and parked underneath the tree. I was a little relieved to see only Mike and Jeremy in the car. I suppose I'd have to meet Claudia someday, but I can't say I was in any great rush about it.

Mike was out of the car first. "This place is hard to find."

Why did he have to say that? Why did the first words out of his mouth, the very first words, have to be negative? Why couldn't he say, "This place is charming," or, "What a pretty neighborhood"? No, he'd had to say, "This place is hard to find."

He wouldn't have realized that he was being negative. If I had challenged him on it, he would have simply said that he was stating a fact.

But this house was also as cute as a little bunny, and the neighborhood was quite handsome. Those were facts, too. Why couldn't he have said those? Why couldn't he have been nice just for once?

Because he was him.

Jeremy was now coming up the steps, eager to show me the ring. It was in a little square plastic pill case that was imprinted with the name of a now-closed pharmacy in East Grand Rapids, Michigan, my hometown. Through its clear lid I looked at the ring that I had been so used to seeing on my mother's hand. It was pretty, a solitaire in a platinum Tiffany setting with a delicate vine pattern engraved around the band. The ring sparkled and the engraved lines were still crisp. Mother's actual wedding band, which my father had kept, had worn thin, but she had taken off this one, her engagement ring, when she worked in the kitchen or the yard.

I started to choke up a little, thinking about her. She had died four months before Mike had left. I was glad that she hadn't known. She would have been disappointed with him and worried about me.

Jeremy took the ring back, still admiring it through the box as if he were afraid to open the lid. "Claudia says that I should get it cleaned and checked. Do you know where the nearest jeweler is?"

"I have no idea," I admitted. I can't say I loved the idea of the lady friend advising Jeremy on matters related to my mother's ring . . . even though it was good advice, better than he might have gotten from either of us. "You'll have to look in the phone book. The phone company gave me a new set. It's upstairs on my desk."

Jeremy went inside, and as soon as the door closed behind him, Mike spoke. "It's hard to imagine him getting married, isn't it?"

It was a relief when we could be civil to each other. "But they're probably as mature as twenty-one-year-olds can be, and she's great."

"I told him that we would still help with his medical-school tuition, and he thinks that the Zander-Browns would do the same."

"It's nice of you to say that *we* are paying his tuition." Our divorce settlement stipulated that Mike would pay the boys' college tuition, but he'd said that he would assume responsibility for graduate education as well. So there was absolutely no "we" about these tuition payments.

He nodded, and for a second I saw a flash of his smile. Mike's smile was something that you noticed most when looking at his—or his sons'—childhood pictures. It was a clear, sweet symmetrical smile without any impishness or mischievousness. It had a purity to it that almost seemed incongruous on an adult face. As Mike didn't have a trace of the glad-handing salesman in his personality—he was an economist—he had no idea of its potential power, so he never smiled for effect. It appeared only when he felt good about something . . . hence I didn't see that smile much anymore.

"I have to admit," he said, "that I am glad that he's not marrying someone who is going to have to take on a lot of debt to finance her education."

"My sense is that her parents have a ton of money."

"I don't know about that," he said.

He was lying. Of course he knew. He would have made it his business to find out.

Mike didn't worship money, but it interested him. It interested him a lot. He was interested in people's attitude toward money, how they had earned it, how they spent it, what role it played in their lives. He was suspicious of people who lived on inherited wealth and contemptuous of those who lived on credit cards. One of his complaints about me—and this one had been valid—was that I had never fully appreciated how much security and comfort he'd provided for our family.

I had no idea how to make amends for that now.

"We didn't say anything to Jeremy," Mike continued, "but Claudia thinks we should give the two of them an engagement party. Some of the Selwyn families, some of the neighbors—our old neighbors, that is, people like that."

"What a great idea." Jeremy had gone to Selwyn Hall, a private Episcopal school near the grounds of the National Cathedral, and I hadn't seen much of those families since he'd graduated from high school.

I like giving parties. I don't get rattled by all the last-minute stuff you have to do for a big party. I don't care a lot about the napkin colors, the platter garnishes, and the centerpieces, but I do care about the food being good and people having a good time. The old house had been great for parties. The rooms were big, parking was easy, and I'd had so much storage space that I could keep lots of things on hand. I wasn't sure how I would manage in the new one. If we could count on good weather, then—

"So," Mike continued, "as soon as Jeremy settles things with Cami, Claudia will be in touch with the Zander-Browns about setting a date."

Oh. *Oh.* The "we" of this party wasn't Mike and me, but Mike and the lady friend.

"She has a big house," Mike explained a little awkwardly. "She can accommodate a crowd, and you and I are both in smaller places now and . . ." His voice trailed off.

If Mike had really thought that he or I or the two of us together should have hosted this party, we would have figured something out, renting space in a hotel or a restaurant if necessary. But apparently Claudia's having the party at her house had seemed right to him, and so I was going to be a guest at my son's engagement party.

Two

The first party for my son and his fiancée at someone's else house? I didn't like the sound of that. Although Cami had spent several weekends with us, I'd never met any of her family. Shouldn't it be me, Jeremy's mother, who got in touch with her mother to set a date for this party? I didn't know what the etiquette books said about this mother of the bride–mother of the groom stuff, but I was willing to bet that the lady friend didn't get to go first, especially when she hadn't even met the bride.

Suddenly the party seemed like a bad idea. "I'm not sure that it will work. Cami and Jeremy are going to be so busy this fall with their medical-school applications and interviews. How are they going to come back here just for a party?"

"It might not work," Mike said evenly, "but let's not give up before we start."

There was the "we" again, the "we" that didn't include me.

It was time to stop thinking of Claudia Postlewaite as "Claudia the lady friend." She wasn't a joke. She was a real person, much more a part of Mike's life than I'd realized. If she was a part of Mike's life, then she was a part of the boys' lives . . . and therefore also part of mine.

More than anything else, I wanted my family to be a family. Yes, Mike and I were divorced, and yes, we'd been really angry with each other, but the four of us were still a family, a "two-household family" was our term for it. I was never, not ever, going to think of us as a "broken home."

So I took a breath. "I'm sure Jeremy would appreciate the opportunity to celebrate with the families of his high-school friends."

Mike looked at me suspiciously. "Appreciate the opportunity to celebrate" was not the way I normally talk, but it was the best I could do on such short notice.

He was still standing at the foot of the three steps that lead up to the narrow front porch. If we had been at the old house, he would have long since been inside. "Would you like to come in?" I asked. "See the house?"

"If you've got time."

"Of course." It might be small, but I was proud of my new house. I wanted him to see it. Zack's friends had been over the day before to help me unpack. Because they were all from the theater-tech crowd, they had arranged the first floor like an artful stage set, pots of ivy accenting displays of my grandmother's Swedish dishes. I'd never had such accessorized decor before.

It had been unfair of me to be annoyed with Mike for saying that the house was hard to find because he had, in fact, been speaking the God's truth. The house was nearly impossible to find.

I had left the city and moved into Arlington County,

the first suburb into Virginia, across the Potomac River. The county's roads were a hodgepodge of eighteenth-century farm lanes, Civil War military roads, and post-World War II developments, twisting around the county's hilly topography. Furthermore, the excellent schools in the northern part of the county made it a very desirable place to live, so every side yard that had been zoned as a buildable lot had sprouted a McMansion, and whenever a small house went on the market, a developer pushed out its side walls and tore off the roof, adding massive master suites, second-floor laundry rooms, and family rooms with coffered ceilings.

My house, a little nineteenth-century farmhouse, had been destined for such remodeling, but the small creek that ran along the back edge of the oddly shaped lot was part of the Potomac River watershed. The neighbors joined with environmentalists to raise enough of a ruckus that the developer gave up with his grandiose plans. He installed central air-conditioning, refurbished the kitchens and bathrooms, and hoped that someone on the planet still wanted to live in a small house.

The house itself was white and L-shaped. From the covered front porch, which was just big enough for a porch swing, you walked directly into the living room, the long end of the L. On the far wall was a fireplace positioned between a pair of built-in bookcases. The kitchen and dining room formed the short end of the L, and the stairs were in the middle of the house.

Upstairs were three small bedrooms and one bathroom. The basement, which was going to be Zack's territory, had a bedroom, a bathroom, and a dark narrow space, which the realtor called a "family room," and it would have been if your family consisted of hobbits.

I had no garage, no first-floor powder room. There was no room for a table in the kitchen, and I had one-fifth of the counter space that I had had in the old house. I would have to use my dining room for dining and my living room for living. People were going to have to walk either upstairs or down when they had to pee. But it was a sturdy, practical little house, and that seemed right for me.

It didn't take long to show Mike around. He did not, as I expected him to, comment on how small the house was or how few bathrooms there were. He praised the work the builder had done. He admired how fresh everything seemed, how nicely arranged the rooms were. I tried not to take that as a criticism of the old house, which had been neither fresh nor nicely arranged. I tried really hard.

He lingered longest in the kitchen. The salmon was coming to room temperature on a white platter. The ginger cookies were cooling on wire racks, and nothing smells as enticing as a fresh ginger cookie.

Mike missed my cooking. Just as I'd gotten used to not worrying about bills for health insurance or car repairs, he'd assumed that all families sat down every night to a perfectly sautéed trout fillet with a citrus sauce or a golden-brown roasted chicken, its cavity stuffed with lemon slices and heads of papery garlic. I'm not the Martha Stewart perfect homemaker. I do not care about presentation or display. I never do any crafts, and I don't care what laundry detergent I use. But I love to cook, and because I understand the science behind cooking—I know what happens to the bonds of a coiled protein molecule when it is exposed to heat, air, or acid—I'm very good.

In the three years since he had left, I'd often invited Mike to stay for dinner. His relationship with Zack continued to be problematic, and the best way for the two of them to see each other was at the house. Mike had also come for all the holidays, Thanksgiving, Christmas, and Easter, and I'd sent him back to his Capitol Hill condominium with lots of leftovers.

I could have invited him for dinner today. There was enough salmon for all four of us. But everything seemed different now. This had never been his house; he had not painted this dining room. Furthermore, he'd had lunch with a person who was going to give a party for my son. We were starting to build separate lives.

So I offered him a cookie.

Jeremy flew back to California the following day, and he promptly proved himself to be every bit as impulsive as his mother. Within hours of his getting back, I got an e-mail from Cami. It was a photograph of her left hand with my mother's lovely ring sparkling on her finger. "I'M SO HAPPY!!!!!!!" the message read.

• • •

Three days later I got a handwritten note from Cami's mother. Rose Zander-Brown had distinctively slanted handwriting, and her stationery was thick and flecked.

She first praised Jeremy, saying how much they liked and admired him. Then she spoke about being eager to meet me, hoping that Zack and I could join them for a weekend at their place on Long Island this fall, possibly Columbus Day. She also hoped that I would understand that she couldn't be firm about the day. She still had two children at home, and she wanted to wait until after she got their school calendars before making too definite a commitment.

It was a perfect letter, flattering without being effusive, politely formal but with the right down-to-earth touch about the school calendars.

I'm suspicious of people who can write perfect letters. It gives them a weapon the rest of us don't have. Furthermore, I've never had much luck with girls who have pretty handwriting and nice stationery. I was never a part of the giggling cluster that gathered around the most popular girl's locker.

But Rose Zander-Brown and I weren't girls. We were two women, two mothers, and the stakes weren't what we were going to wear to the dance Friday night, but the most precious thing ever, our children.

I'm not one to "borrow trouble." My normal workday is full of plenty all on its own, but occasionally I'll start my shift with a bad feeling about a piece of equipment. *You're not going to work right today, are you?* I wasn't always right, but considering that I'd had no evidence for my suspicion, it was surprising how often I was. I had that feeling now. I fingered the letter; the paper was soft with a feathered edge and a roughened pebbly surface. *What kind of trouble are you going to cause me?*

It didn't answer.

Although Zack had first attended Selwyn, where Jeremy had gone, he was now at the Alden School, about to start his senior year. The school had originally been a prim all-girls school, and in those days the first day of school had been marked by the Senior Entrance. The seniors, clad in floaty white dresses, had swept swanlike into the orangerie of the aging mansion while the younger girls applauded admiringly. But since the school had started admitting boys, the event had lost every shred of dignity. The seniors charged into the high-school gym while the underclassmen hooted and cheered.

Each year the Entrance has a theme. It's supposed to be top secret. Maybe some of the moms who were at the school all the time knew what it was, but I wasn't one of them. So as soon as Zack got home from school the Tuesday after Labor Day, I asked him about it.

"We kept it simple," he answered and flipped up one of the straps of his backpack. Pinned to it was a round, white, political-campaign-style button; SENIOR YEAR: ALL TOO BRIEF.

"I don't get it," I said.

"We ran in in our underwear."

I love high-school kids. "Good thing you wear boxers, not briefs."

He grinned. "A surprising number of girls seem to too."

"I bet that was a disappointment."

"Yeah, and then Mr. G. said that all the girls had to wear something on top, even the ones who don't usually wear bras. The debate team tried to argue that that was sexist, but it was a no-go."

"Mr. G." was Chris Goddard, the headmaster of the entire school; the high-school kids interacted with him more than they did with their own principal. "There are laws about indecent exposure," I pointed out. I wished that we could talk like this forever. We were facing a year of constant nagging—SAT prep, college essays, senior projects. First-semester senior year hadn't been fun even with our dutiful Jeremy; it was going to be a nightmare with Zack. "Don't forget we have that meeting with the college counselor tomorrow."

He made a face. "Is Dad coming?"

"Of course."

He scooped up his backpack. "We had another theme before this one. 'Senior Year: It's All Hype.' "

"I don't get that one either."

"HYPe. Capital H, Capital Y, Capital P."

Oh. HYP. Harvard,Yale, Princeton. The three highest-ranked colleges in the country.

"And some girls in the costume department," he

continued, "found this really thin silver fabric that you can see through. They were going to make Harry Potter Invisibility Cloaks. The deal was that Invisibility Cloaks were the only way that most of us could get into those places, but the fabric was pretty expensive."

"Those schools are pretty expensive, too."

"Oh, come on, Mom," he scoffed. "Don't you think if I could get into Princeton, Dad would pay anything it took?"

He was right about that, but even if his transcript showed only his much improved second-semester junior grades, Zack could not have gotten into Princeton. "Let's see what this counselor has to say."

"If he uses the word *package,* I'm walking out."

"Me too."

"So," Mike said to the college counselor eighteen hours later, "how should we be packaging him?"

Zack slumped in his chair and kicked at his backpack. Where were the Harry Potter Invisibility Cloaks when you needed them?

Zack hadn't done well at Selwyn. Small for his age when he'd started in fourth grade, he'd never had the gang of friends that Jeremy always had. Nor did he do well academically. He never brought the right books home from school; he never knew what assignments were due when.

We'd had him tested for everything—auditory processing disorder, attention deficit disorder, sensory integration disorder. You name it, we tested for it, he didn't have it.

These results should have been good news, but Mike was frustrated by the absence of a diagnosis. He was a goal-oriented, problem-solving person. If Zack had a diagnosis, a label, then we could design a protocol and set out to fix him. Even better than a protocol would have been a pill—Ritalin, Adderall, Concerta. Mike kept hearing about how other people's kids had been transformed by one of these ADD medications.

So Mike did research. "Zack's not hyperactive," Mike said. "That's why they missed the diagnosis, but he's impulsive and inattentive."

And if we give him a pill, he will be "fixed." That's what Mike really wanted—a pill that would turn Zack into Jeremy.

Reluctantly I dragged the poor kid in for yet more tests during his middle-school years. The results were the same. One of his scores on the TOVA—Test of Variables of Attention—was borderline, but the rest were fine. Zack did not need to be "fixed." He was Zack, not Jeremy, and the sooner Mike realized that, the better.

Then Mike left, moving out four days before Zack started high school.

Zack's grades immediately got even worse. He started sneaking off with upperclassmen to those kids' parked cars where they would, at best, smoke cigarettes. His teachers were frustrated with him because he would start ambitious projects and not finish them.

The school's athletes shunned him, disappointed that he wasn't going to contribute what Jeremy had. He was miserable. I had no idea how to motivate him to work harder, to care more . . . because I was miserable myself. My mother had died, my husband had left, my younger son was floundering. I had no advice for anyone.

Finally, after an incident that involved storing another kid's Jell-O shots—little pockets of Jell-O made with more vodka than water—leaving them in his locker overnight so that they melted and attracted ants, the school suspended him for three days and strongly encouraged us not to re-enroll him in the fall. He wasn't formally expelled, but the school staff told us that he would be happier someplace else. Both Zack and I agreed.

His horrible grades were going to make transferring a problem. Tense and angry, believing that he was the reason Mike had left, he insisted that he didn't care where he went. Wilson, our local public high school, was fine with him—fine as in "fine, Mom, fine; now leave me alone."

The one school that interested him was Alden. Although its philosophy was as traditional as Selwyn's, the student body, especially in the high school, was very different. The school had a strong arts program, awful athletics, and what Zack had described as a "kick-ass" light board in its theater. This was the single most positive thing he had said in three months.

Apparently the Chair of the Performing Arts Department at Alden had the pull that athletic coaches have at other schools. She went to the admissions office and said, “This is a kid we need.” So he was admitted with the condition that he work with a coach to improve his organizational skills. That helped him some. He also did some self-esteem-building therapy. I have no idea if that helped.

What really made things work for him were the other kids. At many schools the theater kids are a dark bunch, given to risky behavior. But at Alden the best students were those involved in the performing arts. They wanted to go to Juilliard and Tisch, so they kept out of trouble and were determined to get good grades even in their much-hated math classes.

In this case, peer pressure was a good thing. Wanting to fit in is a great motivator for a teen. The theater kids at Alden were not slackers, so Zack stopped slacking. He proved to be unusually adept at the mechanics of the light board and the wiring of the sound system. “Let’s find that new kid,” people were saying when he had been at the school less than a month. “He’ll know how we can pull that off.”

That built his self-esteem far more than any of the expensive therapy did.

His grades during his first year at Alden were erratic, which was an improvement over his Selwyn grades, and by the end of junior year he was doing fine—and not just “fine, Mom, fine.”

Nonetheless, finding the right college for him was not going to be easy.

He'd been assigned to Alden's newest college counselor, Travis Jackson. Travis was very young and very new to his job. I was sure that over the years he would see families far more messed up than ours, but he might not have yet.

"Mr. Van Aiken," Travis said carefully after Mike had asked about packaging Zack as if he were a new species of Fig Newtons, "let's set the goal first. We want to identify the type of school that would be best for Zack; then we'll start talking about individual schools and their admissions standards." He turned to Zack. "What kind of environment do you best learn in?"

We got nowhere. Zack was completely uncommunicative. Travis tried asking him about his involvement with the theater, about his community service, about working with the organizational coach. Zack gave the briefest answers, never looking at the counselor. I knew what he was thinking—that no decent school would want him, the whole "I would never join a club that would have me as a member" thing.

The bell rang, and Zack shot out of his chair, desperate to get out of the interview. Travis followed Mike and me into the outer office. "He isn't always like that," I said, still the mom, still needing to apologize, still needing to explain.

"I'll talk to him alone. He may be more responsive if his parents aren't in the room. And if you take him to visit a variety of schools, he'll get a feeling for what's right for him."

"I'll be taking him," Mike said.

Rather than have the seniors miss class to visit colleges, the school adds a Senior Travel Day to the long weekend in October. Mike had already announced to me that he would take Zack to his college visits. Clearly he didn't trust me to do it.

The two of us headed down one of the paths that skirted the old mansion in which the high-school students took their classes. Mike was shuffling through the brochures Travis had given us.

"It's hard to get excited about these schools," he said. "I've never heard of half of them."

"But a really big or really competitive school—the ones we have heard of—might not be right for Zack."

"He's doing so well now. He can handle anything."

"He is doing great," I said. "But if he gets in an environment where he's just one of six thousand, he may find it hard to keep motivated. He has this burden of years of underperformance. He still struggles with that. It could drag him down."

"Like it does you."

"What?" I stopped in the middle of the path. How dare he say that? How *dare* he? "I hope you aren't saying that *I* am underperforming."

I am an advanced-practice nurse with a specialty in intensive care. I have a master's degree. I am one of the most respected nurses at a major teaching hospital. I was *not* underperforming.

"Not now. Of course not. But when you were his age, you were. You know you were." He took a breath. "Darcy, when you and the counselor were talking about Zack and this coach who usually works with the ADD kids, you said something—Are *you* ADD?"

I started walking again. It wasn't politically correct to say that someone *was* ADD. Attention deficit disorder was something you *had,* not something you were. "I don't see that it's any of your business, Mike."

"When did you find out? Why didn't you tell me? Are you taking those pills?"

I didn't answer.

"Darcy, come on. After we split up, you started getting places on time; you were making lists and not losing them . . . is it because you're taking pills?"

I still didn't answer. Of course I had ADD.

It was ironic, wasn't it? For years and years we'd been testing Zack to see if he had ADD. I'd researched the medications, but I hadn't read much about the diagnostic criteria.

Then, when he had been applying to Alden, the admissions counselor had said that he had some habits similar to—and this phrase seared through me—"even modeled on" ADD behavior. Whose behavior would he have modeled but mine? I borrowed a book from the counselor. I started paging through it on the way to the car. Ten minutes later, still in the parking lot, I knew that I was the one who needed to be tested.

I made an appointment with the educational psychologist who'd tested Zack. My parents had kept all my elementary-school report cards, and the psychologist later said that he'd almost been willing to diagnosis me from the evidence they provided. But he had me take the computerized test. The results were unquestionable, and so I, a woman in her forties, got a prescription for Ritalin.

I was already seeing my nice mom-type therapist, and she had been important. She'd helped me identify the behaviors I had wanted to change and craft a regime to implement those changes, but actually sticking with that regime day in, day out, that had needed Ritalin. The Ritalin alone wouldn't have been enough, but the therapy alone wouldn't have been either.

"Why didn't you tell me?" Mike was close now, his shoulder just behind mine, and his mouth close to my ear. "I thought we were making progress."

I jerked away from him. "I know what you're thinking—the medication 'fixed' me, and I would have been worthy of your return. Well, it didn't 'fix' me. Yes, it made me a better housewife. It made me better able to stay on task while I complete routine chores."

I didn't need Ritalin at work. The intense atmosphere of the ICU kept me focused in a way that unloading a dishwasher didn't.

"But I'm still the same person," I continued, "and even more important, you were totally the same person. You would have found something else to criticize about me. The laundry would have been done, the cabinet doors would have been closed, but you would have found something wrong."

"Darcy, why didn't you tell me? We were still trying to work things out."

"No, *I* was still trying. You had stopped."

"Oh, the therapist." He didn't have a good answer for that.

"My being diagnosed would have fed into your myth that I and only I was the problem. You hadn't learned anything. You hadn't changed. That wasn't good enough."

"You didn't even give me a chance. Why didn't you say something?"

Because I was too angry. And I was tired of being that angry. And tired of feeling that all the choices were yours, that I had no control. Not telling you gave me power.

The pointless, stupid power of a two-year-old.

We were in the parking lot now and had to stop talking. There were three women standing by the side of a car, talking. One of them was leaning against the car; another had set her purse on the hood. They must have been talking for a while. Two more women came out of the middle-school building and went to join the conversation.

I did not understand how women could stand around a parking lot, talking for so long. What did they talk about? After "you bring the juice, I'll bring the cupcakes," what was there?

• • •

I like my work schedule. I work three straight twelve-hour shifts; then I have four days off. The patients benefit from this schedule. I provide better care if I see them three days in a row. Many of them have multi-organ failure and it takes a while to master all the information on their charts. Their families also like seeing a familiar face; it comforts them. My own family had benefited because on my days off I was completely available to the boys.

But when I was on shift, I didn't do much around the house except cook. So, during the three days following our appointment with Zack's counselor, I didn't check my home e-mail. When I turned on my computer Sunday morning, I found a message from Rose Zander-Brown, continuing an exchange we'd started the week before. She confirmed that the wedding would be the third weekend in June and would be an outdoor affair at their house on Long Island. She concluded the message by saying that she and her family were looking forward to meeting Zack and me in D.C. during the Columbus Day weekend.

I didn't get it. Why was this meeting happening here? I thought she was going to invite Zack and me to Long Island.

Then I figured it out. Claudia must be having this engagement party during the Columbus Day weekend.

That was not going to work. I called Mike on his cell phone. "This engagement party—is it the Saturday before Columbus Day?"

"Yes."

I wondered why no one had told me. "The Tuesday after Columbus Day is Senior Travel Day. You and Zack were going to look at colleges that weekend."

Mike paused. He doesn't like making mistakes. One of the unexamined assumptions of our marriage was that I made mistakes, and he didn't.

"Oh," he said slowly, "I guess I had just written that down as being for Monday and Tuesday."

"But most families leave Friday afternoon. That's what we did for Jeremy. Can Claudia move the party?"

"I doubt it. She's already booked the caterer and ordered the invitations. I guess he and I can leave first thing Sunday morning. We'll still have three days."

I decided to talk to Zack before I got too huffy about this. As soon as he got up, I told him. I wanted him to be outraged. *Let me get this straight. We are prioritizing a party over my college search. You wouldn't have done that for Jeremy.*

But anything that spared him time with his father was just ducky with him. "I'm not going to want to go to any of those places anyway," he muttered.

Part of why I'm a good nurse is that I like learning new things. I never pass up a chance to be trained on a new piece of equipment, even if it isn't likely to be on our floor. When the doctors start ordering a new test, I want to know what we're going to do with the information that it provides.

But this curiosity had never extended to an excessive interest in other people's lives. I don't gossip. As a kid I'd never joined the gaggle of girls who giggled endlessly about who liked whom. Once I had my own sons, I had stayed out of the mom-on-mom gab fests about which kids the coaches were favoring or which families didn't supervise their children properly.

So I didn't know much about Claudia Postlewaite. Mike had said that she was a "sewing educator." I'd assumed that meant she taught home ec at one of the high schools. But with this party coming up, I felt that I needed to know more. So I logged on to the Internet, opened the Google search page, and typed in her name.

Thousands of entries popped up.

She was not a home-ec teacher. She was a "custom clothier and pattern designer" with her own Web site. The home page of the site was an intricately designed swirl of soft colors. The picture showed her to be a trim, small-boned woman with delicate features and short, dark hair. I guessed her to be in her early forties, younger than me, but not embarrassingly so.

The Web site had a variety of different pages, which the viewer accessed by clicking on buttons that were pictures of—since this was about sewing—actual buttons, all of them antique, all of them made from shells. One page listed her workshops and trade-show appearances; she seemed to be on the road as often as two or three weekends a month. Another page posted photos of clothes she had made. Sometimes she was sewing for clients, sometimes for herself. The few children's garments were described as being for friends' children, so I assumed that she had none of her own.

There was also a lifestyle/self-help component to her Web site. She had trademarked the term *Managed Perfectionism*, and whenever she raised that issue, she inserted a little picture of a conch shell. She claimed to be standing up for perfectionists, saying that instead of being life-draining and stultifying, perfectionism could be a source of joy. Perfectionists, she asserted, earned their bad reputations because many of them tried to impose their standards on other people, either by judging those people or trying to control them. That, she said, needed to stop.

The individual who managed her perfectionism chose one area of her life in which she and she alone indulged herself. Claudia urged that unless you lived alone, this should not be the cleanliness or orderliness of your house. Your perfectionism would give you no satisfaction if you were forever battling with other people. She herself used sewing in that way. "I almost never cook," she wrote about herself, "and I do not keep a calendar in the glove compartment of my car, reminding me when I'm supposed to have my oil changed. I don't decorate my front door for every holiday or create a new Rolodex card every time a friend changes a phone number. I am not a perfect homemaker. But when I sew, every stitch is perfect."

Her argument was well thought out, but was, in my opinion, hooey.

Perfectionism is an addiction, and addictions aren't so easily managed. What if sewing that perfect seam makes you feel so fabulous that, by God, you just can't resist pulling out a new Rolodex card when a friend changes phone numbers? Then pretty soon you get mad at the rest of the family, who are all cheerfully pigging up the Rolodex.

But I suppose that after so many years of living with an undiagnosed ADD sufferer and a Rolodex that looked like post-WWII Dresden, Mike would have found even unmanaged perfectionism a welcome relief.

You aren't competing with her, I reminded myself. *You don't want to be Mike's wife, lady friend, significant other. Let her deal with his criticism.* Although maybe he didn't criticize her.

The final page on the site was for a blog.

I don't get the appeal of blogs, diaries that people post online assuming that the whole world will care about their new-car purchase or their most recent vacation. There are several cooking-related Web sites that I like a lot, but I never read the blogs associated with them.

But my ex-husband's lady-friend's blog? I was going to read that. I was so going to read that.

I clicked it open. The most recent entry had been posted yesterday. I started to read.

And then froze. She was writing about this party, the party for my son.

I couldn't believe this. No one had told me the date of the party, but here she was posting all the details on the Internet.

It was a sit-down plated dinner for eighty. She didn't like buffets at formal affairs.

Eighty? We didn't know eighty people.

I scrolled through the previous entries. She was, she'd written in early September, so "honored" to have "been asked" to host a dinner to celebrate the engagement of "Michael's son." She wrote as if all her readers would know who "Michael" was.

No one, not his mother, not his childhood minister, no one called Mike "Michael."

She mentioned no last names, but she did talk about how the feted couple were both pre-med students at a "prestigious California university"—which was wrong; Pomona was a college. She also talked about the bride's parents, how successful they were, how they had recently purchased a twelve-bedroom house in the Hamptons.

A twelve-bedroom house? Rose Zander-Brown had invited me to stay in a house with *twelve* bedrooms? And in the Hamptons? I knew I was supposed to be impressed at this mention of the playground of the rich and famous. I had never been there, but Claudia wrote about it as if we all went there all the time, didn't we, darlings?

I went back to reading about the party. Because Cami's real name was Camellia, not the more common Camilla, Claudia's centerpieces were to be camellias. Hardy hybrids provided autumnal flowering plants. And the table linens were . . .

This seemed so strange to me. Yes, when I'd had Jeremy's graduation party, I had talked about the menu to a couple of the women at work who cared about such things, but I hadn't posted my choices on the Internet weeks before the party. Who on earth would care about Claudia's hardy autumnal hybrids?

But after each of Claudia's entries, people could post messages to one another. I opened one of those threads and saw that plenty were interested. Apparently she had a sort of fan club, people who kept up with her activities via her Web site. They were almost like virtual groupies eager to feel involved in her life.

The blog included links to pages in which Claudia described the creation of her dress for the evening. "I wanted the gown to have a slightly Asian feel," I read, "without it seeming to be a costume."

Oh, crap. I was going to have to buy a new dress. Not only was someone blogging about my family, but I was going to have to buy a dress. I wasn't sure which was worse.

Zack got his own invitation to the party. He opened it before I got home. "Will you RSVP for me, Mom?"

"No, you need to do it yourself."

"But what about a tux? It says it's black tie. Can I wear Dad's?" Jeremy had been too broad-shouldered to wear Mike's tux, but Zack had borrowed it for his prom last spring.

"He's probably wearing it . . . unless he's getting a new one." That did seem likely . . . although maybe I was doing Claudia a disservice. Maybe she had managed her perfectionism so well that she didn't care what Mike was going to wear. "So talk to him. Otherwise we'll see about renting one."

Mike was indeed getting a new tux, but apparently Claudia was writing an article for a sewing magazine about adapting vintage clothes, so she wanted to alter old tuxes for Jeremy and Zack.

Zack didn't like this idea. "Don't you think that's pretty stupid, Mom, when I could just wear Dad's old one? I can see her doing it for Jeremy since he can't wear Dad's and he's the main deal for the party, but not me. Nobody will care what I wear."

Apparently that was not true; Claudia did care what he wore. "You'll have to take this up with your dad."

"I tried," Zack said, "but he said that I should cooperate."

"Then maybe you should."

As soon as he went up to his room, I went to the computer and logged on to Claudia's Web site, feeling as secretive as if I were looking for male-escort services. Claudia was not only remaking tuxes for "Michael's two handsome sons," she was refashioning a vintage gown for "our lovely Camellia."

Our? Since when was Cami hers?

My father, out in Michigan, had gotten an invitation. "Well, that was nice," I said. My dad is a sweetheart, and his tux was as vintage as could be. "Why don't you come?"

"I think I'd like to. I've never met Cami, and she's wearing the ring I bought when I didn't have a dime to my name."

Since Claudia had invited my father, she would have invited Mike's mother. I wondered how long it would be before Mike tried to dump the problem of his mother in my lap.

About thirty minutes, it turned out.

"Mother will want to see the boys," he said. He was calling from the speakerphone in his car, and his voice sounded tinny.

"I'm sure that she will."

"She'll be staying at the Ritz with the Zander-Browns."

Claudia lived in Great Falls, a Virginia suburb much farther out than Arlington, where I live. The Ritz-Carlton in Tysons Corner was the nicest hotel in that area. "I'm sure your mother will enjoy being at the Ritz."

Mike didn't reply to that, so I didn't reply to his non-reply.

"Aren't you going to say something?" he asked.

"No." I'd taken a Ritalin twenty minutes ago, so my ability to inhibit—i.e., keep my mouth shut—was coming into its glory.

"Don't you have any ideas about what we should do with her?"

How changeable were his first-person plural pronouns. When it came to the party, "we" was Claudia and him; when it come to his mother, it was me and him, and I'm sure that he would have been happier if he could have used the second person—"What are *you* going to do with my mother?"

Marjorie Van Aiken is a difficult woman. From the beginning of our marriage, she has been aggressive, whining, and annoying. "I'm not going to let you take my son away from me," she'd said in that stupid, half-joking way people use when they want to make a point, but don't want to be held accountable for it. "I've seen it too often. Girls just won't let their husbands go to their own homes."

My family lived in Michigan. I wasn't going to make Mike eat Sunday dinner there every week. Moreover, it wasn't me who kept us from going to Philadelphia as often as Marge would have liked. It was Mike. He hadn't wanted to go any more than I had.

So it was with a fair amount of pleasure that I now reminded Mike that his mother was not my responsibility.

But it was with no pleasure at all that I went shopping for a new dress. Getting dolled up for a big doo-wah event like this engagement party has never been one of my strengths. Even though the loss of appetite associated with Ritalin has left me weighing less than I have since before I got pregnant with Jeremy, I don't trust my taste. I'm often drawn to things that look bright and cheerful, only to find that everyone else thinks that they are garish. Sometimes I don't care what anyone else thinks. But sometimes I do, and a party hosted by my ex-husband's blogging lady friend was a major "care about what other people think" occasion.

When I couldn't put it off any longer, I went to Loehmann's, a big discounter, and instantly found a dress that I loved. It was violet blue with scarlet and magenta poppies. I tried it on, and, thanks to the Ritalin, it fit well. It moved when I walked, brushing against my legs in what felt like an almost sexual caress. It had already been discounted twice, so the price was great.

But I hesitated. Was it a lucky find, or was it double discounted at Loehmann's because no sane woman would ever wear scarlet and magenta poppies? I didn't know. I also didn't know if violet blue was a good color for me. I have light brown hair, hazel eyes, and freckles. The colors other people said looked good on me were kind of boring.

I grew impatient with myself. Why was I having trouble deciding? That should tell me something. And what was the point of a dress that felt good on the legs? I would be wearing pantyhose. So I crossed the street to Lord & Taylor and paid full price on a very acceptable, very boring sleeveless black dress.

I know that I don't look great in black.

Ten days before the party, Mike called again. "Your father sent in his RSVP, but he hasn't done anything about a hotel room."

"Of course he hasn't. He's staying with me. As are Cami and Jeremy."

He paused. "Claudia has Cami and Jeremy on the list for the hotel. Do you have room for them?"

I interpreted that as a criticism of my house. "Yes."

"You do understand that Cami and Jeremy need to be on time. They really have to be there to greet the guests. They can't be late."

"They'll be there on time."

Twenty minutes later he called back. "I just confirmed with Jeremy that he and Cami want to stay with you."

I knew that.

"And so I spoke to Claudia"—he was sounding uncharacteristically hesitant—"and she was concerned that it would be awkward for you, having everyone stay at your house."

"Why would it be awkward to have my father, my son, and my future daughter-in-law staying at my house? There will be lines at the bathrooms, but that's inconvenient, not awkward."

"Oh, well, you know . . . with them all going to the party and all . . ." His voice trailed off, and I got it.

I was not invited to this party.

I felt my mouth drop open. I wasn't invited? How could that be? And why didn't I know?

Zack had opened the invitation, and he wouldn't have done that if it had been addressed to both of us. But even if I had seen only his name on the envelope, it still wouldn't have occurred to me that I wasn't expected to come.

"It did seem a little odd to me," Mike was saying, "but Claudia said that you wouldn't expect it, that divorced people do not expect to go to one another's occasions."

I was speechless. I truly was.

What had we promised the boys? That we would still be a family. And families don't do this.

Or did they? What did we know? It wasn't as if either one of us was on a second or third divorce and so knew the rules, the guidelines for how to be divorced, for managing it perfectly.

Although he wasn't going to admit it, I knew that Mike had made the same mistake as I had. He too had assumed that I would be coming. So far we had been trusting our instincts about when we should go places together, and that had been working well enough. But now we were adding someone else's judgment to the mix.

Did I mind missing the party? I wasn't sure. I could think only about how humiliating it would have been if I had shown up, clueless and uninvited, startling Claudia, forcing her to beg the caterers to squeeze in another place setting.

But even if I didn't mind my staying home, I knew who would—Jeremy and my father. Even the twelve-bedroom Zander-Browns might find it awkward. Cami's family was flying in from New York on Saturday morning. They were coming straight to my house for lunch. "We'll see you tonight," they would say after lunch, and I would smile blandly. "I won't be joining you. Your hostess did not care to invite me."

This wasn't going to reflect badly on me. Claudia was the one who would look terrible. I had the moral high ground here; I was the Offended Against. I could see myself enjoying this every bit as much as going to the actual party. I just wish that I had bought the dress with scarlet and magenta poppies. If I was going to get all dressed up with no place to go, I might as well be in a dress I liked.

I knew that I needed to warn Jeremy that I wasn't going to the party. Firstborns do not like to be surprised. Zack can roll with the punches far better than Jeremy. So, a few days later, when Jeremy called to micromanage which cars to take out to Claudia's house, I had to interrupt him. "You know that I won't be going to the party."

"Mom! Why not!"

"I wasn't invited."

"You're kidding, aren't you?"

"Jeremy, your dad and I are divorced. Why would Claudia invite me to her house?"

"Because the party is for Cami and me, and we want you there."

"Don't be like that," I cautioned sternly, although I was secretly pleased by his outrage. "Don't start being a bridezilla when you're only the groom."

"How do you think Cami's parents are going to feel,

coming to lunch when you aren't invited to the party?"

"Cami's parents are grown-ups. They can handle a little awkwardness."

"But this is just wrong. Dad promised that we would never have to choose between going one place with one of you or another place with the other."

That might not have been a realistic promise to make. "Don't be too hard on your father. This wasn't necessarily his decision."

"But he agreed to it."

As I expected, Jeremy talked to Mike, Mike talked to Claudia, and Claudia girded her loins to talk to me, but Mike did so instead.

"Darcy, Claudia was going to call you, but I said that I would. She truly hopes that you will accept her apologies and come to the party."

I didn't want to give up my moral high ground too easily. "Why would I want to go somewhere that I'm not wanted?"

"It wasn't a case of not wanting you personally. It was more that she didn't understand the situation."

"We have an amicable divorce. What's to understand or not understand about that?"

"Darcy, don't make this difficult. Will you please come to this party?"

Why shouldn't I make it difficult? Wasn't I entitled to be a little snot? I had not been on Claudia's list until she realized that my exclusion would make her look all unmanaged and imperfect. Why should I show up just so that she would look better? There was still time to return my dress.

But what good would sitting at home do me? I wanted to have a good working relationship with Mike. I wanted that for the boys; I wanted it for me. So if Claudia Postlewaite was now an element in this equation of ours, I needed to brush up on my multi-variable calculus.

"Of course I'll come," I said as pleasantly as I could, "and tell Claudia that she doesn't need to call me. It would embarrass us both."

Three

If, like Claudia, you'd seen only a picture of "our lovely Camellia," you would certainly call her lovely. Her cheekbones were high, her features were delicate, and her lips and philtrum—the indentation between her mouth and nose—were finely incised. Her hair was light and cut in a short, feathery style.

But during the three times she'd visited us, I'd never thought of her in terms of her appearance . . . probably because she didn't seem to. She carried herself like a smart girl, not a pretty one. Her expression was alert and focused; her body language was that of someone who is always paying attention, always engaged. She also had a slight hint of anxiety about her, which I assumed was the natural "meeting the boyfriend's mother" desire to please.

She, like Jeremy, was her family's good child,

always asking herself if she had done everything she was supposed to have done. This did make her an easy houseguest. She wasn't moody or unpredictable; she knew how to load a dishwasher and scramble an egg. She didn't expect Jeremy to pamper her. I liked her for that.

But another mother of sons had once given me some advice: "Don't fall in love with your sons' girlfriends."

Apparently that happened to women who were hungry for a daughter. When one of their sons brought a girl home, they were so thrilled to have another female at the dinner table that they grew very attached to her. But then—bingo—the kids would break up, and the mother would never see the girl again. The mother would have no closure, no opportunity to say good-bye.

So when Cami had come to visit, I'd always made sure that there were sanitary products in whatever bathroom she was using; I'd happily answered her questions about why I was doing what I was doing with a particular recipe; I'd taken her on a behind-the-scenes tour of the hospital. Beyond that, I had been cautious.

I felt clueless about this whole mother-in-law/daughter-in-law business. What relationship were Cami and I supposed to have? Mike's mother had hardly set a good example. She viewed me as the enemy, the competition, and I did not want to think that way about any girl whom my son loved.

My mother and my brother's wife had always seemed to get along well. I wished I could ask Mother about it, but, of course, when Dad arrived for the engagement party, he was alone. Mother was dead.

The morning of Claudia's engagement party, Cami came into the kitchen early, dressed in the loose pajama bottoms and little knit tank that she had slept in, wearing her glasses because she wasn't awake enough to put her contacts in. She looked cute and sleepy, a puppy waking up.

My son will be happy with you, won't he? "I bet you're still on California time."

"At least I made it out of bed." She pointed to the cabinet over the dishwasher, asking if the coffee cups were there. "Jeremy says that he can't move."

He can be rigid. He can be overbearing. Forgive him. Work with him. Please don't make the mistakes his dad and I made. "You're being a good sport about this."

"Wait until the people taking the pictures see how pretty my little sister is. They're the ones who will have to be the good sports."

Cami and Jeremy, along with Zack, had to get up far earlier than they wanted to in order to get themselves to Claudia's house. The article that Claudia was writing about their garments was for an important sewing magazine—I learned that from the blog—and she had hired a professional photographer to come to her house first thing in the morning.

Zack's interest in participating in such a photo shoot

was well below zero, and it took me two trips to the basement to get him out of bed. But at eight thirty he stumbled upstairs and headed for the door. I tried to give him a protein bar.

"I hate those things," he groaned.

"You said you like this brand." Otherwise I wouldn't have purchased two forty-eight-bar megaboxes of them at Costco last week.

"I don't know why I would have said that." But he took the bar and jammed it into his pocket, a method of transport not likely to make the bar more appetizing.

The photo session was supposed to take only an hour, an hour and a half at the maximum, and one of the boys was going to call me when they left Claudia's. I was expecting to hear from them by ten thirty. At eleven I called Zack. "Are you on the road yet?"

"No." He didn't sound very concerned. "I think they're done with me and maybe Jeremy, but Cami's still in there."

"What's taking so long?"

"I don't know. There was this makeup artist, and he took forever, but I think Cami enjoyed it."

"Are you going nuts?"

"No, not really. Claudia ordered in a deli platter and a bunch of fruit. Her TV's got a superpremium cable package, and Dad and Jeremy are watching a rerun of last spring's NCAA lacrosse championship. They seem to be happy about that."

We had never gotten more than the most basic cable channels; I hadn't wanted to encourage the boys to watch TV. And a deli platter had to be better than a Costco protein bar. "So what are you doing?"

"Kind of hanging with the photographer and the makeup guy. They've both worked in the theater, so that's cool."

"Would you please remind everyone that Cami's family is supposed to be getting in around noon?"

"Okay. No problem."

Zack had not been looking forward to this photo session. He couldn't see the point of it. Why should he have to get out of bed to go put on "used" clothes? Why did anyone need a picture of him anyway? But he was having a fine time and so were Cami and Jeremy.

When Jeremy was at Selwyn, our house had always been full of his friends. We had one of the "fun" houses. The kids knew that there would always be something to eat and that we weren't going to fuss about mud on the carpet or a broken glass or two. The parents knew that Mike or I would be home and that we weren't going to allow underage drinking.

But this morning Cami and my boys were having a good time at Claudia Postlewaite's. She was the "fun mom" today. I didn't like that. I wasn't going to compete with her for Mike . . . but for my boys? She'd be well advised not to underestimate me in that fight. She might be able to order a deli platter, but that was nothing compared to what I could slam out of even this small kitchen.

• • •

Initially the Zander-Brown family was going to fly to D.C., but in the middle of last week they had decided to drive. Cami told me that her dad didn't like to drive long distances and so—she sounded embarrassed by this—they would probably come with a car and driver. Shortly after noon I saw a black limousine easing slowly down the street. It wasn't one of those huge, stretch prom-night things, but it was bigger than a normal car. It passed the entrance to my driveway—everyone did—but realized its mistake soon enough that it didn't have to turn around. It reversed for a dozen or so yards, then rolled majestically up my driveway.

What kind of family has a second home with twelve bedrooms and goes places in a limousine?

I felt at a disadvantage. They were expecting to see their daughter for the first time in several months, and I had seemingly misplaced her.

I'd had this feeling so often as a kid, the feeling that I had done something wrong, something that I needed to apologize for, but I didn't exactly know what it was. How many moments like this were there going to be between now and the wedding in June? How many times were the Zander-Browns going to have to consult etiquette books and make elaborate adjustments to the seating charts because Jeremy's parents were divorced?

Had I been too impulsive? Should I have, as Mike had said, given the separation more time? Or, at the very minimum, stayed in the old house longer so that I could give Cami and Jeremy a party? Would all this be easier if I were still in my big house with a husband at my side? Had I torpedoed myself with my need to be doing something—anything—with my need to feel in control?

Well, there was nothing I could do about it now. My father joined me on the front porch. He was, as always, lean and dignified. I moved closer to him, glad that he was here.

"So what do we know about this family?" Dad had asked me when I picked him up at the airport yesterday.

I actually knew a fair amount. The Zander-Browns had three children. Cami's sister, Annie, was sixteen, and their little brother, Finney, was eight. Jeremy talked mostly about Cami's father. An extremely successful literary agent, Guy Zander-Brown was an outgoing, exuberant person. "You'll love him, Mom," Jeremy had said. "Everyone does."

Cami spoke of her father with good-humored affection. Once, she was wearing a scarf so beautiful that even I noticed it. "Oh, it's from my dad," she had laughed. "He loves to buy presents, and the more expensive the better."

I'd asked Jeremy about Cami's mother. "I think she's the one who keeps them all on track," was all he'd said.

The rest of my information came from Mike, who had apparently googled them just as I had Claudia.

The literary agency provided a comfortable living; their twelve-bedroom wealth was comparatively recent, coming largely from a few blockbuster clients and a shrewd, aggressive investment strategy that Guy had been pursuing for the last five or ten years. Mike had been interested in that. More interesting to me was a link he had sent me about Rose, Cami's mother.

The link was to an article from the archives of a glossy women's magazine. Written before their son, Finney, was born, it featured Rose and a seemingly perfect life. Beautiful herself, she had two exquisite daughters and a neat brownstone in Park Slope, a gentrified neighborhood in Brooklyn full of artists and writers, filmmakers, doctors, and lawyers. Her days were full of children, friends, and books. She walked her daughters to school in the morning and scooped them up at the playground in the afternoon. Monday mornings she had coffee with the other moms from the school; Friday afternoons they all walked their kids to the ice-cream parlor together. She and her two next-door neighbors had connected their back decks so that they could pop into each other's kitchens without having to go through the long, narrow houses and up and down the front stoops. On Sunday nights she and Guy had drop-in pasta suppers, mingling neighbors, kids, dogs, and clients.

Yet she still had time to work, nestled into a big chair or sitting at her kitchen table, reading manuscripts, looking for the silvery potential in what everyone else had thrown aside. She could spot literary talent anywhere. She had persuaded the mom who wrote the co-op preschool newsletter to write a novel. Her Brooklyn neighborhood was full of people trying to write their first books. They all knew Rose and were eager to get her to read their work.

In the article, Guy had been open about how much the agency depended on her ability. "She has such an ear for individual voices, and she knows how to help authors reach their potential," he was quoted as saying. "I only sell the manuscripts. Lots of people can do what I do. Not many can do what she does."

I don't know why magazines publish articles like this. Are other people's perfect lives supposed to be inspiring? They just make me hate the person being profiled. Sure, you can have it all if you have healthy kids, a husband with a job, and a talent you can use while sitting at your kitchen table. I have a talent. I can get an IV into anyone. It's a good skill, a useful one. I can save people's lives with it, but I can't make a living doing it from home.

I knew that Rose's life had become slightly less perfect after Finney's birth. Cami had told me that he had been born with a midgut malrotation that had required several surgeries. He also had a severe corn allergy and what she termed *cognitive challenges*. I had asked Jeremy about those "cognitive challenges," and he'd used the term *learning disability,* so I had assumed that this was a case of a high-achieving family needing to explain why one of their children had intellectual abilities that were only average. Private schools are full of families like that. God forbid that anyone should have an average child. The least variation from brilliance had to be explained as a learning disability.

I watched as the doors to the limousine opened. Rose emerged first. She was, I saw, slightly taller than me, and her build was much curvier than mine. She had auburn hair, which she had scooped up and clipped to the back of her head, one of those casual get-this-out-of-my-way styles that looks messy unless you have a really great haircut, and apparently she did. She was a very attractive woman, and she had probably been a lovely girl, but a bit of flesh had settled around her chin and jaw, giving her face a squarish look that kept it from beauty.

We shook hands, she first with me, then with my father. Her voice was pleasant, her gaze direct. She was wearing a traditionally cut white blouse, open at the throat, and the cuffs flipped back so that with her dark red hair spilling from its clips, she could have been an idealized portrait of a Scottish laundress, looking up from her washtub, her face flushed from the warmth of the water.

But her blouse was a heavy silk that moved with liquid smoothness. Her tweed slacks didn't have a single wrinkle although she had been sitting for four or five hours. She was wearing the kind of shoes that I can never find, a low stacked heel, a thick, soft sole, but with enough detailing—bands of black suede inset with dark green leather—that the shoe seemed narrow and elegant. From the haircut to the shoes, this was serious money very well spent.

This wasn't fair. People with money were supposed to be jerks. They were supposed to have scary face-lifts and fashion-victim clothes. Then you could feel superior to them. But Rose Zander-Brown seemed to be doing it right. If I were willing to spend a month's grocery bill on a pair of shoes, hers were exactly what I would buy.

Rose was beckoning to her son, encouraging him to come to her. Eight years old, he was small for his age, a little boy with light hair and the utterly perfect skin that only little boys have. He came forward to shake my hand with the earnestness of someone who has been carefully taught.

"Finney starts with an *F,*" he told me. His voice was thick, as if his tongue were a little too large for his mouth. "Phineas starts with a *P.*"

I noticed that he had a small fanny pack around his waist. "Is Phineas your real name?"

He nodded earnestly. "It starts with a *P.*"

"I'll remember that."

He nodded, then realized that he didn't know what to say next. He looked back at his mother anxiously. She mouthed "thank you."

He looked relieved. "Thank you."

"You are so welcome," I answered.

I shot a quick glance to my dad, and he nodded, agreeing with me.

I had misread the euphemisms. This boy did not

have your garden-variety learning disabilities. He truly was cognitively challenged. He was developmentally disabled. He was, to use the most blunt term, retarded.

The Zander-Browns had not intended to mislead us. Cami had brought up the "cognitive challenges" almost immediately, and in an e-mail about his corn allergy, Rose had mentioned them again, noting that Cami had said she'd told us. It was my own Jeremy who had used the misleading "learning disabilities."

And I, of course, had assumed that since these people had money, they must be jerks. I winced with guilt.

Rose touched Finney's shoulder, pointing him in my father's direction, apparently knowing enough about us to introduce Dad as "Dr. Bowersett." Finney again shook hands with assiduous determination. Dad, his forty years as a pediatrician not wasted, asked the boy if he knew what letters were in his name. As an opening line, this was a big hit, and they chatted away about the alphabet. In a moment, Dad was patting his pockets, looking for pen and paper so he could show Finney that his name, "Douglas," didn't have any of the same letters as "Finney."

I turned my attention to Cami's sixteen-year-old sister.

Oh, my. Here was the pretty one. I'm not one for dwelling too much on what people look like, but this girl was exquisite. It was hard to stop looking at her. She was petite, no more than five-two or -three, with warmer coloring than Cami's. Her hair was a perfect strawberry blond, and as she stepped out from the shadow of the oak tree, the sunlight shimmered against the rose-hued highlights in her hair. Despite her short stature, she was an ectomorph; her neck was willowy, her fingers were long, and, although her clothes hid them, I was sure that her femur and her humerus, the bones in her thigh and upper arm, would be elongated.

Unlike Cami, Annie Zander-Brown carried herself as if she knew exactly how lovely she was. Her head was back, her shoulders were open, and her gestures were expansive. She wanted people to look at her; she expected it.

Her clothes were dramatic as well. She was wearing a calf-length skirt and boots. The skirt was complicated with seams that ran around her body instead of up and down as on a normal person's clothes. On top she had multiple layers, a little stretch something, another little stretch something in a different color and with a different neckline, a sheer blouse with more stitching, some scarves and necklaces—too much for me to comprehend.

"What a cute house," she exclaimed after greeting me. Her voice was light but without the squeaky little baby tones some pretty girls affect. "I love the porch swing . . . it must be so much fun to live here." Then she turned to Rose. "Mom, Dad's still on the phone."

This was spoken with a slightly tattletale air.

From everything I had heard of his effusive personality, I would have expected Guy to be the first one out of the car, but he had not emerged yet. The limo's front passenger door was open, and a man's leg was out, with a foot on the ground. It was as if the leg's owner were promising his family that he would be with them in a moment, and in the meantime they could look at his foot. The leg was in jeans, but the shoe was a leather loafer, with heavy stitching that looked seriously expensive.

"We make him sit in the front," Annie explained, as if she were drawing me into a family secret, "so we don't have to listen to him talk on his cell."

She went back to the car, moving with a skipping, almost dancelike step, and rapped on her father's leg as if she were knocking on a door. A second later the front door opened the rest of the way. Another leg joined the first one, and Guy Zander-Brown emerged from the car, slipping his phone into his pocket.

Over his jeans and expensive shoes, Guy Zander-Brown was in a blazer and an open-collared blue shirt. He was not at all tall, but he looked strong, mesomorphic with a muscular build. His salt-and-pepper hair was trimmed close.

"I'm sure my family has told you that this is the kind of rudeness you can always expect from me." His gaze was direct, his handshake firm. "I wish I could tell you that they're lying."

I meet successful men in the hospital all the time, but once they're in the ICU, either as a patient or as a family member, they have to accept that they don't have as much control as they'd like. Some of them turn into bullies; others try to cling to a confidence that rapidly becomes thin and mechanical.

Guy Zander-Brown had already logged his ICU time. His son's struggles had probably weathered him in an interesting way, teaching him how desperate and powerless a person can feel. He seemed completely genuine, not at all smarmy or overbearing, but successful, confident, and energetic. In lieu of formally greeting my father, he joined in the alphabet conversation, looking over Finney's shoulder at Dad's piece of paper, and pointing out that "Guy" had a *g* and a *u* like "Douglas" and a *y* like "Finney."

I hadn't even had a chance to apologize for Cami and the boys not being here when Zack's car turned into the drive. Jeremy was driving, Cami was sitting in the passenger seat, and Zack was in the backseat of his own car. I wondered how that had happened.

As soon as he saw Cami, Finney dashed to her. "Cami, Cami, that boy . . . that boy over there"—he gestured toward my father—"he doesn't have an *i* in his name. Just like Mommy and Daddy, he doesn't have an *i*."

"I hope he doesn't mind that too much." Cami's hug lifted Finney off his feet. Then she set him down and pretended to examine him. "How can you have grown so much in two months?" She kissed him again, then hugged her parents and introduce them and Annie to Zack.

Zack, God love him, took one look at Miss Annie

Zander-Brown and was struck dumb. He was seventeen; she was sixteen. He was still awkwardly skinny; she was confident and radiant. He would have been very happy to have Harry Potter's Invisibility Cloak so that he could look at her without anyone knowing it.

Fortunately for him, she was more interested in her sister's makeup. "Your eyes look awesome," she gushed to Cami. "How many different shades of shadow do you have on?"

I looked more closely at Cami's eyelids. They did look a little like *National Geographic* pictures of the Grand Canyon at sunrise.

"You should see this dress," Cami was saying to Annie. "It's unbelievable. It's like wearing a waterfall. Claudia says it's a bias-cut silk."

"Oh, how interesting. I hope you aren't taking it back to California. Rachel's little brother's bar mitzvah is black-tie. I could wear it to that."

"I thought you already got a dress for that."

"But it's not a bias-cut waterfall."

Rose touched my arm. "Please don't listen to them. If you don't have girls, you'll never understand."

The driver had opened the limo's trunk. "So, Mrs. Zee, you wanted the ice chest and that big white box?"

"The big white box, yes, please, but the ice chest you can wait a minute on."

I didn't have a clue what the big white box was, but I could guess that the ice chest was full of corn-free food.

Rose spoke to me quietly. "I hate being a nuisance about this, but—"

"No, no," I interrupted. "If this is about Finney's corn allergy, I understand completely. I saved all my labels; I can show you my recipes."

"Jeremy kept telling us not to worry, but I'm a 'food-allergy mom,' and that's what we do, worry."

I knew that corn is one of the most difficult allergies to manage. Corn syrup is used in an extraordinary number of packaged or processed foods, and corn-starch appears even in many medications.

"Cami told me that Finney has been wanting to go to McDonald's," I said, "so we're having hamburgers and french fries. I made the buns and the ketchup. I got peanut oil for the french fries. I found a Jewish family who still had some kosher-for-Passover Coke." Observant Jewish families, I'd learned, avoid all grain products during Passover, so in the spring the Coca-Cola Company produces a small run of Coke that uses cane sugar instead of the cheaper corn syrup. "I also made the cookies and the ice cream."

Rose drew back with an involuntary gesture.

I guess I had overachieved on this meal. I'd told myself that I wanted to be nice, that I wanted to show Rose that our family understood the needs of her family. Instead I was probably coming across as terminally needy, so desperate for approval that I'd made my own ketchup.

"I like to cook," I was now apologizing. "And I like challenges."

"Jeremy said that too."

Jeremy and Zack were already climbing the stairs, black vinyl garment bags folded over their arms. I waved everyone inside. The driver followed us, carrying a very large package wrapped in glossy white paper and tied with an elaborate silver bow. Its size was daunting.

"Don't worry," Rose said to me. "We did not bring you the Taj Mahal as a hostess gift." She signaled to Annie and the girl handed me a perfectly straightforward gift bag—in fact, I recognized the design; her kids' school must have sold Sally Foster gift wrap too. Inside was a pair of very interesting handmade candles, white with spirals of buff. It was the sort of "anyone will like this" gift that I can never find, at least not at a price I'm willing to pay.

"Cami, this box is for you and Jeremy," Rose said.

"It's heavy." Finney said. "Very heavy."

"What fun. I love presents," Cami explained. She tested a corner of the box. "Oh, Finney, you're right. It is heavy. What is it? Who's it from?"

"I'm not going to tell you what it is," Rose said, "and if you read the card, you'll see it is from Jill Allyn."

"Oh." Cami suddenly was less happy about the gift. "Did she really make you bring it down here? Is that why you had to drive down? Because of this?"

"And Annie's clothes," Finney said. "Annie brings lots of clothes. Some of them are Mommy's."

"That's not big news, Finney," Annie said. "Everyone knows that."

Cami pulled Finney to stand next to her so that they could unwrap the gift together. I guessed that "Jill Allyn" was the novelist Jill Allyn Stanley. That article about Rose had mentioned her as one of Rose's "finds." I hadn't read any of her books, but patients' wives or mothers frequently had one of them at the hospital because it was what their book clubs were reading.

Cami and Finney were being careful with the paper, discussing which piece of tape to loosen next. Every so often the sun would catch the ring on her left hand, sending a glittering splatter of light against her little brother's shirt and the wall behind him. Finally, Jeremy suggested to Finney that it might be fun just to rip the paper. Finney brightened. He liked that idea. So he gave the paper a yank. It tore with a delicious crispness, revealing the box for a massive espresso machine made of copper and hammered aluminum.

"Wow." Jeremy crouched down to look at it more closely. "This is something. I bet it makes great coffee."

Cami had a more realistic eye. "But it's so big. I don't know where we'll put it. Mom, we didn't register for anything like this. How are we going to get it back to California?"

"We'll drop it at a shipping place," Rose told her.

"It would have been nice if Jill Allyn had done that in the first place."

"Oh, you know her. She thought it would be fun for you to have a gift today."

"Let's not worry about it right now," Guy said briskly. "We'll take it back to Park Slope and worry about it there."

"Is it okay if we leave it there for a while?" Cami asked. "We really don't have room for it in our apartment."

"It's not like we do either," Annie said bluntly. "Come on, Cami, Mom is always after you to throw stuff out because we don't have enough storage space. You know how pissed off you got last Christmas because we were storing stuff in your room."

"I was pissed off," Cami said, "because you had your clothes all over my bed. I didn't mind Dad putting a couple of boxes in the corner."

"Girls." Rose was warning them not to bicker. "We'll take the machine to Mecox Road. That's where we're storing all the wedding things."

"Oh, right." Annie turned to me. "We have to be the only family in the world who views our house in the Hamptons primarily as an enormous closet."

Dad had started the grill when we'd first spotted the limo, so he and Jeremy went out to cook the burgers. As Cami and Rose helped me put the rest of lunch on the table, Finney waited patiently in a corner of the dining room. Once everything was ready and he'd been told where to sit, he looked to his mother to find out what he could eat.

"You can have whatever you want," she told him. "Jeremy's mother made everything and she was very careful."

He looked at me. "Very *very* careful?"

"Very very *very* careful," I assured him.

"Thank you," he said and instantly looked at Rose, wanting to be sure that she noticed him remembering his manners.

After being properly congratulated, he set to work, eating with a steady, determined joy. He was so absorbed in the food that several times he started to hum, but Cami, who was sitting next to him, would lay her hand on his arm and he would stop.

The time went quickly. Guy took charge of the conversation, and it was lively and interesting. No one described the trips that they'd been on or told long stories about people the rest of the group didn't know. Finally Rose caught Guy's attention and lifted her wrist, tapping her watch.

"Oh, lord," he groaned and leaned back in his chair to look out the dining-room window. "The car's probably been out there for an hour. We need to get moving. We have to eat again in two hours." They were meeting Mike, Claudia, and Mike's mother for afternoon tea at the Ritz-Carlton.

"Finney, you should use the bathroom before we go," Rose said. "Ask Jeremy where it is."

Obediently, Finney went upstairs. I heard him moving around, looking in the bedrooms. I wondered if he had forgotten Jeremy's directions or if he was just curious about the rest of the house. When he came down, he spoke hopefully. "Lunch again first?"

"You can have a snack in the car," Rose said to him.

"Okay," he said agreeably. "But Mrs. Van Darcy. I like her food. She makes good food."

"That's certainly the truth," Guy agreed and rumpled Finney's hair. "You have good taste, Mr. Finney. We'll certainly know where to find you if you ever run away from home."

Finney giggled, probably responding more to Guy's tone than his actual words. But the words did give me an idea. I spoke quietly to Rose. "Would Finney like to spend the rest of the afternoon here? We're not doing anything special, but it has to be better for him than tea at the Ritz."

Rose paused.

I understood. She couldn't be used to this, leaving Finney at other people's houses on the spur of the moment. Between his allergies and his cognitive disability, she couldn't just leave him someplace and hope for the best.

"Cami will be here," I reminded her.

"Okay . . ." she said slowly. Then she waved a hand. "What's wrong with me? His sister, a nurse, and a pediatrician. Of course it's okay. Thank you. He will be thrilled."

Finney brightened immediately when being asked if he wanted to spend the afternoon at Jeremy's mother's house. "And sleep here? I want . . . no, no, ask a question . . . May I sleep here? Please. Mrs. Van Darcy."

I glanced at Rose. Clearly she, not Guy, made these decisions. She nodded. "There's a sofa bed outside

Zack's room," I said to Finney, "if you want to sleep there."

Annie was just returning from her bathroom trip. "Sofa bed!" he told her eagerly. "I'm going to sleep on a sofa bed! Outside Zack's room. A sofa bed."

"You're staying here?" Her voice was edged with envy.

The envy surprised me. Annie hadn't made a great impression on me. I don't like vain people, and clearly she was very vain. I would have thought that a room at the Ritz would be much more to her liking than my small house, but clearly I was wrong.

"Do you want to stay too, Annie?" I asked as if I still lived in a big house. "I have no idea where you'll sleep, but we'll find someplace."

"Really?" She too looked delighted. "I can sleep with Finney, I don't care." Her bracelets jingled as she turned to Rose. "Can I, Mom? Please."

"If it's all right with Darcy," Rose said, "but you have to work on that paper."

"I will. I promise I will."

Rose looked as if she believed that exactly as much as I would have believed such a promise from Zack.

"This is quite a big treat for you, young man," Guy said to Finney. "But, Miss Queenie, I suppose you'll want all your luggage."

Apparently "Miss Queenie" was his endearment for Annie. "Oh, come on, Dad"—her smile was teasing—"it's not that much."

As they went off to unload the luggage, Rose picked up her purse. "Finney has an EpiPen in his fanny pack."

That was a question as much as a statement. She wanted to be sure that I knew what an EpiPen was. Of course, I did. It was a single dose of epinephrine in a spring-loaded syringe. Carried by people with severe allergies, it was a life-saving device, designed for self-injection in case of anaphylaxis.

"We haven't taught Finney to use it yet," she said, "but he always has it on him. And here's a backup." She handed me a slim case that she had taken out of her purse.

Back outside, I caught Dad's attention and pointed to Finney's fanny pack, mouthing, "EpiPen." He nodded. He'd already guessed that.

We watched the limo carry Guy and Rose off to the Ritz. "Darcy, Annie was just telling me," Dad said, "that your house reminded her of their grandparents' cottage in the Adirondacks."

"Annie!" Cami exclaimed. "How can you say that? The cottage was falling down. All the ceilings had water stains, and there were mice in every closet."

"It doesn't look the same," Annie acknowledged, "but it's cozy like the cottage, with just one place to sit so people have to be together. You remember how we always played games there."

"I have games," I said. "I don't have water stains or mice, at least not yet, but I do have games."

So that's what we did the rest of the afternoon. Cami and Jeremy had planned to study, Annie was supposed to be working on a paper, and Zack had to be doing something—dear God—anything, on his college applications, but instead we played games.

Annie wanted to play the card games that they had played with their grandparents. I found the cards and everyone started to gather around the table. Finney waited for one of his sisters to tell him where to sit, but my dad patted the chair next to him. "Let's be a team, you and me."

The games were simple and easy to learn. Annie was enthusiastic, teasing, flirting; it was clear that she wanted everyone to have a good time. I'm not much in the flirting department, but I'm a good sport. If she wanted people to have fun, I would help. As soon as I had a good hand, I slapped down my winning cards with PG-rated trash talk. Then everyone got into the spirit of inane and pointless competition, and we had a grand time. Zack roused himself from his Annie-induced stupor and was enjoying himself, provoking Jeremy to the point that Jeremy, in fun, hooked his elbow around Zack's neck and rubbed his knuckles across Zack's skull. When they were kids, Jeremy used to do this to him . . . although not in fun.

Perhaps because the playground at his very expensive, very specialized school was highly supervised, perhaps because he had no built-in tormentor in the shape of a brother, Finney had never seen "noogies" before. He was fascinated. First he wanted Jeremy to demonstrate them on him. Then Jeremy obediently bent his head and let Finney curve his thin arm around Jeremy's neck.

Who had the "fun" house now?

Four

Around five o'clock Guy called, saying that he was going to send the car for all of us; he and Rose would catch a lift with Mike when he came to the hotel to get his mother. I didn't protest. I had never shown up at a party in a limo; this seemed like a very good time to start. Maybe I could read about it tomorrow on Claudia's blog.

Everyone, even my boys, took it for granted that Claudia and I knew each other, but we'd never met. I wasn't looking forward to our meeting. What on earth would we say? So I decided to take a Ritalin. I don't usually take them late in the day—I have too much trouble going to sleep—but if I took one, I would be more controlled. I could better endure tedious conversations; I would be less likely to blurt out something that would offend someone, embarrass myself, or both.

I had to give Claudia credit for one thing: my guys looked absolutely great in their vintage tuxes. Broad-shouldered and light-haired, Jeremy appeared elegantly assured, a character out of *The Great Gatsby*. Zack's tux glided over his sharp angles, giving his frame maturity and dignity. With his longish black hair and fair skin, he looked mysterious, even a little sinister. Twice I saw him glance in the small mirror that hung near the front door. He liked the way he looked.

Finney was wearing neat gray pants, his fanny pack, a white dress shirt, and a little crimson tie. He had dressed in Zack's basement bathroom and was very happy to report that Zack had been able to tie his tie for him. He told each of us about it, how Zack could tie a tie just like his father could. He now considered Zack his very dear friend, something that clearly made Zack uncomfortable.

That was one problem with the private schools Zack had attended. He had never been in classes with "mainstreamed" students—kids with various kinds of disabilities who joined the traditional classes for a few hours a day. The benefits to the mainstreamed kids probably had to be assessed case by case, but getting to know their part-time classmates as individuals broadened the outlook of the so-called normal students.

But Zack hadn't had that experience. To him, Finney, sweet, earnestly well-behaved little Finney, was unpredictable and unknowable. I watched unhappily as Zack drew away from the boy, leaving my father, as we waited for the girls, to carry the conversation about knotting ties.

A few minutes later, Cami floated down in a sleeveless, pale rose satin dress that drifted and clung to her in a Jean Harlow way. She looked spectacular. Dad met her at the bottom of the stairs. He took her left hand, the one with Mother's ring, and tilted it toward the light. He looked down at the ring for a moment, then lifted her hand to kiss the back of her palm.

"Jeremy's grandmother said that she did everything with her left hand for the first month she had that ring."

"I did too," Cami said. "Jeremy didn't tell me at first that it was her ring in case I didn't like it, but I loved it right away."

"She did, too."

Dad's face was soft. He was thinking about Mother. I couldn't stand to. Everything would have been so much better if she had been here.

We were now all waiting for Annie.

Jeremy was getting tense.

"Annie is late. Very late," Finney said. "It makes Mommy mad."

Cami had already been upstairs once. "I'd go again, but when I try to rush her, it just gets worse."

Jeremy looked at his watch again. Finally he looked at me. "Mom, could you do something?"

It had been a long time since he'd asked me for help. Sometimes I felt as if he'd drunk his dad's Kool-Aid and thought of me as this huge screwup. I could endure that from Mike, but not from one of the boys.

I went upstairs. The two sisters had decided that Jeremy should move into the second twin bed in Dad's room, and Annie could share the double bed with Cami. That bed was now covered with stuff—clothes, scarves, I didn't know what-all. Annie was at the mirror, a chem lab full of makeup spread out across the top of the bureau.

Any hospital nurse knows how to disguise controlling behavior with faux helpfulness. “Let me help you gather up this makeup,” I said, starting to shovel things into her makeup bag as I spoke, “so you can finish in the car.”

She shot me a resentful look. She clearly didn’t like me manhandling her makeup, but she was too well brought up to stop me.

We were hardly out of the neighborhood when Jeremy’s phone rang. It was Mike, wondering where we were. He was going to blame me for our being late. I wished that I didn’t care.

The atmosphere in the car wasn’t exactly party hearty. Jeremy was uneasy about being late; Annie was unhappy about being rushed; Cami was worried about the seat belt wrinkling her dress; and I fretted with the alone feeling that I got when I thought about my mother being gone. After a few minutes Finney started to look anxious. He wanted the people around him to be happy, and we didn’t seem to be cooperating.

Shortly after we passed through Great Falls village, the driver turned into a development of huge suburban McMansions. The houses had three-car garages and elaborate curbside mailboxes. I supposed they also had high ceilings, grand foyers, and huge kitchens. Houses like this were supposed to make the owners feel grand. But how grand could you feel when the house next door was almost exactly like yours?

Claudia and Mike and Rose and Guy were in the front hall, forming an informal reception line. Rose and Guy immediately detached themselves to go talk to their kids. Mike spoke to my dad; that left me with Claudia.

As I knew from the picture on her Web site, she kept her dark hair very short, the kind of style that looks good only on women with good skin and closely spaced, narrow features, both of which she had. I'd be afraid to wear my hair that short—I'd worry that I was trying to look half my age—but this crisply defined haircut suited her. She must have had a lot of confidence in her ability to judge things like that.

"I'm Darcy," I said.

Her eyes flicked up and down, judging my dress, probably dismissing it as boring. Her earrings were pearls surrounded by something sparkly. I had no idea if they were real.

"The tuxes you fixed for Jeremy and Zack," I heard myself say, "were great. They looked fabulous."

"Thank you."

I waited a moment, expecting her to continue. She didn't. The even, small features of her face were pointed in my direction, but her pale blue eyes were focused at a spot beyond my left shoulder. Once she had assessed my dress, apparently there was nothing about me worthy of her gaze.

I'm hardly the Queen of Social Interaction, but I knew that she should have said more: *Thank you, but they are such handsome young men that they would look well in anything . . . it was a pleasure to work with them . . . how sweet of you to say so.* But she wasn't saying anything else. She'd spoken and now it was my turn.

"It's nice of you to do this. Your house is lovely."

"Thank you."

This was some kind of great conversation. I wondered how long we could keep it up, me paying her compliments, her thanking me. Before I could invite her to marvel at the fact we both had *a*'s in our names, I felt a warm hand brushing my arm, drawing me away from Claudia.

It was Rose. Her dress was dark green with a neckline that flattered her curves. She had green sparklies in her ears and around her wrist, and I was willing to bet that they were genuine emeralds. I'd thought her eyes were brown, but I now saw they had green highlights.

My eyes were sort of greenish. Maybe I should wear emeralds.

"I've just talked to the girls." Rose's voice was warm; she sounded happy. "They had such a good time this afternoon. Guy is thinking that we missed all the fun."

"I had a great time too." I got the EpiPen out of my purse and gave it back to her. "Finney's okay, isn't he?"

"He's amazed at how many men can tie a tie. I'd never thought about it, but he's only seen Guy do it, so he thought only Guy could do it. But Zack can, Jeremy can, and your father can. You have a very talented family on your hands." Then she grew sincere.

"Darcy, I can't begin to tell you how unusual today was for me. I may be overprotective, but I can't help it. To walk into someone's home for the first time, and then just two hours later to feel that Finney is going to both be happy and be completely safe, that doesn't happen for me, it just doesn't."

This was nice to hear. It really was. I was almost embarrassed to be so pleased.

Outside the hospital I was never entirely sure if other women liked me. They probably did, but I was never sure. I still had, according to the nice mom-type therapist, too many layers of defensiveness and too much fear of rejection left over from growing up as an undiagnosed ADD tomboy.

Could it be different this time? The closeness, the sisterliness, that other women talked about . . . my mother and I'd had that in the end. Could I have it again, with this woman, the mother of the child whom my child loved?

I wanted to ask her about Finney. I wondered what his prognosis was. And how had she managed? Did she still have the perfect life described in the magazine article? Or had she had to come up with a plan B?

"Oh, Rose." Claudia was suddenly with us, lifting her arm so that her hand was close to Rose, but not quite touching her. She had a pearl bracelet around her wrist. "Could you come with me? There's someone I'd like you to meet."

There was a murmured apology, a rustle of fabric, and I was suddenly alone.

I felt dismissed. I stood, feeling blank for a moment, then forced myself to move out of the foyer.

Both the living room and dining room had been cleared of furniture so that the caterers could set up a bar, tables, and chairs. As Claudia's Web site had promised, the centerpieces were camellias—those hardy autumn hybrids—and the linens on the tables were pale rose, the color of Cami's dress.

The rooms felt empty. We weren't the only people who were late. A side table just inside the dining room held the cards that would tell us which tables to sit at. Very few of the little envelopes had been claimed yet.

I went looking for Mike's mother. She was hovering near the entry to the kitchen. We exchanged a vague and distant hug. As always, her clothes and hair smelled of cigarette smoke.

"Isn't Claudia's house lovely?" she exclaimed. "It's so organized, so clean. Have you seen the towels in the powder room?"

Claudia was giving a party for eighty people. Even I would have put out fresh towels in the powder room . . . if I'd still had a powder room.

I looked around, longing to find something wrong. Having kids in private school and visiting the homes of the other families had taught me the snob's way to judge a house—not by the grand foyer, the high ceilings, and three-car garage, but by the art.

Claudia didn't have art; she had interior decoration. Her walls glowed with some subtle and no doubt wildly expensive paint job. Her windows were draped with folds and swags of subtle, shimmering fabrics. The only major art piece was a kimono-like garment mounted in a large pewter-toned frame.

Okay, so I could be a snob about that, but this woman had built a business that had bought this house and paid for those window treatments. Could I have done that on my nurse's salary? Not hardly.

Mike admired people who started their own businesses, who had what he called an entrepreneurial spirit. I didn't have such a spirit; Claudia apparently did.

I wasn't sure what to do with myself. Claudia was keeping Guy and Rose close to her. Mike was making awkward conversation with my father. More and more people were arriving now, bringing gifts, apologizing for being late. They hadn't realized how long the drive would be.

I recognized almost everyone, which meant that few people were here because of their association with Claudia. I was startled at how many people from Mike's professional world had been invited. He and two other economists had a consulting firm in which they provided damage-assessment estimates, especially in environmental cases. His partners and the various lawyers who hired them were amicable enough, but when Mike and I'd been married, we hadn't socialized with them much. I wondered if they had been surprised to be invited to this affair.

It was good to see Jeremy's high-school friends, especially the guys on the crew team. They were clearly happy to see me; they hugged me, called me "Mrs. Van" as they had in high school. Their mothers also came and talked to me, touching my arm, asking me how I was. "We never hear from you," one after another said.

That was true. Mike had left me three months after these boys had graduated. I was embarrassed; I had felt like a failure. I wasn't about to call the crew-team moms and stage a pity party for myself.

I also didn't know these women as well as they knew one another. Crew-team parents get to know one another while standing around the banks of the river during the day-long regattas. But I spent the regattas on the water, driving one of the motorized boats that the judges and safety officials rode in. I was one of the few parents who had enough experience and the necessary certification to drive a launch, so everyone was always grateful to me. But I hadn't gotten chummy with the other moms.

It had been the same when the boys were in Scouts. I had been the one willing, even eager to dig out my hiking boots and get the lifeguard training. So I went with the boys on their outings instead of going grocery shopping ahead of time with another mom.

Promising the women that I would call, that we would get together, I excused myself, saying that I hadn't picked up my table assignment yet. As I went back toward the front hall, I saw another crew-team mom, Beth Vindern. Her son Josh had been the coxswain of Jeremy's boat.

I greeted her, asking about Josh.

She ignored my question. "You did know that David and I separated, didn't you? The invitation came to both of us."

"I did know," I said, suddenly remembering that I had heard that somewhere, "and I was sorry to hear about it, but this isn't my party. I didn't see the guest list."

"Oh," she said. "I suppose that that will happen to me too. *She* will be inviting my friends to parties."

I didn't know the details of the Vinderns' split. Clearly there was another woman involved. I wondered how I would feel if Mike had left me for someone else. Probably a whole lot worse.

I looked across the room. Claudia was escorting Rose and Guy to the tables. Seeing her at a distance, I noticed what a long torso she had; there was length between her clavicle—her collarbone—and her pelvis. It made her walk seem both graceful and authoritative. She also had great posture, which must have been a challenge considering how much time she spent at the sewing machine and the computer.

I knew, from her Web site, that her dress was "seafoam"—"light green" in my lingo—satin. I don't know if it was deliberate, but whenever you looked at her seafoam satin, your eye then went to Cami's rose satin, and vice versa. That they were in these pale, gleaming colors made it clear that the two of them were the stars of the show.

It was deliberate. It had to be.

Beth followed me to the table where the seating-assignment cards were. They were in alphabetical order. I picked up my envelope and, since it was close to mine, handed Beth hers.

"Did you know that these are technically called 'escort cards'? Like anyone is going to assign us escorts," she said bitterly. "What do you want to bet we're at the losers' table?"

I certainly hoped I wasn't at the same table as Beth. I didn't want to spend the evening with someone so bitter. "I imagine I'm with my father." I pulled my card out of its envelope. I had been assigned to table 9.

Beth was at table 9 as well. Dad hadn't picked up his card yet so I reached across the table and opened his. He was at table 2.

Within a few moments it was clear that Beth was right. If there was such a thing, table 9 was definitely the losers' table. There were two couples who knew no one—one pair was Claudia's neighbors, and I never figured out how the other couple was connected to anyone, but obviously the husband did not want to be there. The other four of us at the table were divorced women.

As soon as everyone was seated, Mike and Guy made toasts. Mike praised Cami, Guy praised Jeremy, and both of them thanked Claudia for hosting the party. I might as well have not existed.

I thought I didn't care about crap like this. Apparently I did.

Hospitals are hierarchical places. The attending physicians are over the residents, who are over the interns. As an advanced-practice nurse, I can legally do more than an RN, a registered nurse. The RNs, in turn, have more authority and status than the LPNs, the licensed practical nurses, etc. etc.

Short of getting a PhD in nursing and a faculty appointment to teach other nurses, I am at the top of the nursing ladder. And my status at the hospital doesn't come just from my credentials. I'm really good. I know what I'm doing. Even the doctors know it. All I have to do is say "Doctor?" in a cautionary voice, and everyone in the room stops.

Once Mike started making good money, he'd asked me if I wanted to quit work. I hadn't considered it for a minute. Work was the one place where I felt completely confident, where I felt respected and valued.

But tonight was as if I had shown up at the hospital having lost my nursing license. No one would know what to say to me, what to do with me. I wouldn't fit in; I wouldn't belong. Someone else had been hired to do my job, someone with a willowy torso, a risky haircut, and a seafoam-green dress.

This party was celebrating my son's engagement. This was my family. If I didn't belong here, where did I belong?

The waiter was refilling the wineglasses. Since I wasn't driving, I let him top off my glass again and again. I did wonder how the other single women at the table were getting home. They weren't stopping the waiter either, and the conversation at the table was growing sharp.

In response to a question from the neighbor, I pointed out Cami's family. Rose was sitting with Mike at one table, and Guy with Claudia at another.

Across the table, Kate Sheehan, one of the crew-team moms, spoke, directing her comment to me. "So I suppose you've heard the advice given to mothers of the groom?"

"No." I looked up interestedly. I probably needed all the advice I could get.

"Keep your mouth shut and wear beige."

"Beige?" I had never worn beige in my life. "Wouldn't I look like an unbaked oatmeal cookie?"

"Better that than ruin everything for everyone else." The woman whom I hadn't been able to place leaned forward, eager to speak. "The day after Dave and I were engaged, his mom called and said that she had bought her dress and it was royal purple. Just twenty-four hours after our engagement, she had her dress. We needed to plan everything around her wearing royal purple."

"Why did it matter what she was wearing? What difference did it make?"

"We wouldn't have wanted everything to clash with her dress. The pictures would have been awful."

"When my Liz got married," another Selwyn mom spoke with an "I can top that" air, "her mother-in-law said that she was going to wear black. She said that's what she wore, that's what she always wore, and she absolutely wouldn't budge. And that would have really ruined the pictures. She would have just stood out, like this big dark blob."

"Wouldn't a few blobby pictures be worth making her comfortable?" I asked.

"These were the *pictures*."

I hate this worship of photographs. It sometimes seems that people care less about what happens at an event than what the pictures look like. Guests can be drop-dead miserable, they can be ready to smash a wineglass so that they have something to slash their wrists with, but if the pictures are great, who cares? "What did you do?"

"I wore a tobacco brown, my mom wore navy, my sister wore raisin, and so Marian didn't stick out as much. But it was a summer-afternoon wedding. The bridesmaids were in primrose. I had been going to wear aqua and my mom and sister were going to be in lavender and periwinkle. It would have been so pretty if Marian had been willing to wear a midtone green, a celadon or a jadeite. To this day, I can't look at some of the pictures and not get angry."

I leaned to the side as the waiter set down my dessert. It was a showy-looking thing with flying buttresses of spun sugar. To my mind, everyone in the story was wrong—the mother of the groom for insisting on wearing black, everyone else for caring so much. "Then I'll wear beige. I can do that. But I'm going to have trouble if they tell me to wear celadon. I have no idea what that is."

“And the other thing,” said yet another woman. “When the babies come, you have to let her mother go first. My mother-in-law was furious because I wanted my mother as soon as I got home. She spent the first two years of Graham’s life complaining because she thought that my mother got to see him more than she did.”

I had to admit that when I brought Jeremy home, I was much more interested in having my mother come help than Marge. But she was not only my mother; she was also a pediatric nurse.

Dresses and photographs didn’t matter to me, but babies did. I wondered if I would play the nurse card in order to get my hands on a grandbaby as soon as possible. “Cami and Jeremy are about to start medical school,” I said. “Then they have their internships and residencies. We have time to figure out the postpartum schedule.”

“No, no,” the neighbor lady said, now joining the conversation. “You can tell yourself that you’re being cooperative, but watch out. If you set a pattern, if you let her family think you’re a pushover, that’s going to last. I have boys, and their mothers-in-law decide everything—which holidays my sons will be *allowed* to come to my house. Then it never lines up, so I never have everyone together. You know the saying, ‘a son’s a son until he takes a wife.’ You have to be realistic. You’re in competition with her parents. That’s just the way it is. You both want the same thing, the kids to visit you, not the other family.”

I winced. I suppose I did want to be a "fun" grandma. I couldn't bear it if the boys had to drag their families to visit me with the same dread and reluctance we had felt about visiting Marge. That would be awful.

"Don't the Zander-Browns have a big house in the Hamptons?" Beth Vindern asked. "How are you going to compete with that?"

"Darcy has a very big house herself," one of the Selwyn moms put in loyally.

"Actually, I don't anymore." I felt as if someone were sticking pins in me. And of course I was competing not only with the big house in the Hamptons; I was also competing with the premium cable-TV package of the house we were in.

How bitter, how hostile these women were. How could I keep that from happening to me? "Let's go back to talking about me wearing beige," I said brightly. "I'm going to be facing that long before the babies come."

"What about keeping your mouth shut?" Beth Vindern said. "Won't that be even a bigger problem for you?"

She had spoken with the mock-teasing air that Mike's mom specialized in. I hated that. If you tried to defend yourself, the other person would just accuse you of not being able to take a joke.

But what Beth had said wasn't fair. I'm not one of those people who insist on talking all the time, telling long, pointless stories about themselves. Furthermore,

I'm a health-care professional; I am scrupulous about patient confidentiality.

Of course, when someone is being a jackass and keeping everyone else from doing anything, I do try to get the traffic moving. Beth probably hadn't forgiven me for the regatta at which I had told her that her son was absolutely not suffering from hypothermia and she needed to get out of the way of the EMTs who were trying to examine the kids who might be.

I suppose I could have gently explained to her that as a coxswain, racing in a hooded waterproof jacket and long pants, her son was less vulnerable than the rowers in their thin Lycra unitards. I could have drawn her attention to the fact that Josh, although shivering, was coherent and his color was good while two of the rowers, their faces waxy, were growing disoriented.

But I hadn't. I had been quick and blunt. So now, years later, she was retaliating.

Why do people think it is okay to tease me? I hate it as much as the next person. My nice mom-type therapist said that people were trying to get a reaction and that I should call them on it, that I should hold them accountable. *I'm sure that if you knew how critical that sounded, you would not have said it.*

She was probably right. When I didn't react, when I just brushed people off, they kept poking and poking, trying to get a reaction, not stopping until they could tell that they had hurt me. But I couldn't make myself respond; I couldn't let them see that I was hurt. I wasn't going to let them know that they had any power over me.

But they do have power over you, my therapist said, *they do hurt you.*

Yeah, okay, but I didn't have to let them know.

Why don't you stand up for yourself? she asked.

She was wrong. This wasn't about standing up for myself; this was about not letting other people see me sweat. There was a difference. There had to be.

Jeremy's Selwyn friends who had come without girlfriends were all seated at one table, and as the first course was being served, I'd noticed sudden activity at their table. The guys were on their feet, squeezing their gilt caterer's chairs closer. One lifted a chair from the younger-siblings table, carrying it overhead as he threaded his way back to their table. Another scooped up one of the place settings from that table while a third had Annie by the arm, escorting her to the newly laid place. She was laughing and protesting, a lovely sprite in a moss-green dress. You couldn't blame them for wanting her at their table.

This left Zack, although he was a year older than Annie, stuck at the younger-siblings' table, in charge of Finney. He couldn't have been happy, but he was soldiering on. He had his arm propped up on the table, the side of his wrist twisted toward Finney. Finney was trying to reinsert Zack's cufflink. At one point Zack bent sideways, his black hair brushing close to

Finney's head, so that he could observe the procedure and offer advice.

I was proud of him . . . and wished there were some way to let college-admissions committees know about this moment.

Just as my table was trying to figure out how to eat our spun-sugar flying buttresses, Guy came over to me. "Here you are," he said, kneeling so that I didn't have to crane my neck to talk to him. "I hope you're having a good time."

"Of course." What else could I say?

"Finney's about had it. I don't know where the communication breakdown occurred, but the caterer thought he had a peanut allergy, not corn."

Virtually all the dishes had been sauced or glazed. "What did he eat?"

"Salad with oil and vinegar and a fruit plate. Apparently he kept wanting to come sit with you because he was sure the food at your table had to be better."

"That's the nicest thing anyone has said to me all evening."

"I hope that's not true," Guy said gallantly. "But when you decide to write a cookbook, you need to let me represent you."

I had no interest whatsoever in writing a cookbook. "Don't hold your breath."

"I never do." Then he got down to his real business. It was long past Finney's bedtime, and the driver had arrived to take him back to the house. "We knew he would want to leave before we could, so Annie agreed to go with him. That's when we thought we would all be at the hotel. What should she do about getting into the house? And what can he eat? I'm afraid you've become the bell to his Pavlov's dog. He'll see your house and start to want to eat . . . as would I."

"The leftovers from lunch are in the refrigerator. Annie can figure out the microwave, can't she?" I glanced over to the table where Annie was sitting. Rose was talking to her, one hand on the back of her chair.

Annie didn't want to leave. Who could blame her? Eight tall college rowers were fawning over her. Even if a major bribe had been involved in Annie's agreeing to leave, Rose couldn't be having an easy time trying to get her to stick with the plan.

I dropped my napkin next to the dessert plate. Whatever sweets I had at home would almost certainly be tastier than this minicathedral. "Let Annie stay. I'll go with Finney. My father is probably ready to leave too." He had been seated next to Mike's mother. "If Finney's comfortable with us, we can put him to bed."

Guy was looking at me, his bright eyes assessing.

"I won't feel like Cinderella," I assured him.

"Then that will be great," he said. He was going to take me at my word, not wasting time on "are you sure?" polite mumbo jumbo. He went to tell Rose and get the EpiPen. I found Claudia and thanked her. For which she thanked me. We were getting good at that.

She glanced down at her wrist. Her pearl bracelet

was an interesting little evening watch. She was checking the time.

If she had been anyone else, I would have told her that I liked her watch, but undoubtedly she would have thanked me, and I'd again be standing here, trying to figure out what to say. So I moved off to the younger-siblings' table and reminded Zack that he and Mike were leaving for their college visits tomorrow and they had a six a.m. flight. I was offering him an excuse in case he wanted to leave early. He nearly trampled me to get to the door.

Needless to say, Zack was not happy the next morning. He didn't want to get up at four thirty. He didn't want to visit colleges. He didn't want to be with his father. But he had to do all three.

Cami and Jeremy were going back to New York with the Zander-Browns, so the car returned mid-morning to pick up the kids for the return trip. Finney went dashing outside, eager to show his parents the tie around his neck. "The grandpa . . . Doctor . . . Doctor Bow-wow . . . he stood behind me, and I put my hands on his. Like this." Finney launched into a full-body, air-guitar version of a four-in-hand knot, his arms waving as if he were signaling aircraft.

Typical family chaos followed. Annie couldn't find the little bag with all her earrings. Guy's cell phone was ringing. Rose noticed that Annie's school back-pack was still exactly where it had been on Saturday; she hadn't worked on her paper. Cami hugged me, telling me that she'd known we would love Finney. I got the rest of the Kosher-for-Passover Coke and gave it to Finney. He thanked me. Then Rose thanked me. Finney tried to decide if he wanted the Coke in the trunk or in the car with him. Then Guy and Annie thanked me. Finney thanked me again. Finally, Rose got them all into the car.

Dad put his arm around my shoulders as we watched the car pull away.

"That seemed like a success," he said. "Your mother would have liked them."

That was true. She would have been drawn to Guy in the way everyone was, and she would have approved of the way Rose was bringing up her kids. But what would she have thought of Claudia? That's what I wanted to know.

I took Dad to the airport that afternoon, and things seemed very quiet when I got home. It would, I realized, be the first night that I had slept alone in this house.

That was something I would have to get used to.

I stripped the sheets off Dad's bed, put them in the washer, and tried to figure out what to do with the leftovers that had accumulated in the refrigerator. I opened my laptop and searched on my favorite Web sites, but found no useful advice about what to do with two-day-old grilled, corn-free hamburger patties.

I was kidding myself. I wasn't online to do culinary research. I was there to check out Claudia's Web site, to see if she had written up a description of the party. I typed in her URL and clicked on the link for the blog. The most recent post was from the Thursday before the party, in which she had warned her readers that she wouldn't be posting until after the event.

I scrolled through some of the replies posted since Thursday. People were wishing her the best, saying that they were sure the party would be wonderful.

Maybe I should post: *Hey, folks, I was there, and it sucked. Everyone was late because she lives so far away from everything, and she tried to poison a very sweet little boy . . . but everything was beautiful, and she had gone to a tremendous amount of work, and everyone, except for me, seemed to have a good time.*

I got up and switched the sheets from the washer to the dryer. I gathered up the towels from Zack's bathroom and started those. My laptop was in the dining room. On my way to the kitchen, I hit the Refresh button, but it was still Thursday in Claudia's Web site world. I threw out the hamburger patties and put the leftovers container in the dishwasher. I wrapped the buns and froze them so that I could throw them out next month. The sheets wouldn't be dry yet, so there was no point in going to the basement. I hit Refresh again.

And there it was, a new message, posted while I was throwing out leftovers.

She thanked everyone for their kind thoughts and was sure that their good wishes were behind the party's great success. She said she was amazed at how satisfied she felt; creating an evening for others to enjoy could be as satisfying as completing a new dress from a pattern you've designed yourself. She went on about the guests, the "high-profile Washington journalists" and the "powerful K Street lawyers," people she described as "our" friends.

Our? How many of those people had she met before the night of the party? Only that one neighbor couple who had been seated at the losers' table with me.

The final paragraph was marked with the conch shell she used whenever talking about her trademarked Managed Perfectionism. She acknowledged that one incident had happened that could have spoiled the evening. An appropriate meal was not prepared for a guest with severe allergies.

Don't expend energy trying to assign blame, she wrote. *Blaming doesn't solve the problem. Nor does dwelling on the mistake, offering endless apologies. You'll ruin the evening for everyone else. Give yourself ten minutes to fix things, but no more. Do the best you can and then send flowers in the morning.*

Well, damn. That was good advice, sensible, practical, well expressed. I didn't want Claudia to be sensible and practical. I wanted her to be shallow, superficial, and pretentious. I wanted to be able to dismiss her in the way she seemed to be dismissing me.

If she were dismissible, she wouldn't be dangerous.

Zack came back from his college visits feeling worse than ever. He and Mike had gone to some big schools that Zack might have gotten into—the universities of

Michigan and Wisconsin—and some smaller ones, Beloit and Kenyon, for which he didn't have a prayer. It was a toss-up which he loathed more at the moment, the schools or his father.

Travis Jackson, his school counselor, called me Wednesday afternoon. "He needs to visit a college by himself. Let him try to imagine himself being a student there." He recommended that we have Zack drive himself up to Stone-Chase College, a small liberal arts school about sixty miles north of D.C. Travis thought we should do this right away. He would set up the appointment at Stone-Chase and make arrangements with Zack's teachers.

As close as it was, I had never heard of Stone-Chase College. It wasn't a place that D.C. private-school families send their kids.

"It's only a visit," Travis said. "It's a friendly place, and the campus is beautiful. He needs to start feeling more positive about the college experience."

So Zack spent Friday up there. "How did you like it?" I said as soon as he came home that afternoon.

"It was okay," he said.

Normally a comment like that from Zack came with a shrug, a physical disclaimer asserting the unimportance of whatever was being discussing. *Sure, it was okay, but what a stupid-ass thing to care about.* But this time he did not shrug.

"People weren't totally stressed out like they were at those other places," he continued. "They weren't all full of themselves, either."

This was extremely high praise.

We had been here before, when Zack, miserable at Selwyn, had visited Alden and its "kick-ass" light board. Alden had been right for Zack. I was very encouraged by his response to this Stone-Chase place.

"How competitive are the admissions?" I asked, a tactful way of finding out what his chances of getting in were.

"They're cool," he said. "They seem to be all about ignoring freshman grades if you can just show that you've gotten better. In fact, you'd think that they actually liked people who had shit to figure out. The lady I interviewed with said that there was no question about my getting in. It was just a question of how much money I'd get."

"Money?" There was no way that Zack could qualify for financial aid. We hadn't even picked up the forms.

"It's merit money. They discount the tuition when they want somebody. And the more my SAT scores go up, the less Daddy will have to shell out."

He said the word *Daddy* with fierce sarcasm. He wanted to thumb his nose at Mike. Right now he would have loved not to take any money from him at all.

"Dad doesn't mind paying the tuition," I said urgently and truthfully. "You shouldn't pick a school because of the money. What do you like about the place?"

His answer was vague. He was done talking.

As soon as he left for his Friday-night prowls, I picked up the material he had brought home. All schools make themselves sound great in their brochures and catalogs. I couldn't figure out what he found so appealing about Stone-Chase. Monday morning I called school and left a message for Travis Jackson.

Travis called me after he had had a quick conversation with Zack. "I imagine what appeals to him is that Stone-Chase has a good track record for getting these late bloomers or kids with mild learning issues into medical school or dental school."

"Medical school? Zack?" I couldn't believe that I had heard him right. "Medical school?"

"They don't go to Harvard or Hopkins, but they go to perfectly respectable schools and do become doctors if that's what they want."

Because he has my memory for concrete facts and is nimble-fingered enough to be good in a lab, Zack had always gotten his best grades in science classes; but he had never said anything about wanting to go to medical school. In fact, he taunted Jeremy for being such a grind.

That evening, in as neutral a tone as I could muster, I raised the issue with him.

"Not medical school." He grimaced. "God, no. Who would want to do that?"

"Okay." I let the subject drop, but when I was doing the dishes later in the evening, he wandered into the kitchen and started opening and closing one of the drawers. Slide, thump; slide, thump; slide, thump.

When my Ritalin is wearing off, as it was now, repetitive sounds drive me crazy. I was about to tell him to stop when he spoke.

"You know, next door to the old house, Dr. Taft—did you ever see some of his before-and-after pictures? They were pretty incredible. And Dr. Cheryl, I loved going there."

Andrew Taft, our former neighbor, was an oral surgeon specializing in maxillofacial trauma. Cheryl Schwartz had been the boys' pediatric dentist. Her patients stretched out on brightly colored kid-size examining chairs and emerged laden with balloons, stickers, and neon pencils. Kids who had to get Novocain shots got their faces painted. Except for a higher standard of cleanliness, her office had a lot in common with a circus.

Did Zack want to be a dentist? I'd had no idea. He had gone trick-or-treating as a cowboy, a fireman, and a Power Ranger, but never as a dentist.

"So you're interested in dental school?" I asked. My long-haired, skateboarding, recovering-slacker son . . . a dentist?

"Not necessarily." He wasn't looking at me. That meant that he wasn't telling the truth. He *did* want to go to dental school. "But you know how Dad was always yelling at me because I was 'closing down my options.' So this is just keeping an option open, but there's no reason to blab about this all over Kingdom Come."

"I wasn't going to, but why the secret?"

"Oh, you know . . ." Now he was back into the shrug mode. "There's a pretty big dork factor in that career path."

"Let me at least tell Dad."

"Why would you want to go and do that?"

"He won't ride you so hard if he knows."

"Okay . . . if you have to."

I called Mike later the evening. The idea of Zack's becoming a dentist surprised him too. "But even if we accept that as a working premise," Mike said, "it doesn't mean he has to go to a place we've never heard of."

"It's named after two Marylanders who signed the Declaration of Independence."

"What earthly difference does that make?"

"None, I guess."

There was no question that Stone-Chase didn't have the prestige of the schools that Jeremy had applied to. The average SAT scores of Stone-Chase students were hundreds of points lower than those at Pomona College, where Jeremy was. Instead of being from the top 10 percent of the best high schools in the country, the Stone-Chase students came from the top third of their classes in midsize public schools. It had no national reputation.

"I know you think I'm being a big snob," Mike said. "But college is also about making contacts; it's about being around people with a sense of possibility. A lot of kids at these regional schools have a provincial attitude. They assume that after college they'll go back home."

"He's not going to make any useful contacts if he hates the place."

Fortunately, Cami and Jeremy were handling their medical school applications with all the discipline, motivation, and efficiency that Zack lacked. I was glad of it. Every few days Jeremy would send Mike and me an updated spreadsheet, recording the status of all their different applications. Each school had its own set of hoops that applicants had to jump through, and a person had to be pretty obsessive to keep track of each little step. Of course, most people want their doctors to be meticulous about details, so perhaps the process made some sense. Not a lot, but some.

I couldn't stop reading Claudia's blog. Even when she didn't post, other people did. Clearly she was a celebrity in this world of people who sewed for themselves and others. They were interested in her; they coveted her approval. Every few days she would refer to one of the comments, mentioning the writer by name, praising her insight into whatever sewing or design issue was being discussed. Before the day was over, the person singled out for the praise would reply, genuinely thrilled at having been noticed.

This was a world I knew nothing about, not just the sewing part, but the whole online-community thing. Claudia's followers were women who knew one another and cared about one another even though they had never met. I didn't get it.

Even stranger was Claudia's being at the center of it, and she seemed as open and warm as any of them. I couldn't reconcile this with the woman in the seafoam-green dress who wouldn't look me in the eye. I didn't want other people to like her. Yes, she had great posture, a risky hairdo, a premium cable package, and an entrepreneurial spirit, but people at the party Saturday night—Mike and my boys, Cami and her family—shouldn't like her. They should like me.

Five

I got a thank-you note from Rose. Folded inside was a drawing by Finney. An Egyptian-like stick figure with a triangular skirt carrying an object the size of her blob-shaped head. The object looked like a brown UFO with a red midline, but underneath it Rose had written, "Mrs. Darcy's hamburger with ketchup." Finney had used brightly colored markers; Mrs. Darcy's lips were as crimson as the ketchup, and her eyes were cobalt buttons. Just as my own boys had done at his age, Finney had worked with a heavy hand, bearing down so hard that the ink had bled into the paper. I put the drawing on my refrigerator door. This was what my house had been missing, little-kid art on the refrigerator door.

I'd looked at the drawing before reading the note.

After thanking me for lunch and the great time her kids had had, Rose invited Jeremy, Zack, and me to the Hamptons for Thanksgiving and some heavy-duty wedding planning. She would also, if it was all right with me, like to invite my father.

I love Thanksgiving. It's my favorite holiday. I love cooking for it, and I'm thrilled that no one expects me to buy gifts or create charming craft projects with gold spray paint and fake snow. My grandmother had given me her big white tablecloth, and I used it at Thanksgiving. However well it got laundered, it would always have several faint amoeba-shaped reminders of gravy stains and some pinkish splatters, the result of cranberry sauce dribbling off a spoon. I didn't care. I saw enough clean white linens at work.

So, go to the Hamptons for Thanksgiving? Was this what the women at the engagement party had been warning me about? That I would never again have my family at my house for a holiday?

But to refuse the invitation made no sense. Rose and Cami had a lot of decisions to make about the wedding during the Thanksgiving weekend. Cami wanted Jeremy there, and that's where he wanted to be. So, if I wanted to be with both of my sons for my favorite holiday and—as important—to have the two of them be with each other, I had to let go of the whole mitochondria-DNA tablecloth thing.

I checked with Zack and then called Rose. "Of course you can invite my dad, but you have to let me bring some of the food."

"Only some of it?" she asked. "Guy and Finney are going to want you to bring everything. But first, tell me what your family does about holidays. Do you celebrate them with Mike and Claudia, or do you split the time?"

Oh, crap. It wasn't enough to renounce my grandmother's tablecloth. I still had the Mike-Claudia issue. I didn't want them there, at least I didn't want *her* there, but it didn't seem right not to have Mike. He'd celebrated every holiday with the boys and me, even after he'd moved out.

"Actually," I said to Rose, "this is the first time we've had to deal with that. Mike only met Claudia this summer."

She paused. "You're kidding."

"No. They met in June."

That surprised her. "I got so many e-mails from Claudia before the party, and she was so chatty and friendly and so excited about the wedding that I assumed she would be the one I'd be dealing with during this process. Once I got here, I realized that I had it wrong, but *June?*"

"Until Saturday she had only met Jeremy once, and I hadn't met her at all." I could hear how tight my voice was. All through the planning of the engagement party Rose had thought that I didn't matter?

"I don't know what to say," Rose said. "She gave me the impression that their relationship was very established. But I can't invite Mike and not her, not after she put on that party. So, do I invite neither of them or both of them?"

I knew what was right. If Claudia wanted to be part of the family, I should treat her that way. I should welcome her. I should be saying to Rose, *Yes, by all means, invite both of them, put them in a room next to me, and, if I'm lucky, the walls will be thin and I can hear them having sex.*

"I can't tell you who to invite to your house and who not to," I said instead.

"I don't know why not. Everyone else does," she said bluntly. "You try having a big house too many people want to visit. We bought this place last May, and at one point during the summer I felt I should be circulating my guest lists for public comment. So you need to do better than that. Tell me what you want me to do."

"I don't know. The boys and I have never celebrated a holiday without Mike. On the other hand, having him in a room down the hall with another woman . . . I suppose I need to get used to that."

It wasn't really about sex—or if it was, I was too deeply in denial to admit it—it was about another woman having the right to be at a holiday gathering with my family. Was that part of Claudia's plan in hosting the engagement party—to box us in so that we had to include her in everything? If so, it had worked.

"Well, you don't have to get used to it on my watch," Rose said briskly. "I'll invite them, but I'll make reservations for them at a nearby inn."

"Oh." I thought for a moment. Rose apparently did think it was about the sleeping arrangements . . . but even so, it was a good plan. Mike and Claudia would be there, but not all the way there. There would be something slightly second-class, B-list about their invitation. I probably shouldn't have liked that, but I did. "Thank you," I said to Rose. "Thank you." I wasn't used to people making allowances for my feelings . . . probably because I usually pretended that I didn't have any.

My father decided to come as well. He had never been to the Hamptons, and he liked to go to new places. "And I can still write prescriptions," he said. "I'm bringing my own EpiPen."

When Mike found out that my father was coming, he called me. "What should we do about my mother? Should we say something to Rose and Guy about her?"

So we were a "we" again. "Mike, we're their guests. We can't invite our own relatives." If I was indeed locked in a lifelong battle with my son's in-laws about holidays, Mike's mother was the last prisoner I would ask to be exchanged.

"But they invited your dad. Why did they do that?"

"I don't know," I said, although I did. People liked my dad, and he knew his way around an EpiPen. A more perfect guest the Zander-Browns couldn't have found.

"I know that this is at their house," Mike complained, "but this is our family holiday too. I don't like how fragmented things are becoming. If you hadn't sold the house, we could at least have Christmas there and we could control who was invited."

And if he hadn't moved out on me, all kinds of things would be different. He was the one who had started the fragmentation, not me.

He and I had imagined that we would be in the old house forever. We had seen ourselves hosting huge Thanksgiving dinners and having Christmases with so many grandchildren that brightly wrapped presents would spill across the living-room floor far beyond the branches of the tree.

Of course, we'd never thought about how we were going to accomplish this, how we were going to keep our boys and their families always coming to our house, and only our house, for holidays. I suppose the safest way would have been to encourage them to marry orphans or women who loathed their own families. The worst way, of course, had been for us to have divorced and sold the house.

Claudia's blog was getting boring. She apologized for how much space she had devoted to her personal activities and launched into a discussion of the challenges of machine quilting with metallic thread. Metallic thread would provide sparkle to holiday projects, and with the proper needle . . .

I'd never registered with the site. Registering would have given me the right to purchase her patterns or post comments, neither of which I wanted to do. Registering would have also given whoever administered the site access to my name. I wondered if Claudia could find out who the nonregistered "guests" were. My user name was nursemom23. The boys had picked it; the 23 meant nothing except that twenty-two other women wanted the world of cyberspace to know them as "nursemom." At least I assumed they were all women.

If Claudia did have a list of her lurkers and stalkers, would she know that nursemom23 was me? That would stink.

Rose and I were exchanging daily e-mails about Thanksgiving plans. She had been planning on getting most of the dishes from a caterer whom she trusted not to use corn products. But I kind of got in the way of that. I volunteered to take care of the sweet potatoes, the mashed potatoes, the cranberry relish, and the pies. Oh, and the green beans and, if they didn't mind, the ambrosia salad. I apologized for the salad. "It's Kool-Whip, coconut, canned mandarin oranges, and minimarshmallows. It's 1950s cuisine at its worse, and we can't let Finney near it, but we always have it at Thanksgiving. It's our worst family tradition."

She laughed. "Guy grew up on food like that. He'll love it."

Then, a week later, she e-mailed me, saying that Claudia was going to bring the pies.

Claudia was bringing the pies? She hadn't mentioned that on her blog.

I make a fabulous pie. Even Mike's mother says that no one makes a piecrust like I do. People are always asking me for my recipe, and of course I give it to them, but the secret isn't in the ingredients. It's the technique as well as understanding and respecting the molecular structure of different fats. I cut the shortening into a finer crumb than the butter. Once I add the water, I hardly even breathe on the dough. I'm not vain about much, but I am about my pies.

This was far too important an issue for e-mail. I called Rose. "Are you sure Claudia understands about Finney's allergies? Don't you remember what happened at the engagement party?"

"I don't think she's the sort of person who makes the same mistake twice. She's already talked to the pastry chef."

The pastry chef? She was going to *buy* these pies? We were going to have store-bought pies on Thanksgiving? Don't they take your citizenship away for that? "But you've said yourself how easy it is to forget. Some people automatically dust their bottom crust with cornstarch." I did that when a fruit filling looked particularly runny. "They may do it without thinking. They may not believe her. They may not take her seriously."

Who was sounding like the food-allergy mom now?

"I suspect," Rose said carefully, "that Claudia is very capable of making people take her seriously."

Of course she was.

"Is there something you aren't telling me?" Rose asked.

"No, no. I just like making pies, that's all."

What a liar I was. This was about more than pies or even Finney's health. It was about my role as the Pie-bringer Queen. Claudia was trying to dethrone me. First she had left me off the guest list and then had put me at the losers' table. Now she was bringing the pies. Why hadn't the divorce agreement covered things like this?

Since I was hauling only slightly less food than a family setting out on the Oregon Trail, I was driving to the Hamptons for Thanksgiving. In order to beat the traffic, I left Washington before dawn on Wednesday. Zack had morning classes; he would fly up in the afternoon.

Everything I had read about the Hamptons commented on the light, how clear and crisp it was supposed to be. This light had lured artists to come out from the city and to turn garages and sheds into studios. But I, good midwesterner that I am, noticed how fertile the soil was. The crowns of trees were broad and spreading. On either side of the highway were the cultivated fields, now fallow for the winter. Many of the farms had roadside market stands. Most were boarded up with sheets of plywood, but some were still open, selling decorative gourds and the peach jams and strawberry preserves made from the summer's harvest.

Guy's assistant, Mary Beth, had sent me directions that were easy to follow. I took the Montauk Highway, then turned left on Mecox Road just past the watermill. I passed the inn where Claudia and Mike were staying. It looked quaint and historic. Then the road bent to the left, then to the right. Some of the houses were also quaint, charming places with shingles and porches, nicely sized for second homes. But many of the houses were new, and their massive roofs loomed over the ten-foot privet hedges. I passed a house under construction; its yard was rutted with tire tracks and its walls were wrapped with Tyvek, the white protective material emblazoned with blue lettering. Immediately beyond it was the Zander-Browns' place. I slowed, found the break in the privet hedge, and then turned up a long gravel drive.

Because Cami and Annie had talked with such enthusiasm about their grandparents' rustic cottage in the Adirondacks, I was unconsciously expecting this house to have that kind of charm, despite its twelve bedrooms. But I was wrong. This house was very big, very formal, and very, very new.

Built from pale stone and cream siding, it was laid out in an L. My house was an L too, but other than that, my little Virginia farmhouse had nothing in common with this chateauesque creation. It had three visible stories, and the interior of the L formed a gravel-covered parking court. Two sides of the court were enclosed by the wings of the house. The remaining two were fortressed by low stone walls. Big stone planters—dish-shaped instead of the conventional urns—sat on top of the wall at careful intervals, and there were two similar planters on either side of the front door. The planters held several varieties of ivy, but, this being November, they looked a little sparse.

A two-seater metallic-blue BMW with a couple of big dents in the fenders was carelessly parked in the courtyard, managing to block any car that might be parked in the three-car garage. I pulled in close to one of the stone walls, hoping to stay out of the BMW's line of fire. I felt sure that it wasn't Rose's car. It was much too small to hold her share of the Oregon Trail load of food.

There was a small door near the garage. It was recessed and half hidden beneath an eave. I suspected that it led to the kitchen. I am a kitchen-door person, but since I didn't know who had driven the BMW, I went to the main door. It was ornate, with leaded side windows and a fan light. The doorbell appeared to be part of a correspondingly elaborate intercom system. I pressed the buzzer, and as I waited for a response, I peered through the window, seeing a wide front hall tiled in an icy marble. The walls had little niches for sculptures. All of them were empty.

A clicking emitted from the intercom. I pressed down on the little switch marked Speak, said my name, but got no reply. I tried the door even though the clicking didn't sound as if it had unlocked the door. And it hadn't. The door was locked. I spoke into the intercom again and got some more clicking. Clearly, the person inside didn't know how to work the intercom. I buzzed once more and went back to the side panel to continue my peering.

The stairs were wide and curved elegantly. My guess was that the main part of the house was laid out like a center-hall colonial with the living room on one side of the hall, the dining room on the other, and the kitchen and family room running along the back. Finally I saw the hem of a skirt descending the stairs. I stepped back so as not to be caught peering through the glass. A minute later, a woman opened the door. It was Jill Allyn Stanley, the novelist, the donor of the oversized espresso machine.

She looked older and more tense than in her photos. Thanks to some more Internet snooping, I now had a sense of her career—lots of early promise that had plateaued into a steady "good enough" kind of success. Wonen's book clubs read her, but she didn't get movie deals or big foreign sales.

"Are you Mariposa?" she asked me.

"Uh, no." She certainly wasn't guilty of ethnic stereotyping. No one had ever before wondered if I was named Mariposa. "I'm Darcy, Jeremy's mother."

"Oh, dear." She seemed to pay no attention to my introduction of myself. She looked even more tense. "Mariposa came two days ago, but I was working and I just couldn't have people cleaning, so I told her to come back today."

"Mariposa is the cleaning lady?"

"Yes. I had forgotten that she always came on Mondays. You don't think she will mind coming back a different day?"

How on earth was I supposed to know that? But it was hard to imagine that in an affluent area like this, the cleaning ladies had lots of free time right before a holiday weekend.

"I really need her to come back because I can't figure out the dishwasher. But maybe she'll come later on." Jill Allyn obviously decided to pursue hope as a strategy. She put her hand on the banister, ready to go back upstairs. "But if you don't have anything else to do right now, could you look at the dishwasher, see if you can get it to work?"

"Is it broken? Do you know where they keep the tools?" Give me a pair of needle-nose pliers and I'll try to fix anything. I frequently can't, but I enjoy trying.

"Tools? Oh, no, no, no. I don't think there's anything wrong with it. I just don't know how to work it. And Rose gets her knickers in a twist about people leaving their dishes all over." And with that, she went back upstairs, leaving me standing in the hall by myself.

I had been right about the layout of the house. On my left was what had been intended as a formal living room. It was furnished in more pale colors; it looked like a model home, although it lacked the accessories and the little unifying pots of ivy that had turned my house into such a showplace. The dining room, to my right, had—I counted—twelve chairs around the table and another six against the wall.

Behind the living room was a library with floor-to-ceiling shelves on three walls. Only one bank of shelves was full of books; the rest were empty, but there were still boxes and boxes obviously waiting to be unpacked.

Then, as I had suspected, the back of the house was open. The kitchen was at one end and informal eating space was in the middle; at the far end, a U-shaped arrangement of three pale leather sofas faced a huge flat-panel TV that hung over the fireplace like a painting. The whole space felt vast and impersonal.

There were several sets of double glass doors along the back wall. I opened one and went outside. A swimming pool was covered with a carefully fitted tarp. An elaborate outdoor grill had been built into a stone enclosure. A broad lawn extended to a marshy swath of reeds. Beyond those reeds was the ocean. I couldn't see it, but I could hear the steady murmur of wind and waves.

I went back inside, closing out the sound of the ocean. This was a beach house? To me, a summer home ought to be a glorious jumble, candy dishes full of unknown keys and paper clips, garages stuffed with croquet sets and kids' bikes, cabinets full of old board games, their boxes bleached and flattened. There should be a leaking shed with a wooden canoe, a stack of bushel baskets, and a rotary lawn mower. In that mess would be a sense of possibilities, ways to have fun, suggested by generations of other people having fun.

This house did not look as if anyone had ever had fun in it.

I found a very elegant half bath underneath the stairs. It was immaculate, but the roll was out of toilet paper. There wasn't even the empty cardboard tube. Apparently someone—Jill Allyn, no doubt—had taken the whole roll, not caring about the fate of others. Fortunately I had a little packet of Kleenex in my pocket. I washed my hands, dried them on my jeans—there was no towel—and then went into the kitchen to address the dishwasher issue.

Most people, when they can't figure out the controls on a dishwasher panel, discover that after they have loaded the dishes and wrestled with the soap dispenser. Jill Allyn Stanley had apparently had a defeatist attitude from the get-go. She hadn't put a single dish into the dishwasher. The counter was covered with teacups and crumb-studded plates. There were crumbs by the toaster, streaks of dried tomato sauce on the counter near the microwave, and little rectangular tea-colored stains all over. Apparently Jill Allyn drank a lot of tea and always put her used tea bags on the counter before throwing them in the trash . . . although she didn't always put them in the trash. A few sat on the counter, dried and slumped over, looking like desiccated mice.

Although the dishwasher had a variety of options for how and when to wash dishes, it was otherwise perfectly straightforward. I loaded it quickly, found detergent under the sink, and started it. I wiped the counters and closed the cabinet doors.

Although it was a million times bigger, this kitchen reminded me of the various time-share condominiums that Mike and I used to rent for family vacations. Everything was immaculate and impersonal. The dishes were white with a ribbed rim. The water and juice glasses had a similar ribbed design. The pots and pans were all from one manufacturer; they were still shiny, looking as if they had hardly been used. There were no coffee mugs printed with corporate logos, no fiesta-striped pitcher purchased for a margarita party, no stray serving dish left behind after a neighborhood pot luck.

I had always enjoyed cooking on our family vacations. All four of us would go to the grocery store together. With everyone piling things into the cart, we would have way too much food; at the end of the week, we would line up the uneaten apples and unopened boxes of crackers in hopes that the maids would take them.

I hadn't taken a real vacation since Mike had left. That was something I needed to figure out how to do.

Leading out of Rose and Guy's massive kitchen was a hallway that led to the garage and the door I had noticed earlier. As I went down it, I snooped. To my immediate left was a big pantry with a second refrigerator. Across from that was a built-in desk with a computer monitor and assorted devices that provided music, security, and internal communications. Recessed storage cupboards lined the desk side of the hall, while beyond the pantry was a back staircase, followed by another half bath, less elegant than its front-hall sister but possessing a full roll of toilet paper. The hall ended with a door to the garage. At right angles to that was the door to the parking court. Just inside that door were perhaps ten plastic pots of gold- and rust-colored mums. I moved them a bit and then unloaded my car, putting the contents of my cooler in the pantry refrigerator.

I was just finishing when I heard the little door open. I went down the hall to meet Rose. She apologized for not having gotten here before me. "I hope that Jill Allyn was at least mildly welcoming." She sounded as if she thought that there had been no chance of that.

"She thought I was the cleaning lady."

"Jill Allyn thinks everyone is her clean—Wait a minute. Why did she think you were the cleaning lady? Mariposa and her sister come on Mondays. We told Jill Allyn that when she said she wanted to come out early."

I explained about Jill Allyn's sending Mariposa away.

"You aren't serious, are you? The house didn't get cleaned?"

"It looks fine," I tried to say, but Rose wasn't listening. She was angry, and I didn't blame her. She jerked out the keyboard on the house computer, keyed in a code, and spoke into the intercom. “Jill Allyn, I’m here.” She was forcing her voice to be pleasant. “Could you come down and move your car so I can unload?”

We both looked at the intercom speaker. There was no answer, not even the bewildered clicks I had heard at the front door.

“I’m not sure she knows how to work the intercom,” I volunteered.

“It may be more than that,” Rose said darkly. “I’ll bet she isn’t where she’s supposed to be.” She tried a different code and spoke the same message. “Do you have friends who are this annoying?” she asked me while we were waiting to see what would happen. A moment later came the futile clicking as Jill Allyn tried to respond.

“No wonder those mums are sitting in the hall,” Rose said. “Mariposa was bringing her son, who was going to plant them.”

“Rose . . . Rose . . .” Jill Allyn called from the front of the house.

I followed Rose through the kitchen and out to the front hall. Jill Allyn was bending over from the railing. “I’m in the middle of a paragraph. I’ll drop my keys down and you can get someone else to move the car.”

Her aim was so bad that if I hadn’t spent years and years playing catch with my boys, the keys would have ricocheted off the wall, chipping the paint.

“Sorry,” she apologized for her bad throw. “Just bring them back up when you’re done, okay?”

No, that wasn't okay. "I'll leave them right here." I pointed to one of the empty sculpture niches.

She looked blank for a moment, as if she had never heard of a parking attendant—which apparently I now was—being so uncooperative. "All right," she said and started to move away.

"Wait a minute," Rose called up to her. "Don't go. You need to change rooms. I know that both Guy and Mary Beth told you when you wanted to come out early, that you needed to stay in the room over the garage."

"They said that, but it made no sense." Jill Allyn leaned back over the railing, her hair falling forward. "No one else was here, and I work so well in the front room."

"I understand," Rose acknowledged. She was having to speak with her head tilted back. "But now everyone is coming, so you need to move."

"I know that, and I will. I definitely will." Jill Allyn sounded a bit like Zack when he talked about his college applications. *Oh, don't worry. I'll get to them . . . just maybe not today.*

Rose picked up on that. "I would appreciate it if you could do it now."

"It doesn't have to be this minute, does it? I'm in the middle of a scene . . . and my stuff's all spread out. So if you need a room this instant, it'd probably be easier for you to reassign things a bit. I'm just suggesting that because it would be easier for you if you did it that way."

"That's not the issue," Rose said. "We have people coming who have never been here before, and Guy and I would like them to have rooms with views."

"If you're going to bring Guy into it, what do you think he cares about—me finishing this manuscript or who sleeps where? What's gotten into you?" Jill Allyn's voice was edged with contempt. "You never used to care about things like this."

"Maybe, maybe not. But I would like you to move."

"And I am going to . . . just not this very second. *I* still have work to do." She emphasized the *I* as if to say that Rose no longer had work to do. She flicked her hand, dismissing the issue, and then disappeared from the railing. Rose said nothing.

I was astonished, not just at Jill Allyn's phenomenonally bad manners but at the fact that Rose had caved. She had given up, let Jill Allyn have her way.

If Jill Allyn had been a superimportant "offend at your own peril" client, then Rose wouldn't have raised a fuss in the first place. But to take a stand, then back down . . . that didn't fit with the impression that I had of Rose. She'd seemed confident and poised. She'd struck me as reliable and straightforward, qualities that mattered a lot to me. So why had she let herself get into an "I'm more important than you" spitting match, and why had she let Jill Allyn win?

I followed her back into the kitchen. "If this is about me or my dad having that room, we don't care. We really don't."

"I know that," she said with a sigh. "I'm sorry you

had to witness that scene, but when it comes to Jill Allyn, I must have some sick inner need to punish myself. I can't think of any other reason why I put up with her. She and I have a long history—we were moms on the playground together—and sometimes it gets ugly like that."

"The way she was talking . . . that sounded like working-mom versus nonworking-mom crap. You work at the agency, don't you?"

"No." Her voice was tight. "I haven't really worked since Finney was born."

"Oh."

She turned her back to me and started fiddling with the toaster cord, tucking it behind the appliance. "You have to understand . . . he changed everything for us. He had his first surgery when he was a week old, and then he had a total of four. After he was finally able to start on solid foods, he was a mess until we figured out the corn allergy. Then we had to come out of denial about the fact that his issues weren't only physical. So, no, I haven't been working."

"I wasn't judging you," I said instantly.

"Other people have."

My guys had been healthy—thank God for that—but I'd seen the toll that a chronically ill child takes on a woman: the nights in the hospitals; the frustrating days of waiting for doctors to return phone calls; the research that never agreed with other research; the anxiety, the depression. It was hard to reconcile what I knew about such women with the glossy magazine article about Rose Zander-Brown who discovered new literary talent at her kitchen table.

Rose probably couldn't reconcile them either. She must have felt like a different person.

"Do you miss working?"

"Not at first. I was too busy and under too much stress. Everything was so complex—there were so many different issues—it all took over my brain. I don't regret the choices I made, not at all. Finney's doing so much better than anyone ever thought he would."

"And you have to give yourself a lot of credit for that."

She nodded. "I know that. But that orientation to the world, that practical, problem-solving, list-making, completely left-brain stuff, has spread. Like with this house, I didn't want to come out here and have to do more housework than I do in Brooklyn. We were supposed to have someone living here all the time and so on weekends we would just walk in with however many guests, and dinner would be ready. But Guy also thought that it would be a great way to support new writers. They could live here rent-free with a small stipend as long as they kept the lightbulbs changed and went to the grocery store before we came."

"That didn't work?"

"Hardly. We bought the place in May, and we've already been through two different caretakers. The first woman was fine when we came out here with a bunch of Annie's friends. But then over the Fourth of

July, we had a big party with people we knew professionally—editors and such—and she finally told me that talking to them was more important to her career than helping me in the kitchen. She thought that they wouldn't take her seriously if they saw her as kitchen help. Of course, I wanted to ask her if that meant that no one was taking me seriously, but I didn't want to know the answer to that one. So then we had two young guys—they were a couple—and they were pretty good, but we showed up Labor Day with two other families, and they had done nothing because they were both on deadlines, and couldn't imagine that anyone would think that going to the grocery store for *me* was more important than their work. And to top it all off, these people go back to the city and tell everyone that I'm a complete bitch. Just exactly what I set out to be in life—the boss's bitchy wife."

The nurses on the OB floor complain about the doctors' bitchy wives, coming in demanding the best rooms because their husbands are on staff. I wouldn't want anyone talking about me that way.

"How does Jill Allyn fit into this?" I asked. "She's the important, moneymaking client and you're the freeloading wife?" Some nurses pay way too much attention to what cars the doctors' wives drive and what jewelry they wear.

"That's what Jill Allyn would say," Rose agreed, "except when she needs to be my dearest friend. In the old days, she was our most important client. When we started the agency, we used to pride ourselves on taking manuscripts that no one else knew what to do with and making them work. Money was only one of the ways of gauging how you were doing, and we usually pretended that it was the least important. Then Finney came, and Guy felt powerless. The one thing Guy could do was make sure we provided for Finney. Making money started to count a lot. We—he—took on a different kind of a client. I'd been the one with the eye for the quirky, literary project that would get great reviews; he could spot the one that would get a movie deal. He turned out to thrive in a higher-stakes world, not just in the publishing deals but also in our own investments, so even after Finney's trust was set up, he kept going, and now we have this." She waved her hand around the marble foyer.

"So Jill Allyn's not as important as she used to be?"

Rose gave her head a slight shake. Her auburn hair swung around her neck. Her earrings were gold, but nothing fancy. "We've got some authors with seven-figure deals, and she's not one of them. In her heart, she knows that, so she uses the friendship to make herself seem important. She works it from both ends. She invites herself out here because she's our dear friend, our neighbor back in Park Slope, and then she won't change rooms out here because she's a client facing a deadline."

"Let's forget about her and get to work."

Rose had been leaning against the counter. She straightened, ready to get on with things. "But how," she asked lightly, "am I to forget about the fact that we wouldn't be working at all if Jill Allyn hadn't dismissed the cleaning lady?"

The house was, in fact, quite clean. Apparently Mariposa and her sister came out for a full day every Monday whether or not the Zander-Browns had come the preceding weekend.

I moved Jill Allyn's car. Rose pulled hers into the garage and we unloaded quickly. Then Rose took me up the back stairs to the room over the garage where I would be staying, now that Jill Allyn was squatting in the room originally intended for me.

It was a big, bright space, but the view to the front was of the road. The windows on one side looked down on the parking court. The other side faced the construction project next door. Furthermore, the dormers, necessary to the house's external grandeur, left the room cut up and difficult to furnish. There was no unbroken wall for the bed, so it was angled into a corner, protruding awkwardly.

"The people who built this house fired their architect and their first builder," Rose explained. "The second builder tinkered with the plans, and this is one of the results."

"Other people lived here? It seems so new."

"They never moved in. They split up two weeks before they were supposed to. We saved a ton of money, and they had already chosen all the furniture, so we could move right in."

"So you didn't choose any of the furniture downstairs?"

"God, no. I can't stand all those noncolors. I keep meaning to do something with the place, but once I get out here, I never seem to have the time."

Rose turned back the coverlet on the bed. Seeing that there were no sheets on it, she crossed the room to get a set from the closet. "I should make Jill Allyn do this."

"It's just making beds," I said. I had already stripped off the coverlet. "It's no big deal."

There are women who take care of their homes because they love the results—the peaceful, orderly rooms, the fragrance of home cooking. Not me. I like the process. I like the moving, the stretching, the lifting involved in housework. I don't care too much about what my house looks like; my kitchen is always clean and my beds are always made because I don't like to sit still.

But Rose got satisfaction from neither the process nor the result.

I'm not the most spiritual person on the face of the earth, but like most people who work in hospitals, I believe in institutions—schools, Boy Scouts, swim teams, the March of Dimes, organized religion. When I was pregnant with Jeremy, Mike and I joined a church and started hauling ourselves there every Sunday. I frequently volunteered to teach one of the youth Sunday school classes. As a result of that, I knew my Bible stories, one of which was the Mary and Martha story.

Mary and Martha were a pair of sisters. Jesus and

his followers came to their house. Martha set to work, preparing the food and doing whatever else was the New Testament equivalent of planting the mums and changing the sheets. Mary listened to Jesus preach. Martha appealed to Jesus, saying that she needed Mary's help. Jesus came down on Mary's side, saying that Martha was fretting too much.

I don't know what Martha was expecting in appealing to Jesus for support. Men always pretend that housework isn't important. But other than that, I had complete sympathy for her. If you divide the world into Marys and Marthas, I'm an off-the-charts Martha. I'm a doer, not a thinker. Given a choice between sitting at someone's feet listening to theology and being in the kitchen peeling carrots, I'd probably skip the chance to hear the Only Begotten Son and put myself on vegetable duty instead.

But Rose was a Mary, an intellectual, a scholar. Finney's birth had made her a Martha . . . and any decent woman would have done that for her child—but somehow the Martha-ness had taken over every aspect of her life, and here she was making beds while Jill Allyn wouldn't come out of Mary-dom long enough to move her car.

We finished the bed. I checked the bathroom for towels and toilet paper. It had both, but the lightbulb was out.

"The new ones are in the pantry," Rose said, "but let's do your dad's room first. It may need lightbulbs too."

There were three more bedrooms on this level, all of them facing the back of the house. Jill Allyn's corner room was over the kitchen; the master suite, which took up nearly half the floor space, was at the opposite end. Both of those doors were closed. Between them was the room for my father. Although less than a third of the size of the room over the garage, it had its own small balcony, a big, comfortable reading chair, and a view of the ocean. From these rooms you could see past the reeds and marsh and over a small bay to the ocean and its endless waves. I could see why other people would want a view like that, but I'm a mid-westerner. I'd rather look at a plowed field or an orchard of blossoming fruit trees.

There were lightbulbs, towels, and toilet paper in Dad's room, but no soap or wash cloths.

"Every room probably needs something," Rose said sighing.

The third floor could be reached only by the back stairs—another result, Rose said, of the original owners firing everyone who had any design sense.

This level was laid out like a college dorm, a long center hallway with four low-ceiling bedrooms on either side. Some had private baths; the others shared one with the adjacent room. This is how the house managed to have twelve bedrooms; eight of them were a little like a Holiday Inn Express.

"The family who built the place had two nannies," Rose told me, "and all their friends traveled with at least one. One way to throw your weight around is to insist that your nanny not only have her own room, but a private bath as well."

Those folks weren't going to be able to visit me. "Do people get pissed off when you put them up here instead of on the second floor?"

"You have no idea," Rose answered. "If I had any sense, I'd just have people draw straws when they walked in. Now let's make up Finney's bed and then leave the sheets out for everyone else to do their own."

We counted out sheets and checked the bathrooms for towels and toilet paper. Rose searched for missing pillowcases while I went to the pantry to get lightbulbs. Jill Allyn was apparently in the kitchen because as soon as I started making noise, she came to the pantry door.

"Lightbulbs," I said, lifting a package to explain what I was doing.

"No one likes her anymore."

I stopped. "I beg your pardon?"

"Rose. No one likes her anymore."

It takes a lot before I am speechless, but I was now. How could she possibly think that this was an appropriate thing to say?

"She used to be interesting. She was the first person I ever let read any of my manuscripts. But once Finney was born, she changed. She became a different person. For years that's all she could think about—Finney this, Finney that. It's really boring. I'm the only one who still sticks by her."

If this was "sticking by her," Rose probably would

have been better off being abandoned. "Don't you have children?" I asked.

"Yes, Jean-Paul. But I didn't stop working when he was born."

And Rose hadn't stopped working when Cami and Annie had been born. I had met dozens and dozens of women with special-needs children, and the only ones I judged negatively were the ones who hadn't changed, the ones who went on as if their lives were still the same.

"And now she's gotten so grand-dame-ish just because she has a big house in the Hamptons." Jill Allyn turned to go, then paused. "Oh, by the way, Jean-Paul is getting in late this evening. You're going back upstairs, aren't you? Will you be sure Rose knows that that's when he's coming?"

I doubted that Rose knew Jean-Paul was coming at all. His name had never come up when we had been sorting out sheets. Was this a hotel where people could invite their own families if they felt like it? It was a good thing that Mike hadn't known about that, or we would have been struggling to figure out where to house his chain-smoking mother.

"So will you tell her?" Jill Allyn repeated.

Jill Allyn had obviously labeled me as an easy mark. She had gotten me to clean up her dirty dishes, move her car, and give up the good room. But advanced-practice nurses are not easy marks. On the whole, we are pretty tough cookies. "No," I said. "You need to tell her that yourself."

"She must know," Jill Allyn said as if excusing herself from that duty. "I mean, she has to have figured it out. I'm here, where else would he be?"

Six

As we hunted for something to plant the mums in, I did tell Rose that Jill Allyn's son was joining us. As I suspected, this was the first she had heard of it. Having dropped out of college, Jean-Paul lived in Montreal, and that he wanted to be with his mother for each and every holiday was not an inevitable conclusion.

The Wednesday-afternoon transportation schedule was so complex and ever-changing that keeping track of it should have, Rose said, qualified as a thesis for an advanced degree in event planning. But by dinner that evening twelve of us were gathered around the table—the five Zander-Browns, the four of us Van Aikens, Claudia, Dad, and Jill Allyn. Jill Allyn's son didn't make it. He had missed his plane and, instead of rebooking himself, had gone back home.

"I bet he didn't even go to the airport in the first place," I overheard Annie say to Cami. "He hates his mom."

"You shouldn't say things like that," Cami reproved.

"But it's true."

Despite my covered wagon full of food, I had not brought a hostess gift. Claudia had. From a large flat box Rose lifted a table runner that was shimmering with amber, rust, and bottle green. There were twelve matching placemats and napkins. Claudia had made them. "Cami told me that you use white dishes here," she said.

"We do. These will look beautiful." Rose examined the items with a flattering interest. "It's nice to have something out here that isn't so desperately bland."

Claudia explained that although she had quilted the table runner and twelve placemats with gold metallic thread and although the amber layer was silk organza, everything was still machine washable. The pattern for the quilting lines was derived from a—

This was as extreme as my making my own ketchup. Was Rose a prize that Claudia and I were competing for? Did the winner get an invitation to stay in one of the four good bedrooms?

If so, I had a head start. I was already in one of those rooms—the worst of the four, it's true, but Claudia wasn't even in the house.

Yet.

For our Wednesday-night meal, a nearby Italian restaurant, carefully schooled in Finney's allergies, delivered a massive amount of food. Determined to compensate for being deprived of my pie opportunities, I had brought a pumpkin roll for dessert—it was a light spongy cakelike thing that I had baked in a jelly-roll pan and then filled with sweetened cream cheese.

Claudia might be able to quilt with metallic thread, but I could bake without corn products . . . and more people appreciated baking than metallic-thread quilting. I cut the pumpkin roll into twelve slices, and Cami passed around the plates.

"There's something terribly wrong with this," Guy said after his first bite.

I looked at him in surprise.

"You only made one. What *were* you thinking?"

Indeed, Finney had already finished his slice and was eyeing his mother's. "No," she said to him. "I love you with all my heart, but this is mine."

"Don't look at me," Guy added. "I'd take a bullet for you, my boy, but I'm not giving you my dessert."

I was about to slide my plate across the table to Finney, but my father had beaten me to it.

We had used paper plates so the cleanup went quickly. Claudia was loading the glasses and utensils into the dishwasher, and—no surprise—she was one of those people who washes the dishes before putting them in the dishwasher. We had a babysitter like that once. The girl would load the dishes after serving the kids macaroni and cheese, and in the morning I would start unloading the machine thinking that the dishes were clean, and only after I was halfway through would I realize that the machine hadn't been run, and I'd have to try to fish stuff back out of the cabinets.

See, I have servant problems too.

The adults were now standing around trying to decide whether to make another pot of coffee; the kids were talking about what DVDs they had brought.

There was a home theater in the basement, and they were all going down to watch a movie.

I didn't like that idea. I wanted us all to do something together.

I had no idea what the Zander-Browns' definition of quality family time was—for all I knew, they memorized Shakespeare's sonnets together. For me, if I couldn't convince people that cleaning the garage would be a happy, meaningful activity, I wanted to play games, preferably active, noisy, chaotic games.

And this garage was already way too clean. I thought for a moment. There had been a big Costco pack of flashlights in the pantry, and the weather wasn't at all that cold—at least it wouldn't be once we started moving. "Okay," I said, "who's up for flashlight tag?"

"Flashlight tag?" Jeremy sat up. "We haven't played that in ages. We used to love it, didn't we? Come on, Cami," he said, "you, me, and Finney are going to kick some major butt."

"Have you forgotten what Mom's like when she plays?" Zack said loyally. "She's ruthless."

"And I taught her everything she knows," my dad said.

"So who's in?" I said. "And no one is allowed to say that it's too cold."

Hands went up. At first Annie didn't raise her hand, but after Cami's "oh, come on, it will be fun," she said she would play.

Jill Allyn had stood up, but not because she wanted to participate. "I'm going back to work."

That was fine with me. She didn't seem much of a team player.

"And I'm afraid that I don't have the right shoes," Claudia apologized, gesturing down toward her feet.

I hadn't noticed her shoes before. If Rose wore shoes that I wasn't willing to pay for, then Claudia wore ones that I wasn't willing to walk in. Hers were narrow and pointy with stiletto heels and a little bow.

"Maybe we can find you a pair," Guy said to her. "Annie?"

"I wear a six, Cami a seven, and Mom an eight." Annie was apparently the one who knew everyone's sizes. "And I think Jill Allyn wears an eight and a half or a nine. We're bound to have something to fit you."

"No, I'm fine here, but thank you," Claudia said politely.

Mike had been standing up. He would have the right shoes. Never wanting to miss a chance to play a sport, he always had golf clubs, tennis and squash rackets, a small gym bag, and various athletic shoes in the trunk of his car.

But he sat back down. He felt obligated to stay inside with Claudia.

This was the first time I'd been conscious of them as a couple. They hadn't sat next to each other at dinner. I hadn't seen them touch each other or exchange a private conversation.

They were a couple. I knew that. But I wasn't going to think about it now, not when I had a game of flashlight tag to lead.

Jeremy and Zack wrestled the flashlights from their stiff plastic packaging while the rest of us got our coats. We trooped outside, leaving Rose to be polite with Claudia and Mike. It was a clear night, and we called to Rose to switch off the outdoor lights. Without streetlights, which were apparently not allowed on these once country roads, or the neon glare from businesses, the sky was like a children's picture book—inky black and filled with stars.

Dad, Zack, Annie, and I played against Cami, Jeremy, Finney, and Guy. Even though we were cutting Finney a lot of slack, I liked our team's chances. Annie didn't have much stamina, less even than my father, but she was quick and sly, good attributes in flashlight tag.

We had a great time. We started with one set of rules, switched to another, then modified those. Finney was not the only one who was confused.

Rose came out to watch for a moment. Dad and I tried to get her onto our team. "No, I should go back in."

Oh, screw them, I wanted to say. *I know what you want. You'd rather be out here with us.* But then Zack shouted at me to come help him rescue Annie.

We finally went in, tired, happy, full of talk about who had done what to whom. I was careful not to look at Mike. He would have loved playing as much as I did. It must have killed him to stay inside.

Guy and Rose took Finney up to bed. "So, Darcy," Guy said when they came back down, "is this what it means to be one of the 'fun moms'? That's what we learned about you at the engagement party. Jeremy's friends said that you were one of the fun moms."

"But not," Zack pointed out, "one of the 'cool moms.' No one called her a 'cool mom.' A fun mom, yes; a cool mom, no."

"What's the difference?" Guy asked. "And make it good. I like linguistic distinctions."

"The cool moms let you drink in their houses and the really cool ones buy the booze for you."

"And the really *really* cool ones," I put in, my Ritalin having long worn off, "have sex with your friends."

"Mom!" Zack was revolted. "We don't want to hear about that."

"And I don't have anything to say because I'm not even one of the ordinary cool moms."

"Ivan Coren's mom went down on Tim Beauchamp," Annie said evenly.

Everyone looked at her, shocked. "Annie, do not repeat things like that." Rose was firm.

Annie shrugged her pretty little shoulders. "Everyone knows it."

"We're getting off track here," Guy said. "This was a discussion of our language's lexicon. Darcy, you are our authority on this. What's involved in being a fun mom?"

"I have absolutely no idea. If I was a fun mom, it was by accident."

"That's probably it," Cami said. "The cool moms

are the ones trying to be your friends, the fun moms are just fun by nature."

"So the cool moms are trying to hold on to their youth?" Guy asked.

"And we fun moms," I announced, "have never lost ours."

"So, Mom," Annie challenged, turning to Rose, "what kind of mom are you?"

"A food-allergy mom," she replied instantly, something she wouldn't have said if Finney had been in the room. "After that I am a submarine mom. You've heard of helicopter moms who hover all the time. I am a submarine mom. I see all, I know all, I'm always there . . . you just don't know exactly where."

Annie grimaced. "I was afraid of something like that."

Early in this conversation, Claudia—being no type of mom at all—had started collecting the stray glasses and other debris. When she was finished, she glanced at her watch and did not sit back down. Mike understood the signal. He got up and turned to Zack and my dad. "Do either of you want a lift back to the inn, or were you going to catch a ride with Darcy?"

Zack spoke without thinking. "Oh, no, we're staying here. Mom is too."

There was a pause, an awkwardness, as Claudia and Mike realized that they were the only ones not staying at the house.

Claudia knew that the house had twelve bedrooms, and she could count. She knew that there was room for

Mike and her. Now it was her turn not to have been invited. Was she going to put that on her Web site?

Rose had told me that the house had a strong wireless signal, so I had brought my laptop, putting it on the bleached-pine desk that sat between two of the dormers in my room. When I got up there at the end of the evening, I checked to see if nursemom23 could get online. She could.

The only new things in my inbox were ads. I sent a quick message to my brother, saying that Dad and I had arrived safely, something that would not have occurred to him to worry about. I went to weather.com and checked on tomorrow's forecast. I couldn't think of any recipes I needed.

Oh, stop pretending. You don't care about the weather.

I typed in the URL for Claudia's Web site and went to the Projects page. Placemats, napkins, or a table runner, I learned, always make a lovely hostess gift. She had elected to make all three for an "upcoming Thanksgiving visit to the Hamptons." She had dyed silk organza amber and was layering it and quilting it over . . . I stopped reading and skipped ahead.

She wrote that white dishes were to be used at dinner so she had also chosen a fabric that had . . . I skipped that paragraph too.

The final picture was of a table set with all twelve placemats and napkins. A color-coordinated flower arrangement sat in the middle of the table runner. The plates were white, but they weren't ribbed, and the table in the picture was darker than the one in the Zander-Browns' house. Claudia had ordered flowers, set her own table with the placemats that she was giving to Rose, taken a picture, and posted it on the Internet, two days before she had given the placemats to Rose.

My ambrosia salad was as gag-o as ever, but the rest of the food at Thanksgiving dinner was great. While we were eating, Guy got the conversation around to the idea of self-branding, which had, at first, sounded to me like a masochistic activity not suitable for family conversation, but instead proved to be a marketing concept. A person—presumably one with an entrepreneurial spirit—developed an instantly recognizable identity for him- or herself on the order of Coke or All-Temperature Cheer.

Jill Allyn dismissed the concept, saying that your work ought to be enough. Mike, to my surprise, said that he and his partners had brought in a consultant who had helped them brand themselves as well-meaning, no-tricks, smart guys.

"But isn't that what you are?" I asked. "Don't you feel like you're playing a trick to get people to think that you don't play tricks?"

He shrugged; and that was my last contribution to the conversation, because the person who knew the most about this was Claudia.

She had customers and clients, the people who purchased her patterns, attended her workshops, or came to her for custom clothing. She'd built her business on all of them, especially the custom clients, having an experience that was serene but also purposeful and energized. Saltwater currents suggested that experience, and so she had developed a brand around such imagery. All the "visuals" associated with the brand were derived from a conch shell. The color palette of her stationery, her Web site, and her home came from the shell. She had found a font in which the *s* mirrored one of the lines in the shell, and she had used that not only on the stationery and Web site but for the house numbers beside her front door.

I thought about her Web site. Whenever she wrote about Managed Perfectionism, she tagged the passage with a picture of the shell.

She was still talking. Her professional wardrobe—the one she wore when she was giving workshops—was "edited" to reflect the shell. When she wanted to be the most obvious about it, she told us, she wore a nubby raw-silk blazer in the golden tan of the shell's rough exterior with a blouse of a pale, glowing pink. When she wore blues and greens, she chose ocean hues. Her jewelry was pearls or handcrafted necklaces of sea glass.

Annie was fascinated. "The color you're wearing now . . . that's oyster, isn't it?"

Claudia was in tailored trousers and a blouse with an open neck and a high stand-up collar. Both were in a pale fabric that I assumed was a heavy but liquid silk. The only color was a washed-out-green belt and a necklace with small greenish stones floating on a thin silver wire.

"What about navy and black?" Annie continued. "Don't you wear those?"

"Generally not. But if I have to wear black for a funeral or such, I'll use shell buttons and wear fresh-water pearls because they look closer to nature."

The shoes in which she hadn't been able to play flashlight tag last night had been a sandy taupe with a bow of weathered blue. Her watchband was an intricately braided hemp. Now that she spelled it out, I could see how these added up to a picture of an empty windswept beach on a cool day.

"Do you ever get tired of these colors?" Rose asked. "Don't you ever want to kick back and wear fuchsia or lime green?"

"No. I like subtle colors, and this is my professional wardrobe. If I felt the need to wear red and purple polka dots at home, of course, I would."

She said that with a complicit little smile as if to imply that we all knew that no sane person would ever want to wear red and purple polka dots anywhere.

"Do you go to the beach a lot?" Cami asked.

"I don't really have the time."

I was willing to bet that she didn't have the desire either. So far I hadn't seen any evidence that she had outdoor interests. This shell-ocean theme was something she had picked because she liked subtle colors. It didn't have a thing to do with her real self, whatever that might be.

What would my brand be if I had one? Nursemom23? Magenta and scarlet poppies on royal blue? Ritalin Queen? I was clearly too late to be Pie-bringer Queen; Claudia had already infringed on that trademark.

The pies were fine. They were certainly beautiful. The outer edge of the Dutch apple pie consisted of tiny circles of crust individually cut and overlapped. Even if the bakery had a machine that cut the circles, it would have been a ridiculous amount of work. In the center of the pumpkin pie were pieces of crust cut in the shape of autumn leaves. I wondered how the baker had done that. If you put the leaves on when the pie went into the oven, the filling would lap up over the edges. But if you put them on later, they might not brown.

For store pies they were excellent . . . although I probably shouldn't call them "store pies." They were more "boutique pies," and they were probably better than a lot of people's homemade pies, but they certainly weren't better than mine.

As we were cleaning up after dinner, I noticed Mike trying to get my attention. He was standing at the far end of the family room with Jeremy and Zack. I went over and stood between the boys, linking my arms with theirs, pulling them close to me. It felt normal, the four of us standing together, a unit within a larger group, a family.

But within moments Claudia joined us, standing next to Mike. She slipped her hand into his arm, curving her fingers around the sleeve of his navy blazer. Her fingernails were filed into ovals and polished with a light pearly peach. The cuff of her oyster-colored silk blouse slipped down her wrist, revealing her braided hemp watchband.

He's mine now. I belong here too.

He glanced down at her. I didn't know if he'd been expecting her to join us, but he seemed okay with it.

"Listen," he started, his voice heavy.

Zack immediately flinched, and I reminded myself that this wasn't normal anymore. "Be careful, Mike," I cautioned him. It wasn't super-duper nice of me to criticize him in front of Claudia, but he was about to make a jackass of himself. "No one is going to take it very well if you issue a bunch of orders."

Mike shot me a quick, hard look, but he didn't argue. "Okay, then take this as some strong encouragement."

"All right," I said, trying to sound mild. "We'll listen."

"You know that Friday and Saturday are going to be spent on wedding plans."

I nodded. Rose had begged everyone to enjoy Thanksgiving and not start fretting about the wedding until Friday. Mike and Claudia were not going to be around. First thing tomorrow morning they were driving to Philadelphia to see Mike's mother.

"I spoke to Guy," Mike continued, "just sorting out

what we would pay for—and it's clear that some very serious money is going to be spent on this wedding. When they said that everything was going to be here, I assumed that it would be a low-key home wedding, but—"

"Dad—" Jeremy interrupted. He didn't want to hear any criticisms of Cami's family.

Mike held up his hand. "And it is not our place to question their decisions. This is more than a family wedding for them; they have their own business and have obligations to Guy's professional associates. But even if that weren't the case, it isn't our place to judge what they're doing. We can say that we wouldn't spend this on one evening, but on the other hand, if I had made his kind of money, I would be damn proud of myself too. I'd probably want people to know it."

That wasn't true. Mike was not a grandstander. Being proud of himself would have been enough for him.

"The only one of us," he continued, "who has the right to say anything is Jeremy, and, son, I would advise you not to."

"I don't want Cami upset," Jeremy said. "That's all I care about."

"And nothing will upset her more than feeling as if she's caught between you and her parents."

"You don't have to worry about me," Zack said. "I'm staying out of this."

"And I'll keep my mouth shut too," I promised.

"So are we done here?" Zack asked.

"If you go help with the dishes," I said. "You too, Jeremy."

He grimaced at me, but moved toward the kitchen. Jeremy looked at us suspiciously for a moment, then followed his brother.

Claudia was still holding Mike's arm. She turned closer to him, clearly speaking to him and only him. "Have you resolved the rehearsal dinner?"

"Not yet," he answered, his eyes quickly shifting to me, then back to her. "I was about to bring it up."

"Then I'll go rescue the boys."

She did just that, going into the kitchen and waving Jeremy and Zack off from the chores I had assigned them. I don't care what kind of mom you are, you don't do that.

And what was she doing calling them "the boys"? They were seventeen and twenty-one. I could call them "the boys," Mike could, my father could, even Mike's mother could, but everyone else should respect their maturity.

I turned back to Mike. He was looking a little troubled. "So what's up with the rehearsal dinner?" I asked. "That's the groom's family's deal, isn't it?"

"Apparently so, and Claudia has offered to help plan it. I think she would like to. Is that all right with you?"

Not really. "I'm sure she'll be a lot better at it than I would be."

"It won't be like the engagement party. Your name will be on the invitation."

I knew that he was planning on paying for everything himself, and the stubbornly proud tomboy in me didn't want my name on anything I wasn't paying for. On the other hand, I was sure that I couldn't afford Claudia's very refined choices.

"Okay," I said. "I'm out of line here—"

"One of your strengths."

I stopped. Was I out of line so often that he could mock me about it? "That was a horrible thing to say."

He blinked. "Well, no, it isn't horrible. It is a strength—that you're willing to say things that no one else is willing to, things that need to be said."

"That's true, but that's not what you meant. You were being critical, and you know it." I started to walk off. I had just been trying to help. Let Claudia screw up. See if I cared.

He grabbed my arm. "Come on, Darcy, what were you going to say?"

If Claudia screwed up, I might not care, but Jeremy would. I took a breath. "Okay . . . it's about Claudia's Web site. My guess is that the Zander-Browns won't want anything about the wedding plans on her Web site."

He looked puzzled. "Why would she put anything on her Web site about their plans?"

Because that was what she did. The whole purpose of her life was to have things to post about. "I don't know . . . I'm not saying that she would or wouldn't; I'm just saying that it's probably a bad idea, and, for the sake of all of us, you might mention it to her."

"I can't imagine that she would, but I suppose it doesn't hurt to mention it."

I went into the kitchen. Claudia was at the sink, so I looked for something to do on the other side of the kitchen. The trash can was full. I started to gather up the loose edges of the black plastic liner. Someone had scraped the dessert plates into the can.

The top layer of garbage was crescents of uneaten piecrusts. People hadn't finished their crusts. They'd eaten the filling but left the elaborate outer rim on their plates. All the handling to make those perfect little circles and crimped edges had developed the gluten and made the crust tough.

No one ever left my piecrust on their plate.

Friday morning, Rose commandeered the long table between the kitchen and the family room for the wedding-planning session, laying out various brochures and printouts. She had four copies of many of them, one each for Cami, Annie, herself, and me. I poured myself a cup of coffee and as we were waiting for the girls, I picked up the glossy brochure from the tent-rental company. The photos made the tent look like something out of the boys' old King Arthur books. The white roof slanted sharply down from multiple peaks; it looked medieval and romantic. The interior shots showed a space that was soft and spacious. The company recommended draping the interior with fabric, and in case of inclement weather, windowed walls and canopied walkways could be added. A thinner sheet of paper had been tucked inside the brochure. I glanced at it and then instantly dropped it as if it were radioactive. That sheet was the price list. I looked at it again, thinking I had to have read it wrong. I hadn't.

Mike wasn't kidding. This was very serious money indeed.

Rose had typed up an agenda, flagging the things that we absolutely had to decide this weekend. I was overwhelmed. Not only were there so many different things on the list, but for each item there were too many choices, too many possibilities. The calligrapher had offered eleven sample scripts—some intricate and scrolling, some stately, some contemporary. The printer had at least twenty fonts, seventeen different shades of white papers, at least ten times that many colored papers, and eight ink colors.

But we didn't need to limit ourselves to those fonts, those shades of white, those ink colors. Everything was custom; anything was possible. And that would be true with the rental company, the caterer, the florist, everyone.

We got nowhere. Cami couldn't make up her mind. She wasn't a perfectionist; she wasn't a princess for whom nothing was good enough. Quite the contrary. She loved everything. Everything was beautiful. She couldn't choose.

My responsible, beautiful daughter-in-law-to-be was a ditherer. I hadn't known that about her. I hoped that she wasn't planning on being a surgeon or an ER doc. She wouldn't be able to make decisions quickly enough. She might well end up as one of those internists who drive everyone else nuts because they keep ordering more tests, never committing to a diagnosis.

She consulted with Jeremy, but he knew even less about this than I did. "Whatever you want," he kept saying, "that will be fine with me."

Clearly a major problem was that she didn't have her dress. Without a dress, we couldn't set a theme or a tone. Cami liked Annie's idea of an English cottage garden, to have everything charmingly informal with a glowing mixture of flowers, mosses, and vines. "But what if the dress is really formal?" Cami kept saying. "Then that won't be right."

Cami and Rose had appointments at bridal salons on Monday and Tuesday. Rose was letting Annie skip school to go with them. So we were not going to have a dress today or tomorrow. Did that mean we wouldn't be able to make any decisions at all?

I needed a pill. I glanced at my watch. I couldn't believe it. I couldn't take another Ritalin for two more hours. It sure felt like it had already worn off.

Rose was struggling to remain patient with Cami. "Let's at least settle the portable toilets."

My father and his EpiPen had taken Finney out to explore the town, and Guy was sitting in a big chair at the far end of the family room. This was apparently his concession to Annie's memory of how, in the Adirondacks cottage, everyone sat in the same room all the time. So he sat where we could see him, but since he was working, I wasn't sure how much his presence added.

He was reading manuscripts that someone on his staff had prescreened for rejection. On one side of his chair were two cartons full of the manuscripts. On the other side was a big recycling bin. He would read the first three pages carefully, then flip through the next seven or so. Apparently agreeing with the decision to reject the manuscript, he would take the cover letter and scrawl something across the top. He would put the cover letter in a pile on the carton side of his chair and let the manuscript drop into the recycling bin.

I forced myself back to the port-a-potties question. Except they weren't port-a-potties. They were "luxury comfort stations." Companies brought in trailers with stalls, vanities, and mirrors, just like a restroom in a restaurant. The trailers had electrical connections and sewage hookups so that the toilets flushed and the sinks had running hot water. Some of them were Mafia-grand, white with gold rococo trim. Others were Euro-tech chrome and rosewood.

Why was Rose handling all this herself? Sure, it was easy to make fun of wedding planners, but some of them had to be sensible and efficient.

We were now talking about the music. We needed music for the ceremony, music for dinner, music for dancing.

If this had been a normal wedding, one deejay would have brought three sets of CDs and done it all. But this was not a normal wedding. We were going to have woodwinds at the ceremony, strings at dinner, and a band for dancing, all of them live, all of them needing to be selected.

And even after those decisions were made, Rose would have to read and sign their contracts, then write and mail the deposit checks. She would have to figure out where the musicians were going to be positioned while performing. She would have to remember to have the caterer provide them with meal service. She would have to be sure that they got directions and knew where to park.

Why was she doing this herself? This was not what Marys were supposed to be doing with themselves.

When Dad and Finney came back, we took a break, rounding everyone up for lunch. Jill Allyn monopolized the conversation, talking about a new book that only she and Guy had read, and she got her little digs in at Rose. "It really is the sort of book you used to enjoy."

Cami didn't eat much. She was supposed to go upstairs with a stack of CDs and pick music for at least one part of the event. As Rose and I were finishing the dishes, she came into the kitchen, carrying her laptop, looking uneasy. "Mom, would you look at this?"

"Of course." Rose dried her hands. "What is it?"

"It's an e-mail from Claudia. With pictures of a dress. A wedding dress." Cami set the laptop on the counter and Rose peered at the screen.

"This is pretty." Rose adjusted the angle of the

screen and then clicked on the keyboard. “Oh, there’s a video.”

“Isn’t it nice the way it moves—how it looks so simple when she’s standing still, but then all those layers swirl and float?”

Annie came over to look. “Is there a train?”

“Let’s see if they have a rear view.” Rose clicked some more.

I joined them. All morning Cami had talked about what she didn’t want in a dress.

She didn’t want it to be strapless, but sleeves were sort of frumpy, weren’t they?

This dress had a light drift of chiffon over the shoulders.

She didn’t want a stiff, Jackie Kennedy kind of dress, but she didn’t want it to be sexy either.

This dress was soft and flowing.

She didn’t want something all heavy and beaded, but she didn’t want something superplain either.

This dress looked as if it didn’t have any embellishments, but when Rose enlarged the picture, we saw tiny seed pearls and insets of narrow satin ribbon.

And, above all, she didn’t want a super-Cinderella fairy-princess gown.

Except that she did want that.

Cami was young, just two years out of her teens, and she wanted to look like a princess on her wedding day. But as a literate, ambitious young woman, she knew that she was supposed to think that a princess fantasy was absurdly girlish.

This dress, with its swirling layers, combined the restrained elegance of a Grecian goddess with billowy romanticism.

"What do we have here?" It was Guy. He put one hand on my shoulder and one hand on Annie's to look at the screen. "Now that's one good-looking dress."

"Do you like it, Dad?" Cami asked eagerly. "Do you really?"

Annie and I moved aside so that he could get a closer look. Then there was a lot of back and forth, Cami asking her parents if they liked the dress, if they *really* liked it, while Guy and Rose tried to be supportive and encouraging without making the actual decision.

"It does have the same neckline as my prom dress. I liked that so much." Cami bit her lip. She was making up her mind. Then her features started to blur. She was about to cry. "Oh, Mom, Dad . . . I think I love it. No, I know I do."

When Cami had brought her laptop into the kitchen, she'd been hesitant. She'd suspected that this was the dress she wanted, but she'd been unable to trust her first impression. Now that she had made up her mind, she would never look back.

This was probably how she had fallen in love with Jeremy. She would have been cautious at first, suspicious of her strong attraction. Then suddenly one day, a day that was no different from the day before, she would have been flooded with absolute certainty that he was the one. Just as she would never stop loving this dress, she would never stop loving my son.

Guy went back to his chair while Rose and Cami made plans to see the actual dress. Annie was at the table, lining up the papers and brochures that we had shoveled aside for lunch. Her back was to us; I couldn't read her expression, but it didn't seem like her to be organizing other people's papers.

I went over to help.

"That dress was perfect, wasn't it?" Annie said after a moment; she didn't sound happy.

"I don't know much about fashion, but Cami seems to love it."

"Claudia asked her what she wanted, and I guess Cami could only come up with what she didn't want. So Claudia asked me."

"And you told her?"

She nodded. "That was exactly the neckline I described. I've been borrowing Cami's clothes for years. I know what she likes. I'm not saying that Mom and Cami and I could have found a dress that good, but . . . I don't know."

"You were looking forward to all of you going out together."

"Mom had already talked to me about how I was going to need to help Cami make up her mind. As Dad says, her decision tree can get pretty twisted."

Annie felt cheated. She had wanted to go shopping for the wedding dress.

Did Annie want more of a relationship with Cami

than she had? Wednesday night, Annie hadn't wanted to play flashlight tag, but had changed her mind the minute Cami had urged her to. Annie was also the one who kept recommending that the wedding have a cottage-garden theme. Cottage gardens are cozy and intimate. Had she been looking forward to the appointments on Monday and Tuesday because it would be something that she, her sister, and her mother—just the three of them—would be doing together?

If so, Claudia had robbed her of that.

A family is a system, Claudia, full of equal and opposite reactions. You can't fix a problem in one spot without creating one somewhere else.

Yes, Cami had needed to find a wedding dress, but Annie had needed to be a part of the finding. And what was more important, the perfect dress or the relationship between two sisters?

But finding the dress did make the afternoon much more productive. Cami was now able to imagine herself walking down the aisle surrounded by an English country garden. This made her able to choose a florist. She didn't select the actual flowers, but at least the wedding was on someone's schedule. That was a start.

Even in absentia, Claudia, clearly a Martha Stewart kind of Martha, continued to help. Cami e-mailed her to gush about the dress. Claudia instantly replied with an e-mail so lengthy that she had to have already written it.

"She says that if we're going to go with different shades of camellias," Cami summarized the e-mail, "there are lots of ways to keep pink from being overly sweet."

"So is she saying that the bridesmaids should wear pink?" Annie asked. Cami was having five bridesmaids, with Annie as the maid of honor. "I look horrible in pink."

"She says that . . . well, not quite that. 'Annie might not want to wear pink,' " Cami read, " 'but she will look lovely in a very pale sage.' "

"That's true," Annie agreed. "I do."

So we were on track, and when our little train started to derail over the stationery order, Rose had Cami read off Claudia's cell-phone number from the bottom of an e-mail. Rose called her, and, from Mike's mother's house, Claudia assured us that very pale blush paper, almost a warm ivory, with the embossed camellia was wonderful especially if we used a faded chocolate ink. The mocha we had been considering would be too contemporary.

She gave us a brand.

Guy was back in his chair, still reading the manuscripts. Something was different about the one he had now. He was much farther into it than any of the others, and he was massaging his forehead with the forefinger of his left hand.

Rose finished talking to Claudia and was filling out a form, double checking with Cami each time she made an entry.

Guy was still reading that same manuscript. He was frowning, but still reading.

"Okay, I think that's done," Rose said with relief. "The printer will go with the Edwardian Script font."

"Don't forget to tell the calligrapher to use that number fifty-seven ink," Annie said.

"Oh, yes. Thanks for reminding me." Rose made a note. "Okay, now for the—"

"Rose," Guy spoke up for the other side of the room, "do you think you could take a look at this manuscript? One of the new kids in the office was going to turn it down, and I'm inclined to agree, but there's something in it that keeps me reading. Maybe you'll have a notion of what we could do with it."

"I'll be glad to take a look at it," Rose answered. "Not today, of course. Or even Monday or Tuesday. It won't be until the end of the week."

"That would be fine," he said.

She went back to proofreading the form for the printer. Guy watched her for a moment. Then, the realist that he was, he dropped the manuscript into the recycling bin, scrawling another *no* across the cover letter so that one of his assistants could send a form rejection.

This was all wrong.

I wanted to stand up and scream, sweeping all those glossy brochures off the table, *Stop this, Rose. Stop it this minute. Hire a wedding planner. This isn't what you should be doing. You should be reading that manuscript, figuring out what's wrong and how to make it right.*

What was going on? Finney was settled at a good

school; he had good doctors, good therapists. This could have been the year for Rose to figure out what to do with herself. Instead, she was filling out order forms and choosing port-a-potties. Why?

When I had received my first note from her, I'd had an intuition that there was going to be trouble in this for me. I'd stopped thinking that way. I liked Rose so much, I couldn't imagine how she could ever harm me. But my instinct might have been right. Rose was unhappy, and unhappy people are trouble.

Seven

I was now curious about Rose's family's cottage in the Adirondacks. Annie, in particular, spoke of it with longing.

Friday evening, Dad, Guy, and I were outside, getting the big grill ready so that we could barbecue hot dogs and steaks. While we were waiting for the flames from the piped-in gas to heat the artificial briquettes, I asked Guy about the cottage.

"That is a source of regret," he said. "Maybe if we'd handled things differently we'd be up there now, wrestling with charcoal and lighter fluid. It was a low-tech place."

It had, he told us, been in Rose's family for several generations, having been built as a summer home. Wide porches faced a sloping green lawn and the family's extensive stretch of lakefront. Three years ago Rose's parents had died within a few months of each other, leaving the house to their children: Rose, the oldest; Jack, the only son; Holly, the youngest.

"The three of them loved the place," Guy said, "but it was falling apart. It needed a new roof, the foundation had a ton of cracks, and it wasn't winterized."

The three siblings could not agree on which repairs to make first. Living in Albany, Holly wanted it winterized so that she and her family could use it on weekends all year. Jack cared only about its being available for summer use, but he wanted to upgrade the boathouse, something no one else cared about. "Rose and I were willing to invest both in winterizing the house and upgrading the boathouse, but as little as I know about houses, I thought we ought to do the basics first, replacing the roof, repairing the windows, that sort of thing."

"I do know something about houses," Dad said, "and you were right."

"I figure I was," Guy said. "But then it turned out that Holly and Jack couldn't afford to do any of it, and I wasn't going to bear all the costs without some change in the ownership structure. Maybe I was wrong, but the money wasn't trivial. It would have been cheaper to have torn the old house down and started over."

Holly would not consider Guy's plan. If the cottage belonged to Rose, was Holly going to have to ask permission to go to a place that she had been going to her entire life?

"She would only let us have a controlling interest in

the property if the contract allowed her and her family to come and go as they pleased. But by then Rose and I had an agenda. We want Finney to be able to live independently someday, and Park Slope probably will be the best place, but the cottage was another option. The village was within walking distance, and there are decent enough services. But for that to be a viable alternative, we couldn't agree to anything that would compromise his right to be there whenever it suited him."

To fund the repairs, Rose's brother had arranged to sell a section of the lakefront. After living through one summer of very noisy, disruptive construction, the family found the following year that the massive new house blocked far more of their view than they had anticipated. Furthermore, the new house was frequently rented to large multifamily groups who blocked the shared driveway and trespassed onto the remaining property in order to use the family's private dock.

"All those strangers scared Finney. It was strange because he sees strangers in Park Slope all the time, but he didn't want to go down to the dock even with Rose. Holly and Jack were then willing to have us buy them out, but we didn't want the place either. It was sold a year ago, and we bought out here last spring. I suspect Rose sometimes wishes we'd given in to her sister, but it wouldn't have ended there. If anything had ever not gone Holly's way, she would have blamed Rose entirely."

"Oh, are you talking about Aunt Holly?" Annie was

coming out from the shadow just outside the french doors leading back into the house. "And, no, Dad, I haven't been here forever eavesdropping."

"What did you hear, Miss Queenie?" Guy lifted his arm, and Annie, who didn't have a coat on, huddled close to him.

"Just that Aunt Holly blames Mom and only Mom, but I didn't hear for what. Are you going to tell me?"

"Probably not," Guy said evenly.

"Is it about having to sell the cottage or about taking advantage of Grandma Lily?"

"Whoa!" Guy stepped back and turned to face her. "What's this about your grandmother? Mom never took advantage of her. Anything Grandma Lily did, she did willingly."

"Oh, I know that, but Aunt Holly acted like Mom was guilty of elder abuse." Annie glanced at Dad and me. "I did used to do my share of eavesdropping," she said cheerfully, "so I do know a few things I'm not supposed to."

A *few* was probably a massive understatement.

"Then perhaps we shouldn't know it either," Dad said. "It looks like this grill is ready."

I love my father, I really do, but not listen to this? I wanted to hear the story.

Fortunately, Guy had already started to tell it. He'd wanted to defend Rose. "When Finney was little, the one person Rose completely trusted to take care of him was her mother. I think she trusted Lily more than she trusted me."

"I understand that," I said, nodding. "If one of our boys had been chronically ill, I probably would have trusted my mother more than anyone else."

"More than me?" Dad asked in surprise.

"Yes. More than you, Dr. Bow-wow. You might be a loving and experienced pediatrician, but she was my mother."

Dad thought for a moment. "You may be right. I would have relied on my own judgment. Your mother would have done exactly what you had asked her to do even if she thought you were being too cautious."

"Or too controlling," Annie put in. "That's what Mom has to hear, that she's too controlling."

"And I thought you were going to pretend that you didn't eavesdrop anymore." Guy clamped his hand lightly over her mouth and then continued to talk to Dad and me. "For a couple of years, Lily and John—Rose's parents—kept Finney at the cottage for a week in July and a week in August, which meant that we could do things with Cami and Annie that wouldn't have been possible if he'd been with us. We tried to remember that they needed us too."

Annie slipped free of her father's arm. "But Grandma and Grandpa were exhausted when the week was over, and they didn't want to spend their whole summer running a summer camp, so Aunt Holly claimed they were playing favorites, that they were doing more for Mom than for her. I suppose that was true, but it seems to me that Mom needed more than anyone else."

"It sounds as if," my father said, "your aunt is a classic younger sibling who never thinks she's getting her fair share."

"Then she should have taken Mom's clothes more often," Annie said. "That's what I did. I was always wearing Cami's clothes and swiping her makeup, and now I like her just fine."

We went in to get the steaks. Rose was on one of the pale leather sofas, playing a reading game with Finney. He picked up a card, then pushed it away with a jerk. His shoulders were hunched forward. He was getting frustrated.

And Rose looked very tired.

When Mike had moved out, I felt as if there was a big orange traffic sign around my neck that read ABANDONED AND BETRAYED. Rose had no outward signs of a person abandoned. She was still married; she had people clamoring to be guests in her home. But her close friends had thought she was obsessed with Finney; the would-be writers who had once valued her opinion had lost interest in her; her sister was angry with her. Her mother, the one person she had trusted completely, had died.

She might not be wearing that big orange traffic sign where the whole world could see it, but it was around here somewhere.

Zack and I were leaving after dinner on Saturday night, wanting to avoid the Sunday-after-Thanksgiving traffic. When we were ready to go,

Rose and Guy walked out to the car with us. All the outdoor lights were on, and the flagstone parking court was bright.

"Do you have Christmas plans?" Rose asked. "My sister is supposed to come, but we'll still have plenty of room if you can join us."

"Thanks, but the boys and I are going skiing in Colorado with Dad and my brother's family." We had made these plans last spring before Cami and Jeremy had gotten engaged.

"What about New Year's? Will you be in Colorado for the whole holiday? Would you like to come here for New Year's?"

I could feel myself drawing back. This invitation seemed a little too urgent, a little too intense. Did Rose see me as her chance to have a friend again, a sister?

Other women had needed me. I was certified to drive one of the motorboats in the crew-team regattas; I could be counted on to stop a Cub Scout's spurting blood; when the Teacher Appreciation Luncheon Committee wanted entrées that didn't need to be refrigerated or reheated, they knew I could come up with something great.

Until my mother's last illness, I hadn't seen the difference between people needing me and needing the things I could do. But my mother hadn't wanted me because I was a nurse and knew my way around a hospital. She had wanted me at her bedside because I was me, her daughter.

And now that she was gone, I probably did want

someone to want me that way again. Rose wanted something; I wanted something. Maybe it was the same thing.

"It's sounds like fun. I'll try to make it work," I promised. "I really will."

Jeremy definitely wanted to spend New Year's with Cami and her family. I suggested that he invite her to spend Christmas with my family in Colorado, but he shook his head, saying that she was too stressed about the wedding plans; she needed to be in the Hamptons as much as possible. I let Zack choose for himself. After Christmas in Colorado, he could come home for New Year's if he stayed with one of his friends' families, or he could come to the Hamptons with Jeremy and me. I was surprised, but pleased, when he decided to come with us. So I paid the airline's ticket penalty and changed our tickets so that all three of us could fly directly from Colorado to New York.

When I told Rose that we were coming, there was no trace of the desperate relief I expected to hear. Maybe I had read too much into the tone of her invitation. Maybe she had simply been tired. Maybe I had been the needy one, and that's what I had needed to hear.

A few days later she called me back. "I need to apologize and explain. After I heard from you, I tried to get reservations for Mike and Claudia—"

I blinked. I hadn't known that she was going to invite them. She didn't need to. New Year's Eve was not a 'must do' holiday in our family.

"—And there is nothing anywhere close. They'd be driving for miles and staying in a very ordinary motel. So I had to ask them to stay at the house. It would look so inhospitable not to. They have to know we have the space."

So she had already invited them. She wasn't asking my permission.

And why should she have to? It was her house, wasn't it?

"I hope that this won't be too awkward for you," she finished.

"For *me?* Oh, goodness, I'll be fine. Don't worry about me."

The time between Thanksgiving and Christmas had always been particularly busy for our family because Mike's birthday was in early December. In the three years between his leaving and my moving, I'd always invited him to have dinner with Zack and me. Left to himself, he wouldn't have celebrated the day.

But this year was different. I couldn't invite him without Claudia, and I didn't want to invite her. I didn't have room to store twelve metallic-thread quilted placemats with a matching table runner. So I said nothing, and eventually Mike invited Zack to go to dinner with Claudia and him that night.

A few days before Mike's birthday, Rose called me to apologize for the "Christmas trip," but Cami needed to spend the entire holiday on wedding plans.

"I know. That's what Jeremy said. I never thought that she was coming to Colorado with us."

"Oh, no, not that trip. Hasn't Claudia called you?"

"No."

Apparently Claudia had a notion to surprise Mike on his birthday with a trip to one of the Virgin Islands before they went to the Hamptons for New Year's. She'd called Rose to see if she could get a ticket for Cami.

"She wasn't planning on taking my boys, was she?" I asked.

"She said Mike has them for Christmas."

"For Christmas Day. And Christmas Eve too if he wants. But on the evening of the twenty-fifth, I'm taking them to Colorado to go skiing. We're meeting Dad and my brother Chuck's family."

"Oh, I was supposed to know that, wasn't I?" Rose sighed. "I can't keep track of my own plans anymore, much less other people's."

"And Mike knows about the Colorado trip too."

"He doesn't know anything about the Virgin Islands. It's a surprise. I assumed that Claudia had cleared it with you."

"Well, she didn't. I wonder if I should tell her about it."

"That's totally up to you," Rose said. "I didn't mean to be the intermediary."

Rose had called me as I was walking out the door for work, so I couldn't have called Claudia then. My shifts were particularly grueling, so I didn't think about Rose's call again until the morning of Mike's birthday when I was reminding Zack that he was to meet Mike and Claudia at the restaurant.

"Will Dad pay if I have to put the car in a lot?"

"Of course."

I watched him hoist his backpack and trudge out the door. I wondered what I would have done if I had remembered Rose's call. Would I have gotten in touch with Claudia? I didn't know. Surely it would have been her place to call me. I double checked my e-mail inbox—the messages accumulated while I was working—and there was nothing from her. She must have dropped the plan.

I spent most of the day in the kitchen. A giant blue plywood stork had appeared in the front yard of a family down the street. Although I had spoken to them only a time or two, I prepared three different entrées for them to put in the freezer. The new mother was desperately grateful. The baby was asleep, so I didn't get to hold him, but the mom told me to stop by any-time between one and four a.m.; he was always awake then.

Sooner than I'd expected, I heard Zack's car in the drive, followed by the sound of a second car. I went to the door. Mike had followed Zack home.

Zack started talking right away. "We're going skiing at Christmas with Grandpa and Uncle Chuck, aren't we?"

I nodded. "We leave the night of the twenty-fifth."

Mike followed him up the steps. "May I come in for a minute?"

In the living room, he looked tired and harassed. "When I told Claudia that I'd have the boys for Christmas, she misunderstood. So she made some travel arrangements and hoped to include them."

"Then she's going to be disappointed. She hasn't made any definite plans, has she?"

"Well, actually, yes. She didn't buy their plane tickets, but she has rented a large house in St. Thomas and arranged some activities. She booked us on a private charter boat for a couple of day trips. She's put a lot of effort into this." He did not look at all excited. "Believe me, Darcy, I knew nothing about it . . . so I was wondering if just this once you could be flexible."

I've never known anyone to stick with a "just this once" pledge. "Mike, my dad paid for our tickets. You know there's no way I'm going to tell him that the boys aren't coming."

"What about if they came a few days later? On the twenty-seventh or so. I'd pay for all the ticket changes."

It would probably take them much of a day to get from St. Thomas to Colorado. "Chuck only has the house until the thirtieth. And then we're going straight to Rose and Guy's for New Year's. Mike, this is not going to work. I am not going to truncate my dad's time with the boys . . . or theirs with their cousins."

"Just this once, Darcy . . . please."

"No."

"Dad, I told you this is what she would say." Zack sounded a little triumphant. "There was no reason for you to follow me home."

I winced. Zack should have kept his mouth shut.

"You may be right about that, Zack," Mike said too slowly, too patiently, "but you could have been more considerate of Claudia's feelings."

"Me? What did I do wrong?" The triumph drained from his voice. He turned to me. "Mom, I was fine. Okay, I didn't like it when I saw her sitting there all puffed up—you know how people get when they think they're about to give you the treat of a lifetime and they can't wait until you're groveling with joy—I admit that that rubs me the wrong way."

I knew that about him. He was always surprising me—completely, even deliberately failing when I expected him to do something, but coming through when it never occurred to me that he would. He hated having people expect something from him. The minute he started to smell expectations, he went running in the other direction.

"So I looked inside the envelope," he continued. "She had given them to me and Dad at the same time, and once I figured out why I was looking at a picture of a big house on the ocean, I thanked her, and I was really nice, saying that it looked like a great trip, but that Jeremy and I couldn't go."

I couldn't see anything wrong with that.

"But you didn't have to say it right then," Mike said. "You could have waited and let me handle it later."

"I could have," Zack answered, "but I didn't."

"Let's not make this about Zack," I said. "Claudia made a mistake. I can understand her wanting to arrange a surprise for you, but she should have checked on the boys' schedules first. She should have talked to me."

"It wasn't anything personal," Mike defended her. "She wasn't deliberately ignoring you. She's never had to deal with family situations before."

"She knew enough to call Rose to see if Cami could come."

He paused. "You knew about this?"

Oh, Darcy, why can't you keep your mouth shut? "Only through Rose."

"Then why didn't you do something? Why didn't you call Claudia and stop her?"

"For all I knew, once Rose said Cami couldn't go, Claudia bailed on the whole idea. Why was it my responsibility to get involved?"

"Oh, come on, Darcy. You're not afraid of getting involved. Didn't you call what's-her-name's mom when you were afraid that she and Jeremy were going to start having sex?"

Zack had been trying to ease out of the room, but he was suddenly alert. "You did what?"

"It was a long time ago," I answered, trying to keep the conversation from hopping down this particular bunny trail.

"Have you ever called a girl's mother about me?"

"There's no right answer to that," I replied. "Either you will be mad at me if I did call or offended if I didn't."

He grinned. "That's true, but which is it?"

"I hover less with you than with him."

"You just think I can't get laid."

"Zack!" Mike exploded. "That's no way to talk to your mother."

"Oh, come on, Dad. I haven't done anything wrong here. Claudia screwed up, not Mom or me."

"And if Claudia's really determined to have a happy-family-on-the-beach Christmas," I put in, "why don't you take your mother?"

I had, as I often do, spoken without thinking. If I'd had a reason for making that remark about his mother, it was to make Mike feel guilty. And it would work. So I was expecting some self-justifying phone calls in which he tried to get me to excuse him for not taking his mother. I decided right away that I was going to let him off the hook. *No one knows better than me how challenging your mother can be,* I was going to say. *She is a treat best enjoyed on her home turf.*

But then I heard that Mike and Claudia were taking Marge with them.

I would not have wished that on anyone.

The boys and I had a great time in Colorado. Chuck and his wife have two daughters; Suzanne was nine, Sabine six, and the girls adored their big cousins. All of us, even Dad and little Sabine, skied or snowboarded all day. We ate in every night, preparing everything from my mother's recipes. Her beef Stroganoff used canned mushrooms, dried onion soup, and cream-of-mushroom soup. I thought it was overly salted with a chemical aftertaste, but my father was thrilled.

"This dish brings back so many wonderful memories," he said with a sigh.

In the middle of our family harmony, I had to wonder about Claudia, Mike, and Marge, a threesome vacationing together in St. Thomas. What kind of time were they having? Any ill feelings I had for Claudia didn't justify my sticking her with Marge for a week, and as the boys and I were flying from Colorado to New York, I decided that I wanted to apologize to her.

It would be awkward. She and I had never had a private conversation, and in public we exchanged only meaningless pleasantries.

I was in the middle seat between the boys. *What do you think of Claudia . . . No, no, of course, she's nice enough, but what do you really think? . . . Yes, Dad seems happy, and he's dressing better, but what do you really think? . . . Remember that night she wouldn't borrow shoes to play flashlight tag, what did you think of that?*

Fortunately they were both asleep, and I couldn't badger them into telling me what I wanted to hear.

In New York Guy had arranged for a car service to bring us from the airport. We got stuck in traffic, so we arrived later than planned, but as soon as I got myself settled in the room over the garage, I went to find Claudia, knowing that she and Mike had arrived earlier in the day.

She was in the kitchen, loading the dishwasher. She seemed to have staked this out as her particular job. I didn't like that. She was invading my territory. Surely everyone would agree that the kitchen was mine.

Her nubby gray slacks were, I supposed, the color of driftwood, and the soft yellow of her shirt had to be a color in her conch shell. If I hadn't known about her brand, I would have thought it was a perfectly normal outfit. But knowing that she had been thinking about the brand when she chose that shade of gray made it all seem a little creepy. She had just returned from a week in the Virgin Islands, but there was no sign of sun on her face or hands.

Who was she? I had no idea where she had grown up, who her family was, where she had gone to school. I wasn't a snob; one of our best nurses had come from a trailer park, another had worked her way off the welfare rolls. I didn't care what her background was; it just seemed strange not to know. She must have wanted it that way. She wanted people to see what she had become. She had invented herself; she had created a brand.

What else did she want? Mike, my boys, Cami's family, and this big house in the Hamptons. She was playing musical chairs with me, and she was going to make sure that I ended up standing along the wall.

Suddenly I felt that behind the cool, elegant wardrobe, the real Claudia was a garishly colored Bobo doll, one of those inflatable vinyl clowns whose bottoms were weighted so that when you punched them, they always popped back up, their eyes bulging and their stupid painted-on grins leering. It wouldn't matter what I did to keep this woman from trying to take a place—my place—in my family; she would bounce right back. The harder I hit, the faster she would recoil.

But that did not change the fact that I owed her an apology.

So I got to it. "Claudia, I think that something I said ended up with Mike suggesting you take his mother to St. Thomas. I didn't mean it to. I don't think Marge does very well away from home."

Claudia looked down at the ironstone cream pitcher she was rinsing. "She smokes."

"Don't you hate that?" Marge's smoking had always made our visits to her difficult. When the boys were little, she would go outside to smoke, claiming that she never smoked in the house. But clearly she did—the smell of her curtains attested to that—and the change in routine made her jittery.

"We had to change planes." Claudia's voice was tight. "Flying on December twenty-third is difficult enough, but when you have to find someplace to smoke between flights . . . we almost missed our connection." She fitted the cream pitcher over one of the prongs in the dishwasher and then glanced at her watch. "And that is not the way I travel."

"When you fly with her, you have to change in Charlotte." I was surprised that Mike hadn't remembered that. “North Carolina lets people smoke in airports.”

Claudia picked up a mug, emptied the old coffee out of it, and rinsed it. Before putting it into the dishwasher, she ran a soapy sponge around the rim, then rinsed it again. So much for Managed Perfectionism. This was Perfectionism Run Amok. “Has Marge ever talked about what she wants to do when she has to leave her house?”

I shook my head. “No, but Mike and I split up more than three years ago. She might not have been thinking about that then.”

“Oh.”

That was all Claudia said, but I got it. Was Marge Van Aiken hinting, in that snarky way of hers, that she and her Parliament Lights were looking for somewhere to live? If so, Claudia’s spacious, immaculate house would be appealing.

No one on earth, not even Claudia, deserved that.

But in about thirty seconds my sympathy for Claudia faded. She needed to wake up. A man Mike’s age was a package deal. On one hand, he came with two handsome sons, one of whom was about to marry into a family with a house in the Hamptons. On the other hand, he had a difficult, demanding mother whose long-term care he would eventually have to figure out. Family life was full of the kind of compromises that Claudia Postlewaite probably was not used to making.

First thing the next morning, I volunteered to do a

grocery-store run. I didn't have a car, so Rose went to get the keys to her Mercedes even though I wasn't wild about driving someone else's very big, very expensive car on unfamilar roads.

"Would you like me to give you a lift?"

It was Mike. He must have guessed how I felt.

"That would be great."

I got my coat and purse and went outside. Mike was moving toward the driver's side of his car, and Claudia toward the passenger side. I hadn't known that she was coming.

Mike's car is a little, two-door model. The backseat was a narrow, uncomfortable bench. I'd never seen anyone ride in it. Claudia opened the passenger door, pressed the lever below the seat, and pulled forward on the leather headrest, folding the seat down. She flattened herself against the open car door, her hand still on the headrest, waiting very politely for me to crawl into that narrow backseat.

I'm older than you, I wanted to shriek. *I'm the mother of this man's children. I should be in front, not you.*

But the harder you hit a Bobo doll, the faster it slaps back into place. I might care who sat in front, but she cared more. That would always give her the advantage.

Eight

Mike had knelt down to examine his front tire. He was right to stay out of this estrogen drama. If he'd said one word about my being in the front, I would have instantly launched into a stupid tomboy riff about how I didn't mind having to duck my head, stick my butt in the air, and corkscrew myself into the backseat. In fact, I would have tried to slither my way through the procedure as quickly as possible to make the point that I was more flexible and agile than Claudia.

My nice mom-type therapist had asked me why I felt patronized when anyone tried to help me. Was I confusing help and pity?

After wasting a session protesting that I wasn't, I reluctantly admitted that I probably was. I couldn't stand the idea of people feeling sorry for me. People had felt sorry for my mother . . . because of me.

Grand Rapids, Michigan, is not a small town, but East Grand Rapids, where we'd lived, is. It's a suburb, small enough, affluent enough, homogeneous enough that when "Dr. Bowersett's little girl" spent the day outside the principal's office for mouthing off to a guidance counselor, people heard about it.

And my mother got such sympathy from the other ladies, such polite, triumphant sympathy.

Through all my adolescent garbage, my mother had been loyal and optimistic. She'd gotten exasperated, impatient, even angry with me—she was not a saint—but she'd never given up on me. She'd never thought that I was naughty by nature or that my misdeeds were her fault because she hadn't quit work. It was as if she'd intuited, long before the medical establishment would have supported an ADD diagnosis for me, that my unease with myself and the world was something biochemical, something that I truly could not help.

I'd always pretended that I didn't feel guilty about what I was doing. So what if I didn't want to take the AP classes? So what if my friends' families couldn't afford to live in East Grand Rapids? I did feel bad about how hard I was making things for my mother, but I couldn't figure out how to change.

Years and years later she was diagnosed with pancreatic cancer. It progressed rapidly, and during the final months of her life, in the spring before Mike had left, the person she'd wanted with her was me. Both Dad and Chuck were doctors, but I was her daughter.

Being valuable to her, being necessary to her, eased much of my guilt. I was finally paying her back for how she had stood beside me when I had been determined to push her away. She was the one who'd directed me into nursing, who'd never for one moment let me believe that nurses were just people not smart enough to be doctors.

Frightened by the fact that she was going to die, Dad and Chuck wanted her to have whatever she wanted, and what she wanted was me. Dad was torn about pressuring me to spend more time with her. Chuck was not. He would call me, grim and insistent: "You need to get back out here."

But Mother was in Michigan, and I had obligations at home. Jeremy was a senior in high school; Zack was floundering during his last year of middle school. Even though Mike was still home, the last four months of her life were a nightmare for me. When I was in Michigan, I felt that I should be at home. I missed the Sports Banquet at which Jeremy received the crew team's Coach's Award. I was so disappointed by that; I would have loved to be there. Zack needed me even more than Jeremy did. His reports from school seemed to be getting worse by the day, and Mike was too angry with him to help.

But when I was home, I ached to be with Mother.

Even though I was able to take unpaid leave from work, I was exhausted. Before I left Michigan, I would cook maniacally, filling my dad's freezer with meals he could reheat. I would come back to D.C., stop at the grocery store on the way home from the airport, and cook the exact same meals for Mike and the boys to reheat when I left again. I bought light-bulbs in Michigan and toilet paper in Washington even though it was Dad's bathrooms that needed tissue and the lights in my home that were missing bulbs.

I went home for Jeremy's graduation and then flew right back to Michigan. Mother died a week later. Three months after that, Mike moved out.

Our therapist noted the timing, and in the bland,

nonjudgmental tone that therapists must have to practice, he asked Mike, "How did you feel about the choices Darcy made during her mother's illness?"

Mike looked puzzled for a moment as if he couldn't imagine how that question was relevant. But he was plenty smart, and in a second, he got it. "Are you saying that that had anything to do with my leaving?"

The therapist made a little gesture.

"That's ridiculous," Mike said, then turned to me. "Darcy, it had nothing to do with it. I understood why you needed to be in Michigan, but she died in May. It was more than three months."

"So, Mike, you felt that three months was a long time?" the therapist asked.

"I guess." Mike didn't sound like his usual confident self. "My leaving had nothing to do with her mother's death."

"And you, Darcy . . . did three months feel like a long time to you?"

Hardly. "I still think about picking up the phone to call and ask her something."

"So the two of you had very different perceptions about where Darcy was in the grieving process."

"I wasn't thinking about that," Mike insisted.

When we were walking to our cars after the session, he could not leave the subject alone. He was caught between an apology and a need to justify himself.

During the session I had been inclined to let him off the hook. Of course he hadn't consciously been trying to punish me for how much time I'd spent with my mother. But standing there in the therapist's parking lot, I realized that if there was a hook in his gut, it was right where it belonged.

So he hadn't been thinking about my mother's death. I believed that. But he should have been. Why hadn't he noticed that I was stumbling around in a fog of grief so murky that I felt completely lost?

"It's been a lot to handle," I said. "Mother dying, Jeremy going to college, your leaving. They all feel connected."

He didn't like that. "Come on, Darcy. I'm not the kind of guy who kicks people when they're down."

"Before you flounce around saying that about yourself, you need to be sure you can tell when a person *is* down."

His lips tightened. He couldn't stand to have his judgment or his insight questioned. "Of course I can tell."

"Believe what you want," I said. "You always do."

And that was the last of the therapy sessions we attended together. From then on, Mike started discovering his last-minute scheduling conflicts.

One thing people say about ICU nurses is that we don't process our feelings, that we never discuss the deaths or the catastrophic disabilities, that we just move from one crisis to the next. That's probably true, but I can't imagine why people think that's a negative. If your husband or child were in the hospital with multisystem organ failure, would you want your nurse dragging in, grieving for the last person who had been in that bed, or would you want her alert, optimistic, and rational, focused on your loved one and only your loved one?

Those of us who are really good in the ICU, who can provide great patient care year after year, don't turn into totally different people when we go home at night. Our attitude about our own problems is the one we take to work—fix it if you can, and then move on. Furthermore, seeing what problems the ICU families are facing puts some perspective on your own little deals.

So I was sitting in the backseat of a well-maintained, well-insured car driven by a law-abiding, completely sober individual. Where exactly was the big problem?

I had a lot more sympathy for Rose's problems. Her sister hadn't come for Christmas. "Her son's hockey team qualified for a holiday tournament," she'd told me.

But Annie had checked the school's Web site. The tournament was starting two days after Christmas and had been on the team's calendar all season. Qualification had never been in question. Obviously Holly had simply decided not to come.

So Guy, extrovert that he was, had invited any and all who didn't have holiday plans . . . and people who, on December 22, don't know what they are doing on Christmas frequently aren't the most socially adept beings on the planet. It had not been a fun family holiday.

Rose came into the kitchen to help me unpack the groceries. “We have appointments with the caterer for tastings and at the rental company to try to finalize the linens. And the dishes . . . and the chairs and God only knows what else. I hope you know you’re welcome to come.”

I knew that Claudia would be very interested in everything at the rental company. “Can I go to the caterers and skip the tablecloth thing?”

“Absolutely,” Rose said. “Now I assume Claudia told you what she wants to do with those rehearsal-dinner dresses?”

“No, she hasn’t said anything. I suppose we ought to get started on finding a location and stuff.”

“Finding a location?” Rose had been folding a grocery bag. She stopped and sounded exasperated. “Everything’s almost done. Claudia’s just waiting for us to finalize the wedding menu so that she doesn’t duplicate things. Do you really know nothing about it?” Rose jerked the folds of the bag. “When the two of you don’t communicate, that puts me in the middle, and I don’t like that.”

I grimaced. She had a point.

“I know,” Rose continued, “that when she makes plans and decisions—like with that Christmas trip or now with the rehearsal dinner—you figure that it’s her responsibility to call you, and you’re probably right. But she’s not going to do that. As far as she’s concerned, you don’t exist. She never talks about you; she never refers to you.”

"That's sort of creepy," I admitted, "but I guess that's better than her trashing me all the time."

"Actually, from my point of view, it would be easier if she did trash you. I could discount the negatives, and at least I would have some information."

"I hadn't realized that it was so extreme. I'll try to do better. What's going on with—" I broke off. "No, I'll ask her. Or Mike. He bears some responsibility here."

"Not with what she wants us to wear. I'm sure that's her bailiwick."

Apparently Claudia had a hypothesis to prove—that the aesthetic quality of candid group photographs could be improved if some thought was given to a few garments. Her notion, according to Rose, was that if the dresses of the key female participants included, for example, the same diagonal lines, the resulting photographs would be more pleasing.

"She wants people to dress alike?"

"Oh, no," Rose assured me. "She says that none of the garments would look anything alike, some would be separates, some would be dresses, all different colors and styles, but they would each have this 'unifying diagonal.' "

"This is beyond creepy," I said. "Where are people supposed to find these clothes?"

"She's going to make them all and then write an article about it. With all of us illustrating it."

I couldn't think of anything I less wanted to be

involved in. "I'm totally cool with not existing on this one."

"Too bad. If you're not in on this, then we aren't. I'm not willing to go through another event like the engagement party where you are sitting in Siberia."

I made another face. "You weren't suppose to notice."

"No, Darcy, you're wrong there. I *was* supposed to notice. That was part of the point."

I wondered if Claudia had any idea how observant and shrewd Rose was. "I'm sorry that you have to deal with my family's crap."

"I am too," she said bluntly. "But it's not only you. It took me less than a month in this house to realize that we had handed ourselves a plateful of other people's status issues. Yes, Jill Allyn likes working out here, but she really likes telling everyone that she can come out here anytime she wants, that she's so special she doesn't need an invitation. Then Guy wants to invite all the people who she's trying to make feel bad."

"That sucks."

"Yes, it does." Rose put the bags in the cabinet below the vegetable sink. "I really like you, Darcy, and I hope you like me. But if you want to help me, you'll start fighting your own battles. Don't make me fight them for you."

I didn't like the sound of that. I fought my own battles, didn't I? "I pick and choose." I wanted to defend myself. "I try not to sweat the small stuff. If something is important, I stand up, but this nickel-and-dime, who wears what, who sits where, I try to let that go."

Rose shook her head. "What you are calling 'small stuff' are actually symbols with a great deal of potency."

She was talking like an English major . . . but that didn't mean that she was wrong. I might have pretended that I didn't mind sitting at the losers' table, but in truth, it had made me feel awful. "So what's going on with the dresses? I don't know that I want her making a dress for me."

"You'd rather shop for one?"

"No, Lord, no." But I did feel as if I had been shoved onto a train without anyone asking me where I wanted to go.

"How does Cami feel about all this? Aren't more photographs going to add to the stress?"

"Claudia swears that the photography will be very unobtrusive, nothing more than what we might ordinarily have. And, to be honest, Darcy, Claudia is helping Cami and me a lot. She can look at seven different unity candles and pick the one that will look best with our flowers. I'm inclined to humor her on this."

I didn't even know what a unity candle was.

I was going to talk to Mike first. Claudia might be maneuvering to turn me into a blank space on the canvas, but in truth, she didn't owe me anything beyond basic decency. Mike did.

After lunch I drew him aside. "I just found out from Rose that you and Claudia have made almost all the rehearsal-dinner plans already."

"Well, yes. Claudia said June's a busy time of year out here, that we needed to lock in the restaurant now."

"Shouldn't you have consulted me? Or at least told me what you were doing? It was awkward hearing it all from Rose."

He blinked. "Oh. I just assumed . . ."

"Assumed what? Did you assume I didn't care? Or did you assume that it was Claudia's job to tell me?"

He didn't answer.

I knew what was happening. He was preparing his defense. He was going to tell me all the reasons why he had done nothing wrong. "I don't want hear it, Mike," I snapped. "I don't want to hear that somehow you've done nothing wrong, and this is all my fault."

I started to brush past him, but he surprised me. "No, Darcy, wait. You haven't done anything wrong. I didn't assume that you wouldn't care, and I didn't assume that it was Claudia's job to tell you. To the extent that I thought about it, which wasn't enough, I unconsciously assumed that you would be in touch with her."

"That's not fair," I said. "That's not fair at all. Am I supposed to call everyone you ever have dinner with and welcome her into my family? That's nuts. Why would you ever imagine me doing that?"

"Because it's what you did with my mother." He

was speaking slowly as if he was only now understanding this. "The whole time we were married, you and she always figured out when we were going to get together. I'd just show up."

"Mike, that was with your *mother,* my children's grandmother. I'm not going to make those kinds of calls with your girlfriends."

"No, no, of course not. I see now that I was taking it for granted that you were going to handle it." He took a breath and looked straight at me. "That was wrong. I apologize."

Now I was surprised. I didn't know what to say. It was unlike him to make such a simple, sincere apology.

"So can I show you everything now?" he asked. "I know that Claudia brought all her files."

I followed him into the family room. Claudia was sitting at the table with Rose and Annie. Because her posture was so good and her torso so long, she looked tall when she was sitting. Now that I was a resident of the Commonwealth of Virginia, I knew all about Robert E. Lee, the Confederate general. He wasn't a tall man, but because his height was in his torso, he looked really great sitting on a horse.

But he still lost the war. I hoped that that was a good omen for me.

"Claudia, I want to go over the rehearsal-dinner plans with Darcy," Mike said. "The files are in here, aren't they?" He gestured toward a satchel made from some interesting Oriental fabric.

Claudia was on her feet instantly. She didn't even

look at her watch. “Let me get them. I was waiting to show them to everyone.” Clearly she didn’t like the idea of Mike and me in the corner going over her files and her plans.

They had chosen a restaurant on the other side of East Hampton, selecting it because of its beautiful garden. “I’ve done a mock-up of the invitation,” Claudia said. “And as you can see, I wanted to keep the soft, vintage look of the wedding invitations, but still do something different.”

I would have loved to hate Claudia’s invitation, but unfortunately it was about the coolest thing I’d ever seen. I felt as if I were being handed a passport to travel on the Orient Express. The background was a very subtle, very muted 1920s roadster-type map of the Hamptons. A vellum pocket was sewn onto the map and the lettering was superimposed on the vellum. “Michael Van Aiken, Claudia Postlewaite, Darcey Van Aiken request the honor . . .” The directions and other travel information were on a manila luggage tag inside the pocket.

“It’s not a theme party,” Claudia assured us. “The table cards may be similar to this, but that’s it. We won’t have mini-steamer trunks in the centerpieces.”

Oh. Mini-steamer trunks sounded cute, but what did I know?

We were passing around the invitation. Annie looked at it longer than the rest of us. “Is that how you spell your name, Darcy? Finney would love it if you had an *e* before your *y*, but you don’t, do you?”

I peered over her shoulder. "You're right. That is a typo."

"It's only a mock-up," Claudia assured me. "I'll fix it."

Then we talked about her dresses with their unifying diagonals. She had sketches for everyone's dresses. Mine looked pretty plain, which was just fine with me.

"These are for the dinner on Friday night," Claudia said. "But what about the wedding itself? How are you doing on your mother-of-the-bride dress?"

Obviously she was speaking only to Rose.

"Didn't you tell her, Mom?" Annie said. "We found a dress."

"Really? That's great," Claudia said. "I've been waiting until you got yours before even thinking about mine. Do you have it here? Can we see it?"

Once again I felt as if I didn't exist.

"Of course. Annie, will you run upstairs and get it? This isn't the actual dress. They only had my size in a print, but they can order it in a solid color. I wanted Cami to see it before I did the special-order."

Annie came down with a pistachio-colored vinyl garment bag, unzipped the bag, and extracted the dress.

"Oh, yes." Claudia said instantly. "This neckline wrap is going to be great on you."

She had taken out the hanger and was examining the dress. All I could see was the fabric. It was a print, but very soft and impressionistic, swirls of violets and mauves.

"What's wrong with that fabric?" I asked. "I think it's very pretty."

"I don't wear many prints," Rose said. "Do you ever see mothers of the bride in a print?"

"Not usually, but you know . . ." Claudia was thinking. "Maybe we should wear prints—you, me, and, oh, yes, you too. Darcy."

"I could do that," I said, thinking of the scarlet and magenta poppies that I hadn't bought for the engagement party. I wondered if there was any chance that that dress was still at the store.

"It can't be just any print," Claudia said. "We'll use this one as the model. Soft colors, low contrast, an even balance between figure and ground, soft outlines. If we do that, then Cami and the bridesmaids will really pop in the pictures."

I couldn't think of anything about my scarlet and magenta poppies that would fit Claudia's criteria . . . except maybe the "even balance between figure and ground." I had to exclude that because I had no idea what it meant.

"I'll do my best," I said bravely. "But you'll need to write all that down."

We spent most of December 31 on wedding plans. All the vendors were in place, but an infinite number of decisions still had to be made about exactly which table linens and dishes the caterer should use, how many blossoms should be in each bridesmaid's bouquet, etc. Everything was going to be beautiful. The florist had urged Rose to hire a landscape designer to install a curving flagstone walk that would serve as the aisle. For the ceremony, the chairs would be arrayed in gentle arcs rather than straight lines. The whole space would be turned into a fantasy of cottage garden with vine-covered trellises and archways. The flowers would have a slightly old-fashioned air, camellias and roses, hollyhocks, lilies, and daisies.

Pamela, the florist who was not a florist, mind you, but a *floral designer,* was causing one problem. She did not want to use Queen Anne's lace in the bouquets.

For generations the women in Rose's family had been named after flowers—Lily, Rose, Camellia, Daisy, Violet, Primrose, Holly. There had even been a pair of great-aunts named Iris and Pansy. But by the time Annie had been born, they had run out of names. Rather than name her Petunia, Guy and Rose had decided to name her Anne, after Guy's mother.

Of course, when she turned four, Annie started to want a flower of her own, so her parents had declared that Queen Anne's lace was her flower. That's why Guy sometimes called her Queenie or Miss Queenie. Rose's parents had joined in. They'd stopped mowing a dry corner of the Adirondacks property, and within two years the Queen Anne's lace had taken over.

So Cami wanted the bouquets to be camellias, roses, and Queen Anne's lace. Pamela-the-floral-designer objected. Queen Anne's lace—aka wild carrot—was a noxious weed. Other blossoms could provide a similar feathery texture.

Pamela was, she told us, *extremely* active in the local gardening societies, and one of the *oldest* organizations had recently presented a program on noxious weeds, including Queen Anne's lace. So, as a commitment to the botanical integrity of the local communities, the use of such plants in any way was being *strongly* discouraged.

"We don't intend to cultivate them," Rose said evenly. "We want them in the bouquets, that's all."

Oh, no. Rose needed to *understand*. Truly. Pamela was offering only a little advice, the *littlest* bit. This would get Rose off to *such* a disadvantageous start if people knew that she was insisting on this. Things were done a certain way out here, and of course Rose *couldn't* be expected . . . not at first, but—

Even I, as inept as I was at the nuances of girl fighting, could see what was happening. Pamela-the-floral-designer was trying to lord it over Rose, make Rose feel like an upstart arriviste.

It wasn't working.

"I'm sorry to say this." Rose began gathering up Pamela's various brochures and sketches. "This is a deal breaker. If you want this job, you are using Queen Anne's lace."

Pamela fluttered, her hands fluttered, her eyelids fluttered, her brain probably fluttered. Oh, this wasn't a *job* to her. It was a creative opportunity.

I knew, Rose knew, and Pamela knew that she had already invested hours and hours, if not days, in this wedding. She had gotten Rose and Guy to hire her favorite landscape designer and her favorite lighting designer.

Rose stood up. “I’ve appreciated your time. I’m sorry we weren’t able to agree.”

Oh no no *no*. Rose sat back down, and we listened to another ten minutes of gushing and fluttering while Pamela justified why she was deigning to work with a family so deeply unconcerned with botanical integrity.

On New Year’s Day, Guy and Rose had invitations to three open-houses that they felt obligated to attend, at least briefly. All the hosts had said that houseguests were welcome, but I had no interest in going. I couldn’t imagine wanting to go to a crowded stand-up event where I knew no one. Mike would enjoy such events even less than I, but when he came downstairs in the morning, he was wearing gray slacks and a good sweater. I shouldn’t have been surprised. Of course, Claudia would want to go to these open-houses. She wouldn’t know anyone either, but she could write about them on her blog.

I thought she was overdressed. She had on one of those straight knee-length Jackie Kennedy-type dresses with a little jacket over it. The jacket and dress were woven with twists of her sand-tan-beige colors. When she leaned forward, the lining of her jacket was a jolt of vivid coral. Her shoes were the same coral; the heels were high and narrow, the sides low cut.

But what did I know? I was wearing a fleece pullover that the boys had given me for Christmas.

At the last minute Guy took off the sweater he had

had on under his blazer, draping it over the back of one of the sofas. As they were leaving the house, I asked Rose if she wanted me to take it back upstairs. She thanked me.

I had never been in the master suite before. It turned out to be a very large space with a seating area and doors leading to closets or dressing rooms. But it was nearly empty. The king-size bed was made with an ivory comforter and white pillowcases that didn't quite match. The bed itself had no headboard or footboard. The nightstands didn't match, nor did the two reading lamps. The parquet floor wasn't carpeted, and although there was a loveseat in the seating area, it sat there by itself: there were no tables or lamps to make it usable. The walls were off-white, and there was nothing on them.

For the first time, I wondered about Rose and Guy's relationship. Except for the occasional jokes about what an extrovert he was or how he spent too much money on gifts for her and the girls, I'd never heard her criticize him, and he spoke of her only with respect. I'd never heard them disagree or even bicker.

But I'd also never seen them touch each other.

Nine

It was a relief to get home after New Year's. The women at the engagement party were right: I didn't want to spend the rest of my life celebrating my holidays at my son's in-laws'. It was a bore to get up there, I wasn't in love with the house's cold formality, and I couldn't stand all the nonsense associated with who got what room when.

Above all, I hadn't liked staying under the same roof as Mike and Claudia. They had been staying in the center front room that my father had been in, and all weekend long Claudia kept talking about "our" room. She never said, *I need to get a sweater*. It was always, *I need to go up to* our *room to get a sweater*. Unlike at Thanksgiving, she frequently touched Mike. When he'd been reading the paper at the table, she'd rested her hand on his shoulder and leaned over him, her breast brushing close to his hair. When he'd been sitting on one of the leather sofas, she'd sat down next to him and lifted his arm so that it was around her shoulders. On New Year's Day, when they were waiting for Rose and Guy so that they could all go off to the open-houses as two happy little couples on a happy little double date, Claudia had straightened the collar of Mike's shirt and then kissed his cheek.

We all know you're a couple, I had wanted to shriek. *Yes, you're having sex. We get that.*

But there was no point in talking to a Bobo doll. It would never stop bouncing back, never stop smiling.

We'd gone directly from Colorado to the Hamptons. Zack and I had been away from home for a week and a half. So much mail had accumulated beneath the mail slot that Zack had to give the front door a good shove to get it open. Dropping his suitcase, blocking my path into the house, he squatted and started shuffling through the junk mail, catalogs, and holiday letters, looking for a big envelope with green printing. It was near the bottom of the heap; it must have arrived right after we had left. It was his acceptance at Stone-Chase.

He ripped open the envelope. A fierce joy flashed across his face as he read the letter. He handed it to me.

That he would be admitted was never in doubt. His record was better than their published averages, and, more important, this was the right school for him and he was the right student for the school. What he found so darkly satisfying was the amount of "merit money" he would get. I peered over his shoulder to read the letter. Stone-Chase College would discount his tuition to the extent that his education would cost less than if he went to one of Virginia's state universities. The more money Stone-Chase gave him, the less he would have to take from his dad.

Zack must have e-mailed Jeremy his news, and Cami must have told her parents, because a few days later Guy called me in the middle of the day. "Tell me about this college Zack is so excited about."

Annie was a junior at Berkeley Carroll, a private school in her neighborhood, and apparently her high-school record was even worse than Zack's. The Zander-Browns were hiring a private college counselor to work with her. The counselor had encouraged them to have Annie start visiting colleges. Perhaps being able to envision herself on a college campus would motivate her to apply herself more.

"Stone-Chase may not be a great fit," I said. Its students were earnest, middle-class, even slightly provincial. Annie was trendy and urban. "But it will be an easy place for her to visit alone."

Since Zack's offer from Stone-Chase was "early action" and not "early decision," he didn't have to make up his mind until he heard from the other schools in April. That was one thing Mike was pleased about. Since Stone-Chase wasn't asking for an answer, Zack could wait and see.

But Zack desperately wanted the process to be over. Stone-Chase was his first choice. Why shouldn't he accept its offer? He didn't want to go to those other schools. Why should he give them a chance to turn him down?

Of course, he wasn't going to admit to Mike that he was afraid of the other schools rejecting him. So the two of them fought every time they saw each other. It got to the point that I was almost relieved whenever Claudia was joining them. They didn't fight in front of her.

When I worked the night shift, Zack left for school before I got home. One morning in early February I came home from work and found a note on the kitchen table: "Dad said it was okay if I withdrew my other aps so I did."

I called Mike at his office. "Zack said you and he

worked this out. I know it was hard for you to give in, but really this is the best thing for him."

"What are you talking about?" His voice was sharp. "Zack and I didn't work anything out. If anything, last night was the worst ever."

I reached across the kitchen counter to get Zack's note. I read it to Mike.

"I never said any such thing," he snapped. "Where did he get that idea?"

"Isn't it possible that you said, 'do whatever you want,' or something like that?" When Mike was really angry, he got sarcastic, saying things that he obviously didn't mean. I'd always hated that. How could I fight back?

"If I did say it, I didn't mean it," he said. "And he should have known that."

"But if you're going to say something you don't mean, why shouldn't he act on something he doesn't believe?" I wasn't sure that came out right, but my point was simple: *If you're going to act like a big baby, why shouldn't he?*

When Zack walked in the door that afternoon, he was tense and defensive. He confirmed my sense of what had happened. "Dad told me to go ahead and do it. That I could shoot myself in the foot if I wanted."

"You know he didn't mean it."

"It's too late now. I mailed the letters already, stopped at the Palisades post office on the way to school."

This was a kid who would wait until January 23 to

write his grandfather a thank-you note for a very generous Christmas gift and then leave the note sitting on his desk until mid-March when I would finally address the envelope. But last night he had come home, written and printed seven letters, addressed seven envelopes, and found seven stamps. He was serious.

"Do you send in your acceptance to Stone-Chase?"

"Well, I did sort of not do anything about the U.Va. ap. But I'm not going to school with a bunch of preppies."

Did sort of not do anything. It took me a moment to figure that out. He hadn't withdrawn his University of Virginia application. His defiance of his father had not been complete. In fact, it had been pretty toothless.

The University of Virginia was known as a "public Ivy"—one of the state-supported institutions that aspired to provide an educational environment comparable to those at the Ivy League schools. It had the highest admission standards of all the Virginia state schools, but Zack and I were now Virginia residents. Because of that, the college counselor had said that Zack had a chance at U.Va., not a great one, but if all the stars lined up right, he might get admitted or at least be put on the wait list.

I called Mike again. "He left U.Va. in."

"So he's not such an idiot."

"Mike! Do *not* talk about him that way. You're being a bigger idiot than he is."

"I know, I know." He sighed. "I just never expected to feel so powerless, to have so little influence."

Three years—no, almost three and a half years—and Mike was finally appreciating how much had changed, how much he had lost, when he decided to move out.

Very challenging for the perfectionist, I learned from Claudia's Web site, is attempting something new. If you can't be perfect immediately, you may want to give up. But the person who Manages her Perfectionism should be willing to risk a low, slow learning curve.

So Claudia was going to learn to play golf, one of "Michael's" favorite sports.

Golf? I say that I will do anything physical, but I can't stand golf. I don't mind going to the driving range and whacking away, but all the fiddliness involved in really learning how to play drives me nuts. If you're using a cart, you get no exercise, and a round takes way too long for me.

Time seemed to be moving quickly. Cami and Jeremy had gotten into Vanderbilt's medical school. It was a fine school, but not their first choice. They didn't particularly want to live in Nashville. But just as they were getting reconciled to the idea, the University of Pennsylvania accepted them both. Penn is one of the very best medical schools in the country, and they far preferred Philadelphia to Nashville. I was glad to have them back on the East Coast, and Guy and Rose had to feel the same.

But Jeremy was surprisingly subdued on the phone. "What's wrong?" I asked.

"It's Cami and this wedding," he said. "She keeps saying that planning it ought to be fun, but that it feels like a huge burden for both her and her mom."

I wasn't sure what to say. The caterers were now urging Guy and Rose to cut a door into the back wall of the garage to facilitate the movement of the waiters. "How do you feel about everything?"

"Fine. Fine. Everything's fine . . . except, Mom, doesn't it seem strange not to be getting married in a church? Isn't a wedding ceremony supposed to be religious?"

"Oh, Jeremy." I sighed. My forcing him to go to Sunday school had apparently had some impact. "The time for thinking that is long gone."

"Michael"—again, according to the Web site—surprised Claudia with a set of golf clubs for her birthday. She was taking weekly lessons and was practicing at least thirty minutes every single day even if she was only working with her putter on her living-room rug.

Thirty minutes of nudging a ball along a piece of carpet? I would want to hang myself.

At the end of February the Alden School theater staged one of Shakespeare's history plays. Zack had worked hard on the sets and lights, so I went. Rose had encouraged me to read a summary of the play beforehand and take a copy so that I could keep track of who was coming onstage. "They all enter at the same time, and it's pretty easy to get your Warwicks and your Westmorelands confused." I followed her advice, but fell asleep anyway. At the traditional cast party the following night, several of the seniors brought some marijuana-laced brownies. The kids involved were disciplined, and their prospective colleges were informed. Fortunately for Zack, the school was punishing only the coconspirators directly involved in the manufacture and transport, not the many kids who had known about the plan beforehand.

"Is this a 'there but for the grace of God go I' kind of moment?" I asked my not-entirely-innocent child.

"Not at all," he said cheerfully. "It's a 'there but for the grace of Mom.' No one was going to bake from scratch, and everyone knew that there was no way there would be any brownie mix in this house."

I had always known that there was something morally wrong with using cake mixes.

U. Va. did indeed turn Zack down, so a week before his eighteenth birthday, he sent in his forms to Stone-Chase, telling me that he was going to go to campus for some carnival-type thing the last weekend in April. Mike was remarkably gracious about this outcome, claiming that he'd never thought that there was anything wrong with Stone-Chase; he'd simply wanted Zack to "keep his options open." The peace between the two of them was probably only superficial, but that was better than open warfare.

I invited Mike over for dinner on Zack's birthday. "And I do hope," I said to Mike, "that Claudia will be able to join us."

That was a lie. I didn't want Claudia to join us, and I already knew that she couldn't. I'd checked her Web site and found out that she was going to be out of town that evening.

I don't lie. That had kept my mother going through my teen years; if she asked me a direct question, I would answer honestly. So if I hadn't lied to my mother when I was being stupid and reckless, why was I starting now?

"You want Claudia too?" Mike knew how honest I was; it never occurred to him to doubt me. He paused for a moment. "That's very good-hearted of you, Darcy. I appreciate it more than you realize."

I felt like a heel. I wasn't good-hearted. I was a blog-reading, lying snoop.

Claudia did send Zack a gift, a beautifully wrapped box containing a leather portfolio, more suitable to a graduating law student. But I couldn't blame her too much. Teenaged guys were hard to shop for.

"My gift isn't as well wrapped," Mike said and passed Zack a thick manila envelope.

"Gosh, Dad, some people might say that it isn't wrapped at all," Zack said, but his tone was light. He didn't care about wrapping paper.

"And they would have a point," Mike answered,

"and here's another copy for you, Darcy." He slid another envelope across the table to me.

I had no idea what was in it, but waited to let Zack open it first. He took a thick document out, squinted at the first page, and looked puzzled. "What is it, Dad? I don't get it."

"Just read it."

I took out my copy. *Trust Agreement for Zachary Douglas Van Aiken . . . Darcy Bowersett Van Aiken, trustee . . .*

Mike had set up a trust fund for Zack. "You didn't do this for Jeremy," I said.

"Would someone tell me what's going on?" Zack asked.

"Well, Zack," Mike said, "as long as you're at Stone-Chase and are getting your expenses discounted for academic merit, I will put that amount of money for you in this trust."

Zack stared at him, disbelieving. He probably thought that it was more likely that Mike would sell him off as an indentured servant than set up a trust fund for him.

"You've earned that money, not me. Without this, you reap no benefit from what you accomplished. So the money's yours, and it's not for graduate school. We'll still pay for that. But there are massive strings attached. You can't buy a van and bum around California. It's for a down payment on a house or something like that."

"Wow." Zack still wasn't sure what to say. He was

so used to Mike being angry at him that he didn't know how to react. He looked down at the papers again, almost embarrassed to be moved. "I was talking to a guy whose brother is in dental school, and he says that setting up a dental practice is really expensive."

"Then you would have this," Mike said. "You can use it for anything that your mother approves of."

"Why is Mom the trustee? Why not you?"

I had wondered that myself.

"Because there are the massive strings." And Mike smiled, that wonderful, clear, sweet smile of his. "If you decide you want to fight about it every day from now until you are thirty, you can fight with her."

Money mattered to Mike; it was part of his vocabulary, his way of communicating. This trust sent a signal—he trusted me, and he wasn't trying to control Zack.

And maybe he was even proud of Zack.

Even though I had taken the night shift on Christmas Eve, I was working Easter weekend. Working two holidays meant that I had first pick of the schedule for the rest of the spring and summer, which was good as I wanted to take off a full week for the wedding and a long weekend for Jeremy's college graduation.

Zack hadn't seen his grandmother since the engagement party in October, so he went up to Philadelphia with Mike and Claudia for Easter. He was not looking forward to the trip, but I've got to give Claudia credit. She'd worked hard to find activities that interested him. She and Zack—on their own, without Mike or his mother—spent Saturday afternoon in some strange little art galleries. On Easter afternoon, a new theater was having an open-house fund-raiser, and she'd gotten tickets to that.

Whenever I'd gone to Philadelphia, I'd always tried to distract the boys by taking them outside. We'd go on hikes, play ball, or rent boats. Those were Mike-Darcy-Jeremy activities. Zack had gone along because I'd made him.

But Claudia's plan had been designed to please only Zack, not the whole family. And it worked.

The following week she reported to her loyal Web site readers that she and "Michael" had gone golfing together for the first time, playing nine holes on a short course. They had had a lovely time being outdoors on a beautiful day, and she hadn't made a fool of herself even though, since they hadn't kept score, she couldn't say exactly how she had done.

If she thought Mike Van Aiken hadn't kept score, then she didn't know him. He might not have counted her strokes, he might not have been writing anything down, but in his head he was keeping track of his own game.

Rose called. "Annie went to visit Stone-Chase yesterday, and she loved it."

That was a bit of a surprise. I couldn't imagine Annie being happy in such a nonurban setting.

"In fact," Rose continued, "we got a text message from her late last night, asking if she could stay another day and come home Sunday morning."

"That's nice," I said, and I was about to tell her that Zack had gone up this morning for the college's annual Spring Fling, but her call-waiting went off and she had to go.

I wondered if Rose and Guy knew about this Spring Fling. Probably not. I picked the phone back up and called Zack on his cell.

"Mom." He would have seen my number on caller ID. "What do you want?" He wouldn't like the idea that I was checking up on him.

"I just wanted to let you know that Annie Zander-Brown is on campus," I said quickly.

"I know. I saw her."

Annie was hard to miss. "She's okay, isn't she?"

"Why wouldn't she be? Look, can I go now?"

"Sure. I'll see you tonight. Call me before you leave, okay?"

"Yeah, whatever."

It was a beautiful day, and I went out to work in the yard, slipping my cell phone into my pocket. As often happens when I'm doing something physical, I lost track of time. It was almost two o'clock when my phone rang.

I pulled it out of my pocket and flipped it open. "Zack? What is it?"

"Mom . . . Mom . . . it's Annie . . . she's drinking, she's drinking a lot. There isn't supposed to be alcohol here, but there is. So should I do anything?"

"Did you try talking to her?"

"No. She's with all these guys, they're Greeks, the fraternity guys . . . I can't go. . . . I don't know, she's not my responsibility, is she? But she's making an ass of herself. I mean, what do I do if she passes out?"

"Call a security guard. Or take her to Student Health. She's not a student, but I'm sure they would look at her."

"But she'll get in trouble. I don't want her to get in trouble. I don't want to be a big dork."

I paused. I didn't have a good feeling about this. "Zack, do you want me to come up? I don't mind being the big dork. I can be there in an hour."

"Yeah . . . if you want to, yeah, if you want to."

It took me a little more than an hour to get to Westridge, the little town where Stone-Chase was. As I got close to the campus, I called Zack, and he directed me to the closest parking lot, a few of the best spaces becoming available as families with young children left.

The Stone-Chase campus is always idyllic, with green lawns enclosed by white-trimmed buildings made of rosy brick. Today it was full of people, gathered around fair-type booths. I could "pie a Greek" or "dunk an athlete" if I were so minded. There were also little-kiddie rides, a moon bounce, even a car-crash simulator.

There wasn't any obvious liquor, no beer cans or kegs, but plenty of students were carrying water bottles that didn't look as if they were filled with water. Zack took me to one of the smaller quadrangles. It was crowded, but I instantly spotted Annie. She was trying to dance on the rim of a trash can. She was wearing a Stone-Chase T-shirt as a dress; it was sashed with a man's striped tie.

She was being partnered by a guy who was sitting on the shoulders of another boy. Other kids were trying to help her balance. On the grass around them were a number of thermoses. I doubted that they had been used for coffee.

I made my way through the crowd. "Annie, come on down."

She looked down. "Darcy?"

She let go of her partner and started to lose her balance. I grabbed at her, pulling her toward me so that she didn't fall into the trash can. I caught her under her armpits, steadied her. She was very light.

"Darcy?" She was having trouble focusing.

And then she threw up on me. The other students lurched back, but I held on to her, and she sagged against me, retching, the contents of her stomach cascading down the left side of my body, spilling over on my bare arm—bits of hot dog, shreds of lettuce, pickle relish, sour and sticky.

I lowered her to the ground. She curled up into a ball and moaned. The students kept a safe distance. I knelt beside her. Her breathing was regular, she was pale, but not bluish, and her skin was not clammy. I pinched her and she instantly jerked; her reflexes were still good. She didn't have alcohol poisoning.

"Are you her mom?" one of the students asked almost timidly.

"No, but I know her family."

"Which dorm is she in? We'll help you get her there."

I looked at them. The vomit was drying on my arm. "She doesn't have a dorm. She's not a student here. She's a high-school junior, visiting your college."

That sobered them up quickly. "She told us that she was a transfer. That she had come at the beginning of the semester."

"Oh, come on. You think that she's been here since then, and this is the first time you noticed her?"

They glanced at one another, admitting the truth of that.

None of them knew which girls she was staying with, and Zack didn't either. A couple of the students helped me get her to a dorm room, and she and I had a lovely afternoon. She threw up another couple of times, and then she just wanted to sleep. Pretty soon the girls she was staying with were located, and they crept in, apologetic and frightened. They went to pack up her things, and once she stopped vomiting, I got her cleaned up for the car ride. She rode home with me, sleeping most of the way. Zack followed us in his car.

When we were back at the house, I told her that she needed to call her parents.

"I will," she said. "But not yet. They're taking Finney to an early movie. I'll call them when they get home."

The plan was for Zack to take her to the train station Sunday morning. She had originally taken the train to Baltimore, but she said that she had a credit card to pay for the extra fare involved in leaving from Washington. I reminded the two of them to set alarms—I had to be at the hospital before eight on Sunday morning—and then left them to sort out the arrangements.

Zack was in his basement bedroom playing video games when I got home from work Sunday evening. "You got Annie to the train?" I asked.

He pushed back from his desk. "Actually I drove her up to Baltimore. If she had changed her ticket, her parents would have found out about what happened. So, Mom, please don't tell them. I promised her that you wouldn't tell them."

"She told me that she was going to call them when they got home from the movie."

"And she did call them. She just didn't tell them where she was."

"Oh, Zack, come on, I have to tell them."

"No, no, you don't. Yes, she had too much to drink, but she's fine now. Come on, Mom, please, don't make me sorry that I called you. I promised her."

I supposed that it was no accident that Cami and Jeremy had felt that they needed to go to a California college. They needed to get away from their families.

They were each so tied up with being the "good child" that they couldn't let go of that role without moving across the country.

But Zack was going to be only an hour away. He and I were going to continue to be available to each other. I wanted him to be able to call me. I wanted him to be able to make that transition from childhood to adulthood without having to cross the continent. He needed to believe that I trusted him, that I would let him make his own choices as surely as if he were in California.

But still . . . not tell a girl's mother?

"She doesn't want to worry them," Zack pleaded. "She says her mom is totally stressed out about this wedding, and she hates to cause her more trouble."

I could sympathize with that. I didn't want to cause Rose any more anguish either.

"Okay, I won't tell them," I promised.

Ten

Spending those hours in the Stone-Chase College dorm made it easy for me to imagine Zack living there. If Zack were living there, then I would—and this was something I needed to face—be living alone. Probably for the rest of my life.

I have trouble admitting that I'm no longer twenty-five. I was always stronger, faster, more agile than all the other girls on the playground and a fair number of the boys. I can still pound the stairs down to the Emergency Room when they can't get an IV into a failing baby. I can lift patients and can wedge myself into tight spaces to look at the back of a machine. I'd mind losing those abilities as much as other women must mind the crow's feet and sagging boobs.

I'm as effective at work as ever, but the cost is higher. When I started this schedule of three twelve-hour shifts, I could come home, make dinner, do the laundry, and help the boys with their homework. Now I barely check my e-mail.

And I couldn't live with myself if something happened to a patient because I couldn't get down the hall fast enough.

I had the skills to do a variety of other things—I could help run drug trials for pharmaceutical companies; I could review cases for HMOs or insurance companies; I could even be director of nursing at a midsize hospital. But those were desk jobs; I would hate them, and I would never be as good at them as I was at this.

The one thing that interested me was nursing education. I watched the new nurses. Some were well trained and confident. Others were ill-prepared and didn't know it. Nothing is worse in a hospital setting than people who think they know more than they do. Of course, to get a faculty appointment to teach nursing, I would need to have a Ph.D. in nursing. Thanks to Ritalin, I could flog myself through the first part of such a program. In fact, I probably already had a lot of the course credits. And the research part of a dissertation would interest me, but the actual writing of a book-length manuscript? That was daunting. If I couldn't stay awake during a Shakespeare play, how was I supposed to write a dissertation?

While I made no progress on figuring out what to do with the rest of my life, I did finally solve a more urgent problem. I got a dress to wear to the wedding.

Mike had already been instructed twice by Claudia to ask whether I had found a dress, and if not, could she help? Each time I had told him not to worry. Even though I hadn't then found the dress, I definitely did not want Claudia's help.

I had gone out twice on my own and had not even come close to locating a low-contrast print with soft colors, Impressionistic rather than distinct outlines, and an even balance between figure and background. But I was not as pathetic as Claudia probably thought I was. I did grow up in East Grand Rapids. I have some sense and some experience. I called the personal shopping service at Neiman Marcus and told the representative what I needed.

"Oh, my," she said after I had read off the list of requirements. "I thought I had seen it all. Mothers of the groom have to jump through a lot of hoops, but this . . . I've never heard of anyone getting such very detailed instructions."

"It's not the bride's family who's insisting on this." I wanted to defend Rose. "It's my ex-husband's girlfriend."

"Ah, yes," she said knowingly. "These not-quite family members are sometimes the worst."

She called me back several times to say that she was working on it, that she hadn't forgotten me. Finally she located three dresses, but as she had told me over the phone, only one of them was really right.

I went to the store and tried it on. The background was a pale amethyst; the design was layers of some blurry leaflike things in shades of what she called "champagne and gold" and I was going to call beige. There was something drapey going on at the neckline, but otherwise it seemed a perfectly ordinary dress.

Except for the price. This dress was unimaginably expensive. In a normal year I don't spend half that much on my whole wardrobe. I hated the thought of spending so much money.

"I understand," the saleslady said. "You should definitely go on looking, but remember how hard it was for me to find this." She assured me that as long as the tags were still on the dress, I could return it at any time. "Take this as a backup in case you can't find anything else."

I handed her my credit card.

At least I didn't have to find something to wear for the rehearsal dinner. Claudia had taken everyone's measurements over New Year's, and she was working hard on those unifying diagonals of hers.

The rehearsal dinner was becoming more elaborate by the minute. Although Guy and Rose had told us countless times that we could limit the rehearsal-dinner guest list to the wedding party and family members, many of the other wedding guests were coming to the Hamptons for the weekend, and Claudia was eager to invite as many of them as the restaurant would hold. "She says that we need to remember," Mike told me, "how high a profile Guy has. People won't want to feel slighted."

I didn't know how high or low a profile Guy had, but I did know that the more people at the dinner, the more important Claudia could make herself sound on her blog. I now only occasionally went to her Web site because the blog was entirely about the construction of those dresses. For the first time in her career, she had placed the article with a fashion magazine, not a sewing one, and that was a big deal to her.

Although she didn't mention names or even identify me as the groom's mother, I knew which dress was mine. I learned, along with the rest of the population of cyberspace, that she was sewing bust pads into my dress to compensate for my "youthfully boyish" figure. I am not a modest person, and anyone looking at me closely would figure out that a few bust pads wouldn't hurt, but did we have to talk about it at such length?

May and June were going to be full of rituals. Cami and Jeremy were graduating from college the second weekend in May; Zack was graduating from high school the first weekend in June, and the wedding was two weeks after that.

Jeremy's graduation was the weekend of Zack's senior prom, so Zack wasn't going to California with me. I was also happy to learn that Claudia couldn't go either. She had a professional commitment in Cleveland that had been scheduled more than a year earlier.

Finney was also not going to the graduation. It was unusual for the Zander-Browns to travel without him, but his school was having a little carnival on that Saturday. Rose and Guy knew that if they told him that he wouldn't mind missing the carnival, he would believe them. He was easily manipulated. But it didn't seem fair; he would have a grand time at the carnival. So Rose had arranged for him to stay with a family that she knew through the corn-allergy network. The Zander-Browns had kept their children before; this was the first time Finney was going to stay with them. A family from the school would chaperone him at the carnival. He was excited about the plan even without someone telling him to be.

Mike called me the night before I was leaving for California. "It's about these invitations to the rehearsal dinner." He sounded hesitant.

"What about them?" I glanced at the buff-colored garment bag that Neiman Marcus had used for my overpriced mother-of-the-groom dress. The sight of it did not make me feel very charitable toward Claudia.

Mike said that Claudia had used three different printers, one for the maps, one for the vellum pocket, and a third for the little luggage tag . . . which did not seem like the actions of a person who was managing her perfectionism particularly well. As soon as the maps and the pockets were completed, she'd quickly turned them over to the person she'd contracted to sew the pockets onto the maps and stuff the tags into the pockets. When the final invitations had been delivered to her this morning, she realized that my name was still misspelled.

"She is devastated," Mike said. "She's been on the phone all day, trying to get it fixed. She needs to have both the map and the vellum pocket reprinted, and neither printer is being very accommodating about redoing them in a timely way."

"I thought printing could be done overnight these days."

"Apparently these were pretty complex jobs. The map guy already had to redo the maps once at his own expense."

"So she's used up all her chits."

"I don't know about that," Mike said. "I've told her that she needs to go with a simpler invitation, but she's very passionate about these."

What on earth was this wedding doing to people? I wondered if I was getting as crazy as the rest of them and simply hadn't noticed.

"She was going to call you," Mike continued, "and ask you if you wouldn't mind having the invitations sent out like this, but that didn't seem fair. She wouldn't mean to be difficult, but she cares so much about this that I don't think she would let up until you said that it was okay. So the compromise was that I would ask you."

"I don't love this," I admitted. "It was already a little humiliating to have my name last on the invitation, to be listed after her, and then to have it misspelled; yeah, it does feel like a slap in the face."

"She didn't mean it that way. She really didn't. But I agree with you. I do think she needs to come up with something simpler."

"I didn't say that." Mike standing up for me really made a difference; I was surprised by how much. "You know I don't obsess about things like this. If these invitations really matter to her, then tell her to go ahead and use them."

"You're such a good sport, Darcy," he said with relief. "You really are. She shouldn't be asking this of you."

I noticed his pronoun. *She* was asking this, not *we*.

I hung up and went back to packing for graduation. I wondered if I had given in too easily. Where was the line between standing up for yourself and being a pointless pain in the ass, fighting about everything? I had already insisted on seeing the seating chart; I wasn't going to let Claudia put me at the losers' table again. I wasn't going to let her pretend to be the mother of the groom.

But an extra *e* in my name? I supposed I could live with that. It would, as Annie had said earlier, thrill Finney to see that I was "Darcey."

Very early the next morning Guy Zander-Brown called. "Oh, good, I knew you'd be up." They were already on their way to the airport. "Rose got an e-mail from Claudia about the invitations. Claudia wanted to let us know that you don't mind, but let me tell you, we do."

"It's not that big a deal, Guy. It's not like she left my name off the invitation altogether."

"Nonsense," he said in his brisk, high-energy way. "And this is going to be fixed, Darcy. This is going to be fixed. Claudia's expressing the master copy of the map to my office. I've already got an intern working on it, and my interns are very scary people. They would kill to please me."

"For heaven's sake, Guy, it's just an *e*."

"This is nonnegotiable," he said. "There's nothing to discuss. This is going to be fixed. End of subject. And if you go on protesting, I'm going to assume that you're doubting my ability to make negotiation road-kill out of you."

I could never outnegotiate Guy. "Yes, I would be roadkill. In fact, I'd drive myself straight to the mortician, save everyone the bother of picking up my corpse."

Guy had encouraged me to let his assistant Mary Beth make my travel arrangements so that we would all be staying in the same hotel and could use the same ground transportation. When I tried to give her my credit-card information, she assured me that the family had a gazillion frequent-flyer miles, some of which she had cashed in to cover all the tickets, including mine.

She might well have been lying. I wouldn't have put it past Guy to pay for my ticket, but I have too much sense to pick a fight that I knew I would lose. Mary Beth had gotten my seat assignment, so when I printed up my boarding pass Friday morning, I hardly looked at it, just double checked the time of my flight. It was only when I was actually at the gate that I realized I had a first-class ticket.

Well, well, well. This was nice. Very nice indeed. Free champagne, my own little TV; a blanket thicker than a sheet of copy paper. A person could get used to this.

Mary Beth had instructed me to go to baggage claim even if I didn't have bags. A handsome young man, his blond surfer hair neatly combed into a ponytail, was near the carousel assigned to my flight. He was holding a sign: MRS. VAN AIKEN. He escorted me to a luxurious but reasonably sized car and then drove to a very posh hotel.

We were on the "concierge floor." The bellman showed me how to use my key card to get the elevator to go to that floor and then led me to a cluster of rooms that could have been a one-, two-, or three-bedroom suite. Guy and Rose had taken all three bedrooms as well as the living room. I tipped the bellman and explored my room, checking out the toiletries in the spacious bathroom and rolling my eyes at the prices of the snacks in the minibar. There was a big arrangement of silk flowers on the low table in front of the loveseat. Except that they weren't silk, I realized as I got closer to that end of the room. They were real and, according to the little white card tucked into the foliage, for me from Rose, Guy, Cami, Annie, and Finney.

Fresh flowers to a hotel room? I was going to be here only two nights, and I couldn't haul them back to D.C. in the overhead compartment of an airplane. It seemed like a waste.

But a mighty nice waste.

Ten minutes later I heard Guy, Rose, and Annie at the outer door. They had come out to California early in the day so that Guy could meet with a client while Rose and Annie visited a college.

"How was your flight?" Guy was the first to speak. "And you found Drew and the car? Is your room okay?"

"Everything was perfect, from the champagne on the plane to the flowers here."

"You have to thank Guy for the flowers," Rose said. "They were his idea."

"It was more an impulse than an idea," Guy said. "After we checked in, we were saying how glad we were that you were staying with us, so I called the front desk. And I've also heard from my office. The corrected invitations will go in the mail on Tuesday."

For a moment, this very successful, very dynamic man looked like an overgrown puppy, eager to please.

That was it; that's what explained him. Guy liked to

please the women in his personal life. He wanted their approval. That's why he bought Rose the expensive handbags that she didn't carry: he was trying to please her. That's why his wallet was always open for Cami and Annie: he wanted to make them happy. He was, at his core, playing to an audience of three—his wife and daughters. And now I had been added to the list. He wanted to do nice things for me. Not seduce me, thank goodness, just please me.

I wondered—did Rose give him the appreciation and the recognition that he wanted? She was ambivalent about the luxury of their lives. While rationally she valued the lifelong security that Guy had provided for Finney, a part of her was nostalgic for the days when all the clients could fit into her kitchen for Sunday-night suppers that had to be pasta because that's all anyone could afford. She didn't want to be the rich-bitch boss's wife. Did that mean that she had trouble mustering sufficient enthusiasm for Guy's expensive little treats?

Not me. This luxury was a major deal for me, and I was going to show it. So I took a breath and said my piece. I wasn't used to first-class plane tickets or luxury suites. It was a wonderful treat. I felt very taken care of, very pampered, and I loved it.

A slight flush rose up Guy's neck and his eyes shifted toward the corner of the room. I'd hit the mark.

"Do you ever," Rose asked me, "let other people take care of you?"

"Oh, probably not. It's an occupational hazard

among nurses. We're caregivers. We aren't so great at taking."

"Then practice on us," Guy said warmly. "We'll see that you get used to it."

No, I thought. *Don't take care of me. Figure out how to take care of each other first.*

We had an hour to kill before we were supposed to meet up with Cami, Jeremy, and Mike. Guy went to return some phone calls. With the RSVPs coming in, Rose was starting to work on the seating charts. I offered to help her.

"You can't." She sighed. "But do think of me as being on a suicide watch and promise you'll come into the bathroom and cut my body off the shower-curtain rod before I stop breathing entirely."

I promised to do so and then asked Annie if she wanted to go for a walk.

She agreed, but without much enthusiasm. As we rode the elevator down, it occurred to me that she might be bracing herself for a lecture about her behavior at Spring Fling. I wouldn't have dreamed of doing that. I immediately started jabbering about other things to show her that I wasn't going to.

The hotel was on such a busy street that, once we were outside, it was hard to talk, and I was relieved to shut up. Annie was walking more slowly than she usually did. I don't like walking slowly; it takes the fun out of things. I glanced at her and wondered if she was a little depressed, not just teenaged-girl moody but actually depressed.

We turned down a side street, hoping to find a more pleasant path.

She spoke first. "It's odd to be here without Finney."

"But isn't that less responsibility for you?"

She shrugged. "I suppose so." She didn't seem to care about that. "But we're different when he isn't around. Because of the time change, we got here really early this morning. We checked in and had room service. Mom did wedding stuff, Dad returned calls, and I watched TV. If Finney had been here, we would have set up his action figures on the coffee table or played cards or something. And on the plane, the only time we spoke to each other was when Mom or Dad nagged me about this stupid SAT-prep stuff."

"Oh, honey . . . every parent of a high-school kid is guilty of that."

"No, no." She was suddenly alert, energetic, and urgent. "It's more than that. Everyone's folks bitch about the college crap. I know that, but we're different. I sometimes feel as if our family life is an act we put on for Finney. You know how we're always saying how sweet Finney is? How he always wants everyone to be happy?"

I nodded.

"It's sort of true. But people only need to *seem* to be happy. He can't tell what's real and what's fake. He wants people to seem happy because he gets nervous if they aren't. I'm not blaming him. It's not like he has a choice about it. It's just the way he is. So whenever he's around, we pretend to be happy. We tell jokes and laugh; we act like a real family. But the minute he goes to bed, the curtain goes down, and we all disappear. That's why I love it when you come up, Darcy. You get us all to have fun together, and it's not an act you're putting on for Finney. Even when Finney's gone to bed, we're all still doing stuff together."

This girl wanted more from her family. "Is that why you have such good memories of your grandparents' cottage? Because everyone did things together?"

She nodded. "And this stupid place on Mecox Road just makes everything worse. We never go alone; it's never just us. People are always sucking up to Dad, and Mom has to worry about what we're going to have to eat." She stopped walking. "I've tried, I really have, but Mom and Dad . . . I know it seems like I don't care about anyone but myself, but I've said all year that if they wanted to go out for brunch on Sunday, I'd get up and take care of Finney. Even for their anniversary I made sure that I was going to be home so they could go out together, but they ended up taking him and me with them."

Kids can't save their parents. They can't stop their drug addiction or alcoholism. A ninety-two-pound girl can't restart the heart of her two-hundred-twenty-pound-father no matter how much CPR training she had in Girl Scouts. And, above all, children can't save their parents' marriages.

But some of them sure do try.

"If something ever happened to him"—she was trying not to cry—"we'd all just be strangers."

"Oh, Annie . . . sweetie." I put my arms around her. It was different from hugging my boys. She was smaller than me, petite and delicate. "Maybe things will be better when the wedding is over."

She leaned against me for a moment, then stepped back and pushed her tangle of strawberry-gold curls off her face. "Mom will be less distracted, but the problems will still be there."

She was probably right, and I wasn't going to patronize her by pretending otherwise. "You're very insightful."

She looked up at me. Her expression brightened. "Do you think so? I mean, I know it probably seems like I'm stupid because I get such crappy grades, but I do see things, I notice things. The way people behave and stuff. Nine times out of ten it doesn't get me anywhere; I don't know what to do, but I still notice."

"That's one nice thing about growing up. You get better. Trust me. I don't know what to do half of the time, but that's better than one-tenth of the time, which is how I felt when I was your age."

"Did you really feel this way?" she asked urgently. "That sometimes you understand everything about yourself, but then suddenly there is this little nugget that just doesn't make sense, that you can't explain to yourself or anyone else."

"Yes. I felt that way a lot, but it got better."

"I hope it happens soon," she said with a sigh.

"I hope so too." But I didn't tell her how long it had taken me to understand myself, how long and how many pharmaceuticals.

• • •

The weekend was full of activities. Friday night was a casual dinner organized by the families of Jeremy and Cami's friends. It was an inexpensive, family-style Italian restaurant, and we gathered around long tables. It was noisy and fun, probably like Rose's Sunday-night suppers used to be. Then Saturday was Class Day, with departmental receptions, a class picture, and an awards ceremony, followed by another dinner. We had a brunch to go to on Sunday morning; the actual graduation ceremony would be Sunday afternoon.

During Friday evening and all day Saturday, the tone was exuberant. The graduates stood up and made toasts, telling wild stories about their drinking and their studying, about the embarrassments they had suffered as freshmen and the antics that had nearly gotten them throw out of school. They also laughed about their student-loan debts. They drank toasts to their debts; they made up song parodies about their debts.

I glanced at Mike during the first of these songs. He was sitting forward, drumming his fingers on the table. When he noticed my gaze, he sat back, embarrassed. Then I looked at Guy, and his expression was also private and intense.

These were two men whose offspring were graduating without debt, and they were deeply, silently proud. Neither Guy's big house in the Hamptons nor Mike's flashy little car meant to them what this did.

They had been able to provide their children these educational opportunities.

I touched Mike's arm. "You did good," I whispered.

I would never have done that if Claudia had come.

Everything was easier, more fun, because Claudia wasn't around. I was Jeremy's mom; Mike was Jeremy's dad. Some of the people we were celebrating with probably had no idea that we were divorced.

During the recognition ceremony, Jeremy, to our surprise, got a big community-service award. Many pre-meds do their community service by working with kids who are in the hospital. Jeremy had instead planned activities for their siblings, culminating with a Games Day that pitted, in a noncompetitive way, the siblings of the fourth-floor patients against the siblings of the fifth-floor patients. The professor giving the award cited how much that had done for the morale of the families and the patients.

Mike drew close to me and whispered, "That has your name written all over it. Was it your idea?"

I nodded, and as we watched Jeremy walk up to get the award, Mike drew my hand through his arm. "You did good too," he said.

He would never have done that if Claudia had been there.

I had to wonder . . . what would things have been like if I hadn't moved, if he hadn't met Claudia? Would we have gone on forever as we had the first three years, not together but not really apart either, with him thinking of our old house as his family home and me still making his favorite dishes on Sunday night?

It would have been easy, but it wouldn't have been good. Lurking beneath the comfort would have been too many unresolved issues, too much anger. I'd needed to get a place of my own; he'd needed a relationship with someone who was very different from me. Otherwise we would have simply been marching in place.

But we weren't doing that. We were moving forward. I was, I realized, not angry at him anymore.

I wasn't angry at Mike. This was amazing, incredible. It had probably happened gradually, but all of a sudden I felt as if it were the first day of spring, the wonderful day when you can go outside without a heavy coat.

What a relief it was, not to feel so negative about Mike, the man I had once loved, and to know that he now felt the same way about me. Jeremy was not the only one graduating this weekend. There ought to be diplomas for this too—"The Regents of the University of Marriage and Divorce hereby certify that you are no longer angry."

The class dinner ended early, and Guy invited the other families back to the Zander-Browns' suite. The graduates had been planning to go out to bars afterward, but the lure of free liquor made them decide to come to the suite. Mike and I stopped at a 7-Eleven to buy snacks.

As we were ripping open the bags of chips, Guy said, "And now our resident fun mom will get us started on a game."

He was looking at me. I thought for a moment and suggested charades, something that would have been hard to make fun for Finney.

We divided into teams, and the game soon became extremely competitive, with people putting in obscure, lengthy titles. Our team, which had its share of English majors, offered up *Letters to His Son by the Earl of Chesterfield on the Fine Art of Becoming a Man of the World*, and the guy who got it pretended to vomit in hopes of getting the word *hurl* out of them as a soundalike for *earl*. And since he was a young man, and Annie was Annie, he chose her to pretend to throw up on.

"Not on me," she squealed and shoved him aside. "If you've got to hurl on anyone, do it on Darcy. She doesn't mind."

As soon as she said "hurl," he pointed excitedly at her.

"Girl . . . curl . . . burl," his team shouted. "Earl."

Rose was on my team, but the teams were big enough that she was sitting close enough to Annie to speak to her. "When on earth did you 'hurl' on Darcy?"

"Is it 'earl'?" someone asked. The player nodded vigorously. "It has to have 'earl' in it."

"Chesterfield's Letters," someone else shrieked. "He was an earl."

"At Stone-Chase," Annie said. "During the Spring Fling, when—" she stopped.

"But you said it was twenty words," complained one of the players. "How can it be twenty words?"

The team started laboriously figuring out which words they knew and which they didn't. Rose leaned forward to speak to me. "What is Annie talking about?"

"You need to let her tell you," I said.

Annie was looking at us, worried. She got up. Her team was protesting that that title couldn't have twenty words, and the English majors on our team were insisting that that was the real title. No one noticed as Rose and I followed Annie into Annie's bedroom.

"You didn't tell her?" Annie asked.

I shook my head. "Zack said that he promised you I wouldn't."

"Yes, but—" Either she had forgotten the promise or had assumed that I wouldn't keep it.

"What's this all about?" Rose asked; her voice was stern.

Annie started hesitantly, then ended up telling the story of her misdeeds with some dignity.

Rose was almost speechless. "You were so drunk that Zack called Darcy?"

Annie nodded.

"She might not have been as drunk as Zack thought," I said. "She did vomit, but she never passed out. She was never nonresponsive."

Rose ignored me. “And that’s why you wanted to stay for the extra day?”

Annie again nodded.

“Annie, we will not tolerate your lying to us.”

“I didn’t lie,” she protested. “I said that I wanted to stay because the girls I was with were really nice and I really liked the place—and that was true.”

“But you left out a lot. Darcy having to drive up there, your spending the night with her, Zack taking you to Baltimore . . . Annie, leaving aside the drinking, that’s a huge imposition on other people.”

“I know,” Annie mumbled.

The door burst open. “Annie! Annie!” It was one of her teammates. “We got it, but we’re filing a protest. Come on out.”

Annie looked at her mother.

Rose made a little gesture with her hands. “We can’t deal with this here. It’s not fair to the others. We’ll talk about it at home.”

Desperately relieved, Annie left the room, carefully easing the door almost shut.

Rose and I were alone.

“Darcy, why didn’t you tell me?”

I didn’t have a good answer to that. I sank down on the bed. I was tired, my drink had been too strong, and my medication had worn off ages ago.

“You must know how worried we are about her, how we feel that we know nothing about what she’s doing or feeling . . .”

I had been so happy a few hours earlier, so relieved

to be without the burden of anger, but now it was like my mother was talking to me: *Darcy, why?* She would have been bewildered, disappointed, hurt. And I would not have known how to answer. I would not have been able to explain myself. As Annie had said yesterday, there was this little nugget inside you that you could never explain.

"They asked me not to tell." That was all I could say in my defense.

"Don't you know that I would have protected you? I wouldn't have let them know you told me. I would have figured out some other way that I might have gotten the information. Why couldn't you trust me?"

"I don't know . . . but honestly, Rose, it didn't feel like a trust issue."

"It seems like one to me." She sat down on the other bed. "It's bigger than just this one thing, Darcy. You don't trust anyone, do you? Not really. You never talk about yourself. You're so afraid that someone will feel sorry for you that you act like nothing ever bothers you. You're always making me read between the lines, trying to figure you out."

"No . . . no," I protested. I didn't want to be difficult. She had felt betrayed by so many women—her sister, Jill Allyn, all the women in her neighborhood who had stopped being her friend when she was of no use to their careers. I had wanted to be the one who made that up to her. I had wanted to be her sister, her friend.

"I give up, Darcy." She sounded more exasperated than resigned. "It's too hard. I know you'll change sheets, load the dishwasher, make corn-free ketchup, but ultimately I can pay people to do that. I need more than that from a friend. Managing you, reading you, anticipating you, never having you say what you feel—I could accept that because I believed that we had the mother-to-mother thing, that we would help each other do what was right for the kids."

There was nothing she could have said that would have hurt me more. Nothing. I loved her children, each one of them—Finney, so sweet and vulnerable; Cami, so determined to do what was right; and Annie . . . honestly, of them all, I think I loved Annie the most. She was as vulnerable as Finney. She wanted to love and be loved on a level beyond that of a cognitively disabled eight-year-old. Like Cami, she wanted to do the right thing, but Cami had tasks a person could do. Annie had set impossible tasks for herself; she wanted to save her parents.

I knew what it was like to have a perfect older sibling. I knew what it was like to feel that you didn't understand yourself.

Then suddenly, without thinking, without being aware of having an impulse that I might need to control, I blurted it out. "Rose, have you ever had Annie tested?"

"Tested? Tested for *what?*"

"Oh, God, no, I didn't mean that, not STDs, but for learning issues. Don't you think there's a chance that she has ADD?"

Was I saying this? Was this me talking? I hate

people who make amateur diagnoses, who once they find out that someone in their family has ADD, alcoholism, codependency, anything, they start seeing it everywhere . . . and they don't shut up about it either.

"Of course," Rose answered. Her voice was tight. "We took her to an educational psychologist when she was in fifth grade. She underperforms, that's all. She isn't motivated."

"But, Rose, some of the tests have changed, they've gotten better, and people are understanding girls more and more—"

"Don't you think it breaks my heart to see Annie squandering her potential when she has so much and Finney doesn't? Don't you think I've done everything I possibly could? Are you saying that I care more about this wedding than the welfare of my other child?"

I had not said one word about the wedding. I hadn't even been thinking about it. But that's what Rose had heard. She thought I was judging her for spending so much time on the wedding.

What had I done? After months and months of keeping my mouth shut, why had I opened it now?

I know that you're supposed to say that ADD or any other disability is something that you "have," not something that you "are." But right now that seemed a meaningless distinction. ADD wasn't something I had; it wasn't a new handbag. It was who I was.

I should have never spoken now. This was the first time Rose had traveled any distance without Finney.

She had to be worrying about him constantly. At a time like that, she didn't want to hear about what she had failed to do for another one of her children. My timing had been terrible.

Nonetheless, I did believe that I was right: Annie should be reevaluated in light of the improved understanding of various conditions in girls.

I stood up. "I'm sorry, Rose. I really am. I was wrong not to call you, and I certainly didn't mean to criticize the way you're raising Annie. She's a wonderful girl."

Rose said the right thing—that she knew I meant well, etc. etc.—but she wasn't looking at me. She was not accepting my apology.

Sunday was surprisingly subdued. I wasn't the only one with regrets. The graduates themselves were quieter than they had been on Saturday. They were starting to realize that college was over. Whether it had been grueling or joyous, nothing in their lives would ever be like it again. The immediate friendships, the easy gatherings, the lively, unencumbered fun were over. Some of the graduates were facing the long grind of professional schools, the soul-draining memory work of the first year of law school or medical school. Others were going back home with no greater prospects than the lifeguard jobs they had held every summer since age sixteen. And the debts. No one was joking about the debts today.

Rose was leaving as soon as the ceremony was over, not even trying to find Cami and Jeremy in the crowd. She needed to get home for Finney. The rest of us were on red-eye flights.

I felt guilty as I nestled into my spacious first-class seat. Guilty and sad.

All year long Rose had been reaching out to me, trying to have a real relationship, and I had never responded. "Keep your mouth shut" had been terrible advice. Why had I ever listened to it? Why had I had so little faith in myself?

Eleven

The week before Zack's high-school graduation was full of parties, assemblies, and recitals. Claudia came to several of the events, but I couldn't blame her for how strange and disconnected I felt. The festivities had been taken over by the "lifers," the families whose children had come to Alden as four-year-old prekindergarteners. Zack was, in fact, the newest member of his class, the only student to have been admitted after freshman year.

I went to all the parties, all the banquets. I sat through the performances, watched the slide shows, listened to the speeches, and felt less a part of this school community than I ever had, less connected to the other mothers.

Give me another chance . . . I wanted to beg them. I could be your friend. I could stand around and talk in the parking lot. I would learn to trust you; you would learn to trust me.

But this was the last week of Zack's senior year. There were no more chances. I had failed.

The kids had come to graduation with their cars crammed full of beach chairs and portable beer-pong tables. They grabbed a piece of cake at the reception, handed their diplomas to their parents, and departed for Beach Week.

Mike found me at the reception and invited me to go out to dinner with Claudia and him. I should have gone—that would have been the right thing to do—but I couldn't face how awkward and stilted the evening would have been. It seemed easier to go home alone.

I was surprised at how long the week felt without Zack at home. When people had asked me about being an empty nester, I'd laughed. "I never see him anyway. What difference will it make?"

But it did make a difference. A big one.

My shifts started on Wednesday of that week. One of my patients was a man, a husband, a dad, a failed suicide. He'd lost his job and then made some wild investments, leaving his family in terrible financial trouble. He couldn't face the consequences of what he had done. His suicide attempt had made an even bigger mess because now he was in an ICU bed that cost about a million dollars a minute, and he had stopped paying his health insurance, something his wife had first learned in the emergency room.

Usually I ignore anything I disapprove of in a patient's life . . . if I even know about it in the first place. As unfeeling as this might sound, I can even ignore the fact that he or she is a human being. When someone's heart stops, I don't think of him as a person, a person who is loved and treasured, whose death will devastate his family. I don't even think of his heart. I focus on the monitors. I'm not trying to make this person live so that he can go home to the people who love him. I'm working with everyone else in the room to get that monitor started. It's us and the machine. It wants to stop, and we want it to start. I fight this battle as fiercely as I would if it were Jeremy or Zack in the bed. I have to think of the machine and only the machine because sometimes the machine wins and we lose. Someone's Jeremy or Zack dies, and I can't bear to think about that.

But this man, this suicide, this coward . . . I was angry with him. That was wrong; it could have compromised the care I provided. I had to ask another nurse to change patients with me. I'd never done anything like that before.

The Director of Nursing called me in, asking me if I was all right. "I don't know," I said honestly.

She was a good person, and she cared about me. But she needed me to be okay, she couldn't afford to lose one of her best nurses. So pretty soon I heard myself telling her what she wanted to hear and what I wanted to believe: that this was just situational stress; it would pass.

I could have talked to my father. He would understand, but he would worry. He was still enough of a dad that he would try to fix it. He would offer to pay my tuition if I wanted to go back to school. He would encourage me to go to Africa for a year and help with the AIDS babies. But I didn't want to go to Africa. I needed to fix this in my own way.

I felt as if I were losing everything I cared about. Of course, I'd known that my boys would grow up, but I hadn't expected it to be like this. What if I also lost my job? What if I couldn't be an ICU nurse anymore?

I needed someone to talk to.

I needed Rose.

At least one thing was going well for her. I was getting information about Annie through the family grapevine. The girl was suddenly working hard and doing very well in school.

Obviously I had been wrong about her having ADD. I was surprised, but as a nurse, nothing annoys me as much as a doctor who clings to his first diagnosis even when all the evidence says he is wrong. Apparently Annie had simply been underperforming, and once she set her mind to it, she was able to motivate herself.

Good for you, I thought. *And thank you for doing it now. Your mother needed you to be doing well. It was the best Mother's Day gift you could have given her.*

• • •

Then it was finally here, the week of the wedding.

This was the third time that I'd gone to the Hamptons—although I now knew that if I lived in New York and had any degree of understated cool, I would never say that I was going "to the Hamptons." I would be going "out east."

My other trips had been in November and December, and it was now June. Everything was lush and green. The trees were thick with leaves, and the hydrangea bushes were promising their heavy blossoms. The farm stands were open. Quart baskets of ripe strawberries were arrayed in crimson lines on the weathered plank tables. Bits of dirt clung to the roots of the feathery lettuce while the round heads of cabbage were piled in bushel baskets under the tables. Some stands already had peas and broccoli. I would love to be here in July when the corn and tomatoes would come in, the blueberries and the melons, followed by the fruits of August, the peaches, pears, and plums.

There had to be people who did this right, who didn't come "out east" for status, who weren't burdened by twelve-bedroom faux chateaus filled with professional associates for guests. I could tell by the number of older homes, by the people on the sidewalks with strollers. They came to the Hamptons for the beauty and the peace. They came to be with their families and closest friends. The true heart of these villages was not the glittering fund-raisers that the rest of us read about in the society pages, but what happened inside the houses, behind the hedges.

What had gone wrong for the Zander-Browns? They were good people. Their values were solid; their hearts were in the right place. They had faced Finney's challenges with courage and flexibility.

Was it just the house? Had they simply bought the wrong house in the wrong place? People came to Mecox Road with different expectations than they would have had if they were visiting a rambling cottage in the Adirondacks. In the Adirondacks, you wouldn't have been surprised if someone handed you a wrench and asked you to see if you could get the hot-water heater working. In the Hamptons, people seemed to expect that someone else would have gotten up early, squeezed the orange juice, and gone out for fresh bagels.

But you couldn't blame a house.

The problem was with them as a family. They'd been so open and welcoming to outsiders that there was no longer an inside, a core. Guy kept inviting people to Mecox Road. He should have painted the master bedroom instead.

Claudia was already settled at Mecox Road when I arrived on the Monday before the wedding. She came out to greet me, dressed in what was probably perfect summer-in-the-Hamptons gear, khakis and a white polo shirt, a narrow navy belt, and navy boat shoes, Top-Siders without a single scuff.

This wasn't The Brand. Her white clothes had always been creamy or pearly, not as crisp and bright as this shirt. And these navy accents? Hadn't she told Annie at Thanksgiving that she never wore navy?

Why was she dressing differently? Was she becoming flexible; was she recognizing the difference between a public and a private self? Or was she identity-hopping? *I'm now playing golf and visiting the Hamptons with "Michael," so I'm going to dress that part.*

She reached to help me with my luggage, and I handed her the buff-colored Neiman's garment bag.

"Oh, is this your dress?" she asked. "Can I look at it?" Without waiting for an answer, she lifted the bag higher and unzipped it. "Oh, Darcy, this is perfect. It's absolutely perfect."

She sounded surprised.

"I'm not a total moron, you know," I said. "I can follow directions."

She wasn't used to people speaking so directly. "I thought . . . since you don't like to shop . . ."

"I don't care about the things you care about, but I can respect it when something matters to someone else. I try to cooperate. It's part of playing well with others."

"I didn't mean to—"

I waved my hand, stopping her apology. "It's okay. Is Rose here?"

"No. She sends her apologies. She took Finney to

get his hair cut. She said to tell you that you're in the front corner room on the third floor."

I reclaimed the garment bag and carried my suitcase up to one of the nannies' rooms. My dress for the Friday-night rehearsal dinner was already hanging in the closet. It was lavender, pretty much the color of the dress that Grandma Bowersett had worn to my wedding. The back neckline was low and quite complicated with multiple diagonal straps. From the front, Grandma Bowersett's dress had been more interesting.

I went downstairs. Guy had finally persuaded Rose that, at least during the week of the wedding, she had to have some staff in the house. So, from seven in the morning to ten each night, at least one of Mariposa's two nieces would be with us, keeping on top of the dirty coffee cups and empty toilet-paper holders. A private chef was coming in every afternoon to make dinner and to leave something for the following day's lunch.

Both nieces were now in the kitchen, leaning against the counter, talking softly to each other in Spanish. As soon as they saw me, they straightened and stopped talking. I introduced myself. They answered politely, and we stood there looking at one another awkwardly until I moved out of the kitchen and they resumed their quiet conversation.

They'd been working hard. The kitchen gleamed, and in the family room the morning newspapers were neatly folded. A coffee service had been set up on the sofa table; the cream was covered with Saran wrap and nestled in a little bed of ice.

There were no dirty cups for me to load into the dishwasher, no wadded-up kitchen towels to take downstairs to the laundry. As Rose had said, she could pay people to do the things that I did. I guess I wasn't much use to people who have a staff.

I went outside. What the landscaper had called the "permanent installations" were finished. Flagstone walks now carved lawn into interesting shapes. Low walls and elevated terraces were screened with weathered, white trellises. Moss grew around the stones, and vines climbed up the terraces and spilled over the walls. A cluster of lilac bushes flowered in the sunniest part of the yard, and masses of ferns grew in the shade. Everything looked as if it had been there forever.

The swimming pool was uncovered and filled with water. It was rectangular, but boulders and masses of plantings had been brought in to soften its harsh shape. A massive yew shrub, its thick, twisted branches the result of years and years of unplanned pruning, had been transplanted to balance the borders, and an arching wooden bridge had been built across the pool.

Cami and Annie were standing on the bridge, watching the workmen unload the tents. "This is amazing," I called out as I went to join them. It was the first time I ever remember seeing the two of them standing together.

"Mom said to apologize," Cami said immediately, "about not being here, but she thought Finney needed to get away from the chaos."

"Although we were just saying," Annie added, "that it wasn't only Finney who needed to get away."

"But don't tell her that we said that," Cami added quickly. "She's hoping that we haven't noticed how stressed out she is."

I didn't make any promises. "How are the two of you doing?"

"Fine," Cami said. "I should be writing thank-you notes, but I'm fine."

"Actually," Annie said, "we were wondering if everything doesn't look a little fake. If it's just too perfect somehow. Too much like a stage set."

A bird bath, its stone nicked and weathered, was surrounded by silvery-green lamb's ear. Beyond it were raised beds designed to look like a cutting garden with daisies, sweet peas, gladioli, and cornflowers. The feathery white of the Queen Anne's lace was a background to the colors . . . but the Queen Anne's lace plants were going to be dug up two days after the wedding. Otherwise they would take over, ruining both the local ecology and any chance Rose had of joining a garden club.

I could see Annie's point about everything being too perfect. It was a fantasy of an English cottage garden, purchased and transplanted into the backyard of a multimillion-dollar faux chateau.

"That's not the sort of thing I have a good feel

for," I said. "What does Claudia think?" Claudia was now on the other side of the yard, talking to the landscaper.

"She says that it will look wonderful in the pictures."

And that, I suppose, was all that mattered.

Cami excused herself to go work on thank-you notes. Annie and I watched as the workmen began to unroll the first tent. "I hear that you did just great the last month of school."

"I guess so . . . yeah, I guess I did."

The tent was big, and one of the workmen almost stepped on one of the rose bushes. Claudia and the landscaper went rushing over.

Annie spoke again. "Claudia and Jeremy's dad . . . they aren't engaged or anything, are they?"

It was a moment before I could answer. *Why are you asking? What have you heard? Tell me. Let's gossip like two girls standing in front of our junior-high lockers.*

But that would have been stupid. Gossiping about Claudia might have made me feel better for the moment, but if she and Mike did end up getting married, I had to figure out how we would go on being a family.

"You didn't have anything to do with this rehearsal dinner, did you?" Annie asked.

I shook my head.

"I figured . . . because it's totally bogus. It's completely wrong . . . to get all dressed up on a Friday night. That's not what people do around here.

Rehearsal dinners should be clambakes on the beach. Nobody wears cocktail dresses on Friday night. Getting all dressed up like this is going to look so nouveau. I'm sure everyone's going to think that we're major wannabes."

I looked at her. She didn't have as much jewelry on as usual, but her eyelashes were heavily mascared, curving thickly up toward her eyebrows.

She was right. It suddenly seemed obvious. After a week at work and the long fight with rush-hour traffic, the understated people, the ones who did this right, wouldn't want to put on panty hose and high heels. They would want to slip into their worn, beat-up Top-Siders and go to a clambake on the beach.

I'd never been to a clambake on the beach. It sounded like fun.

But Claudia was a "major wannabe." She hungered for identity, for status and elegance. What could be a greater achievement, a clearer definition of a person, than a dinner in the Hamptons with pictures in a fashion magazine?

I didn't have much to do over the next few days. The first niece arrived at six thirty in the morning, and although I was out of bed before then, all I had to do was plug in the coffee urn which the other niece had set up the night before. She had even unloaded the dishwasher before leaving.

Dad arrived on Tuesday and put himself in charge of Finney. The chef packed them corn-free picnics, and they would disappear for the day. They flew kites, played catch, dug holes on the beach, and perfected their four-in-hand knots.

For all his adult life my father had been a problem-solver. People had turned to him when they had an infected finger or a flat tire. He'd always had whatever anyone needed. Besides what had been in his medical bag, he'd had the pocketknife, the match, the right map. He'd been the indispensable Dr. Bowersett, but he was retired now, living in a duplex in a retirement community. No one needed matches there; too many residents were on oxygen to permit open flames. Nor did they need maps; even the ones still driving never went anywhere new. An experienced RN was on the premises at all times, and physicians specializing in geriatrics were on call. Dad was no longer indispensable, and although he did not complain, he felt as if he had lost a part of himself. Finney gave him a chance to be indispensable again.

But Dad wasn't the only one who needed Finney. When Finney was around, everyone tried to hide the stress. Everyone spoke in bright, cheerful tones. On Monday, the day before Dad arrived, we played crazy eights after lunch and, after the workmen left, freeze tag among the new flagstones and terraces. We did it for Finney, but everyone felt better for the distraction. But with Finney off flying kites on the beach, Rose and Cami could give in to stomach-clawing anxiety.

Each day the fantasy in the backyard became more elaborate. The ceilings of the tents were draped and swagged with hundreds of yards of billowing blush-colored silk and rose-pink tulle. Inside the house, everyone was feeling more burdened by the massive number of details. Gifts were piled unopened on the floor of the home theater; Cami was too overwhelmed to open any more.

I was dreading Thursday, picture-taking day. The photographer scheduled to shoot the wedding on Saturday was of the photojournalism school of wedding photography. His goal was to capture the spirit of the occasion through unposed moments. I had seen his portfolio; the pictures were fresh and creative.

But he did not do posed, perfect headshots. So a different photographer was coming on Thursday to take Cami's formal portraits. I had seen his portfolio too; his pictures were detailed and exquisite.

Of course, such detailed, exquisite pictures would require the hair stylist and makeup artist, scheduled for Saturday, to come on Thursday as well. Guy then thought that as long as those people were coming for Cami, it made sense for Annie to get into her bridesmaid's dress and have her hair and makeup done too. Then they would have formal portraits of the two sisters together.

Then Claudia asked if Cami and Annie could—just for a moment, it wouldn't take long at all—slip into their rehearsal-dinner dresses. A few posed portraits would serve as supplements to the candid shots to be taken at the rehearsal dinner on Friday night. It would be so simple, Claudia assured Rose, that it wouldn't take more than a few moments.

But nothing nothing *nothing* associated with this wedding was simple. There were too many different people with agendas that had nothing to do with Cami and Jeremy getting married.

Claudia's Friday-night photographer was giving her a break on his rates because he wanted his work to appear in the fashion magazine. He wasn't going to share credit with the more established Thursday-morning photographer. So if Claudia wanted posed pictures, he would come Thursday afternoon. She went to Rose again. As long as Claudia was having to go to this expense, then . . .

Each request Claudia made only added a little more inconvenience to the plan, so Rose had said yes to each one. But there'd been so many of those "little more's" and "as long as's" that we were now looking at a screaming nightmare. Cami, Annie, Rose, Claudia, and I, all five of us, were getting our hair and makeup done, putting on our rehearsal-dinner dresses, and transporting ourselves to the actual site of the rehearsal dinner where a dummy version of one of the tables would be set up. There we would all pose for "candid" shots.

Oh, and Finney and Zack were coming to provide the sense of a crowd.

Claudia was out of control. She didn't look it; she was still her neat, trim self, wearing crisply ironed khakis and her newly purchased Top-Siders. She wasn't eating too much, drinking too much, or talking too much. It was her own ideas that she was unable to resist. In her heart, she must have known that each of her requests would burden other people, but each new step seemed so useful that she couldn't tell herself that she'd gone far enough.

Despite my misgivings, Thursday started well enough. The hair stylist and his assistant arrived on time. The makeup artist and her assistant were only fifteen minutes late. The bouquets actually arrived early.

Cami was upstairs when the flowers arrived. Annie lifted the lid off the box. There were supposed to be two bouquets—a copy of the bridal bouquet and one of the bridesmaids' bouquets. They were supposed to be camellias, roses, Queen Anne's lace, and various foliage. There were indeed two bouquets with the camellias, the roses, and the various foliage. There was something that had bursts of little white flowers, but it wasn't Queen Anne's lace.

"This is not acceptable," Rose snapped, flipping open her phone. "I swore I wasn't going to be a monster about every little detail, but we are *not* leaving out your flowers, Annie."

"It's okay, Mom. It doesn't matter."

"It matters to me," Rose said.

Rose spoke very patiently first to Pamela-the-floral-designer's assistant, then to Pamela herself. A mistake had been made. It was small, but it was important to the family, and these two bouquets would need to be remade in the next hour. Rose listened and then muted her phone while Pamela went to check something.

"This is *ammi majus*, what people use instead of Queen Anne's lace. It's even called false Queen Anne's lace, but it's really something called bishop's lace."

"Mom, it's okay," Annie said again. "Cami's not going to notice."

"You're being sweet, Annie, but this woman cares more about what the garden club thinks of her than what we want."

Another person with her own agenda.

Pamela came back on the line. Rose listened, then said, "We have some in the yard you can use if you send someone over who can remake the bouquets . . . forty-five minutes, yes, that will be great . . . yes, yes . . ." The call seemed to be ending when something occurred to Rose. "Wait a minute, how can you have no Queen Anne's lace in your workroom when every single thing you're doing for Saturday, every bouquet, every centerpiece, every little floral doodad has Queen Anne's lace in it?"

Annie and I were quiet as Rose listened again. "You only ordered bishop's lace? You were going to use it in everything? Didn't the contract say Queen Anne's? . . . Yes, I know the contract absolves you if something is completely unavailable, but you can't declare it unavailable simple because you haven't ordered it. . . . No, we discussed that over New Year's . . ."

This conversation could go on forever. The florist wasn't going to let up until Rose agreed to the bishop's lace.

So let the florist try that with Mr. Roadkill. "Rose . . . Rose," I hissed at her. "I'm going to go get Guy. Let him handle this."

I hurried to the library, where Zack was helping Guy unpack the books that he had been meaning to unpack for the last twelve months.

"This could be fun," he said after I explained the situation. "I don't know why Rose doesn't ask me to do more of this." He took the phone from her. "This is Guy Zander-Brown." His voice was entirely pleasant. "I hear that you're trying to give me a bishop when I ordered a queen."

Annie tried to protest that it didn't matter, but Guy held up his hand, silencing her.

Ten minutes later, the makeup artist called out that Cami was coming downstairs. The rest of us hurried out to the front hall.

She looked extraordinary. Her dress was wonderful, perfect for a summer garden wedding. When she was standing still, it was simple and light, but when she moved, it was as if hundreds of little fairies were shimmering around the dress, making it sparkle and dance.

But Guy was not in the hall with us. Still negotiating with the florist, he'd retreated behind the closed door of the library so that Cami wouldn't hear. That seemed a shame. Seeing their daughter come downstairs in her wedding dress was something for which Guy and Rose should have been together.

Twelve

With Cami and Annie ready for the first round of photographs, I turned myself over to the hair and makeup people. I liked what they did with my hair, but the makeup . . . I felt as if I were wearing a mud pack on my face. I wondered what would happen if I turned my head quickly. There seemed a good chance that the makeup wouldn't be able to keep up with me, and I would end up with my eyeballs, nostrils, and mouth facing one way while the mascara, blusher, and three shades of lipstick would be hovered in space all on their own.

The makeup artist gave me a little net helmet that zipped closed over my face. I was to wear it when I got dressed. With this much makeup on, a person needed protective gear.

I have to admit that my rehearsal-dinner dress, even though it was in a Grandma Bowersett kind of color, fit like a dream. I slipped it on over the mesh helmet, and it fell right into place, nestling in the slight indentation that I call my waist. The back was low enough that I could easily zip it up myself, and all those complicated straps did exactly what they were supposed to do without me having to tell them a thing.

I looked at myself in the mirror; Claudia had been right about the bust pads. I don't like the weight or feel of a padded bra, but this padding was inserted between the lining and the interlining—whatever "interlining" might be. I had some curve to my shape without feeling as if I were wearing a pair of diapers on my chest.

Cami's portrait session was going slowly. She wasn't the best of subjects. She was so determined to do what the photographer wanted that she couldn't relax in front of the camera. He was also taking his own sweet time setting up the shots, and between each shot, the makeup artist's assistant darted in to freshen Cami's makeup, which distracted Cami even more.

We were on assistant overload. The photographer had an assistant, the makeup artist had one, and so did the hair stylist. Even the assistant floral designer who had come in to harvest some Queen Anne's lace and remake the bouquets had had an assistant.

With so much assisting going on, we were running late. Claudia had gone to the restaurant some time earlier, and now she was calling to see where we were. Her photographer—and no doubt his assistant—were breathing down her neck, as was the manager of the restaurant. The restaurant had agreed to let Claudia have the photo session in the private room where the dinner would be, but there was another big party in the room this evening, and the manager wanted to get started on the setup for that event.

But we eventually got ourselves and our unifying diagonals there. Zack and Finney were in slacks and blazers with ties carefully knotted by Mr. Finney himself.

"Cami is here for one hour," Rose said firmly. "Her friends are arriving later today, and she needs to catch her breath. Jeremy is coming to get her in sixty minutes."

"Oh, it won't take that long," Claudia said.

But it did.

The session was easy for me. The unifying diagonals on my dress were at my back or at the hem. In every pose, my back was to the camera or I was climbing up a staircase with my hem visible behind someone else's ear. My makeup job was wasted. I'm not sure that my face was in a single picture, and that was also fine with me.

But Cami was already weary from the session at the house; her smiles were stiff and frozen, and within minutes Rose's were as well. This made Finney uneasy. He wanted to hold Rose's hand and press close to her. Unfortunately, her unifying diagonal was a wide line of ivory crossing down the front of her deep chocolate dress. Whenever Finney got close to her, he interrupted the diagonal.

"I thought these people had modeling experience," the photographer grumbled to his assistant, not caring if we heard.

Claudia had worked hard on these dresses and this article meant the world to her, but nobody else cared. I thought longingly about a clambake on the beach.

Jeremy came to pick up Cami, and the manager took that as a sign to start dismantling the table.

"No, no," Claudia protested. She didn't have the shots she wanted.

"You were supposed to be done at one thirty," he said. "They got here at one thirty."

"But—" Claudia had obviously been about to say that that wasn't her fault, but she knew that wouldn't change anything. A waiter picked up the centerpiece and tried to give it to her. She shook her head, refusing to take it. *No, no, I'm not done, it's not right yet. It's not perfect.*

Zack stepped forward and took the centerpiece.

"We still have tomorrow night," Rose reminded her. "These were only the supplements for those."

But nothing was perfect yet, and it had to be perfect. "What about taking some outside?" she asked the photographer.

"Sure, but it will take me a couple of minutes to set up."

Claudia went out to scout sites. The photographer and his assistant began gathering their equipment.

Zack was still holding the centerpiece. "I guess I'll go put this in the car. Hey, dude, do you want to come?" he said to Finney. "You can carry this thing for me."

Finney detached himself from Rose's side and put out his hands for the centerpiece. He concentrated hard as he walked, not wanting to spill any of the water. A minute later Zack returned, glancing over his shoulder, obviously keeping his eye on Finney.

"Finney wants to wait in the car. Is it okay? I'll roll

down the windows and make sure that we can always see the car. And he wants to know if he can take his blazer off."

Rose nodded a *yes* to all those questions, and she and I followed Zack back outside. Claudia and the photographers were setting up under a linden tree.

Even though the photographer had to know that Claudia's goal was to get group shots, he called Annie over to pose by herself. Zack went back to the cars to hang out with Finney. Claudia hovered near the photographer while Rose and I went to sit on a pretty wrought-iron bench, but then we remembered our dresses and so we stood.

The photographer was telling Annie to concentrate, to focus.

Rose's cell phone rang. It was Guy. She put the phone on speaker so I could hear. I had to move close; as pretty as this garden was, we were close to the highway, and the summer traffic made a lot of noise.

Guy reported that the flower situation had been resolved.

For about twenty minutes, the florist had declared herself off the job, which had not flustered Guy in the least. "She was bluffing," Guy said, "because she thought I was. But I wasn't."

"What would we have done if she hadn't been bluffing?" Rose asked. "What if we hadn't had a florist?"

"We would have figured something out," he said cheerfully.

I leaned forward. "Do you have interns who can arrange flowers?"

He laughed. "If they couldn't today, they'd be able to by tomorrow."

Rose was thanking him when the photographer's sharp voice drew our attention.

"You aren't concentrating!" he snapped at Annie. "You aren't—"

Rose flipped her phone shut and stepped forward. "I think we're done here."

"No, Mom." Annie pressed her fingers to her forehead for a moment. "I can do this. I can." Then she looked at her fingers and realized she had makeup on them. "Just let me wipe off my hands and get a drink of water."

"I'll get you some," Claudia said, clearly relieved that Annie was willing to continue.

Annie found her purse, took a tissue out, and then, when Claudia brought her the water, put something in her mouth first.

She noticed me watching her. "It was a piece of candy," she explained, sounding almost guilty. "I thought a little sugar would help."

"It probably will," I agreed.

She went back to work. Rose and I continued to watch. "Annie's being such a good sport," I said softly.

"I'm so proud of her. And look at Zack . . . he's being so great with Finney."

That was true. Finney was sitting in the backseat of

Rose's Mercedes, but Zack had squatted in front of the open door, and they were obviously doing something together. Last fall Zack had been uncomfortable around Finney; now he treated him with an easy brotherliness.

"That's a little better." The photographer had moved Annie closer to the tree. "But get some energy in those eyes."

Rose turned her back. "I can't watch this. Give me something else to think about." It was the first time since California that she'd spoken to me without constraint.

"I'm burnt out on my job."

I don't know where that came from. I hadn't intended to say that. It had just come out.

Rose was as surprised as I was. "At the hospital?" she asked. "How do you know? What are the signs?"

"Oh, you know . . ." I felt like a jerk. What a horrible time to bombard her with my problems. "The usual."

"Have you stopped caring?"

She wasn't being polite. She was interested and engaged. Maybe this wasn't such a bad time. She was probably sick of being a mediocre event planner and ready to do something she had once been very good at—friendship.

"Actually, it's that I've started to care about the wrong things." I explained about the machine and the monitors and how, in a crisis, that's what I thought about, not the patients. "I'm not sure I can wall myself off like that anymore," I explained. "I'm afraid I'm going to start loving ninety percent of the patients and hating the other ten."

"I couldn't sleep sometimes if Guy couldn't place a manuscript that I loved, but if that manuscript had been someone else's child . . ." Rose shook her head. "How concerned are you?"

"If I let myself think about it, I'd probably be scared out of my mind. I can't imagine myself not working in a hospital. But I've got to figure something out. I can't be doing this until I'm sixty-five, it's too demanding physically."

"What are your options?"

I told her about wanting to get more involved in nursing education, but that I would need a Ph.D. "I could do the course work, and I might like the research, but writing a dissertation?" I shook my head. "I don't see how I could close myself up in a room and do nothing but write for months and months. That really scares me."

"It doesn't have to be that bad."

"That's easy for you to say."

"Yes, I'm good at that sort of thing. And that's what's going to make it easier for you. I can save you weeks and weeks by making you stick with a decent writing process. If your outline's solid, you can draft quickly. Then it will just be the sentence-level revisions, and that's really fun."

"Is it?"

"To me it is. And don't ask me if I would do this. I

would be happy to start this very second. Where's a pen? Do you have a pen?"

"Don't act like it's a joke," I protested. "If you really can schoolmarm me through this, then I may have a future."

"I'm very serious. I love working with people on their writing . . . or at least I used to."

Zack's normal writing style was stilted, and the early drafts of his college essays had been nearly unreadable. The ideas were the same in the final draft, but he had manage to sound like himself. The essays were relaxed and natural with his dry wit coming through just as it did when you were talking to him.

Last Thanksgiving he had spent an afternoon in the library with Guy; they were supposed to be unpacking books. At the end of the weekend, few books had been unpacked, but Zack's essays were complete. I'd never asked, but I'd assumed that Zack's essays sounded so much like Zack because Guy had rewritten them.

So if Guy could do that for my kid, Rose could do it for me. It really could work. I could become "Dr. Van Aiken" before Jeremy did.

"You're not looking at anything." It was the photographer again, barking instructions to Annie. "You're not trying."

Rose and I looked up, and in an instant we were moving. Something was wrong with Annie, very wrong. She was flushed, swaying. I reached her first. I caught her, my fingers automatically seeking the artery in her wrist. Her pulse was racing so fast. I didn't like it.

"This isn't my fault," the photographer cried. "You can't blame me for this."

"Annie." I took her shoulders, forcing her to look at me. "When you went to your purse, what did you take?"

"A Tylenol."

She'd said it was a piece of candy. "No, no, it wasn't."

Her eyes darted toward Rose.

When will kids learn that there are far, far worse things than having their parents find out what they've done?

Rose was automatically, instinctively trying to take Annie in her arms. Any mother would have. But I lifted my hand, stopping her. Her face was pinched, and her eyes, brown with those green flecks, were anxious. I tried to send them a message: *You have to trust me.*

She blinked . . . but then she didn't even ask what was wrong. "What can I do?"

"Get lots of water and a bucket or bowl. I think she's accidentally ingested something."

Zack had come racing across the parking lot. I held up my left hand clawlike, as if I were gripping a phone, and punched at it three times with my right forefinger. *Call 911*.

He understood. He was pulling his phone out of his pocket.

I eased Annie to the ground. "Okay, sweetie, it's just

you and me. I'm not going to get mad, but I need to know what you took."

"He told me to concentrate, to focus . . . so one of those pills I got at school . . . from the other kids . . . it was my last one. . . ."

Suddenly it made sense—sickening, horrifying sense. I knew why she'd done so well during the last weeks of school. She'd had meds. But if there'd been a proper diagnosis, I would have heard. "Annie, have you been buying ADD medications?"

"For school . . . not to get high, just for school."

She must have overheard Rose and me at the hotel after graduation. She must have heard me say that I thought she had ADD.

"And what was this one?" I couldn't think of any ADD med that would cause a reaction like this.

"I don't know . . . I checked the others on the Internet, but I couldn't find this one. . . . that's why I didn't take it."

"What did it look like?"

"Pink . . . and round, a pill. Kind of big. Pinker than the Adderall."

A lot of pills were round and pink. Birth control pills, but they were small and wouldn't cause such a reaction. Amitriptyline, aripiprazole . . . I wasn't sure, but maybe they would. Amitriptyline is a tricyclic antidepressant; aripiprazole is an antipsychotic. I didn't know enough about it.

Rose came back with bottles of water and a big bowl. "Is she going to be okay?"

"Yes, but I think she should go to the ER. Zack's called an ambulance." I put the bottle up to Annie's mouth and tilted her head back, forcing the water down her throat. It was cherry-flavored and smelled sickly sweet.

"Can you make yourself throw up?" I asked.

She shook her head. "No . . . I've tried . . . some girls at school do it every day."

"Try. Chug some water and try. Hit the bowl if you can." The emergency room might want to analyze her stomach contents.

She bent over the bowl. She coughed and gagged, but didn't regurgitate. Rose knelt next to her, scooping her hair out of the way.

People had gathered around: Zack, Claudia, the restaurant manager, and Finney, little Finney. He was terrified. His eyes were wide, and his face was so pale that his freckles stood out.

"Oh, for God's sake," I snapped at Claudia, "take him inside. He doesn't need to see this."

Annie gagged again and then gave up, collapsing against Rose. "Oh, Mom . . . I don't feel good."

"Come on, Finney," Claudia said. She touched him on the shoulder, getting him to turn, but as they started to walk, she let her hand fall.

No, no, no. I wanted to shriek at her. *Put your arm around him. Take his hand. Do something. He's scared to death.*

Rose was stroking Annie's hair. "Should I try to make her gag?" she asked me softly.

"I don't think it's worth it."

"Please tell me what happened. I have to know."

Of course she did. And not just for her own peace of mind. She would need to tell the emergency room.

Annie was now feeling too lousy to care what anyone said. "She overheard us talking in California," I said to Rose, "and she's been getting ADD medications from other kids—"

Rose gasped.

"So when the photographer told her to concentrate and focus, she thought a pill would help. But it seems to have been something else. We don't know what."

"Is there any chance . . ." Rose couldn't bring herself to say it.

"That she's done lasting damage to herself? Not from a single dose. She's not hallucinating. I don't think it was anything illegal." I heard the wail of the ambulance siren.

"Is there anything I can do, Mom?" It was Zack.

The restaurant manager was already at the edge of the parking lot, flagging down the ambulance. For a moment, the linen-service truck blocked the turn into the lot, but the manager slapped the panel of the truck with his palm, and the driver gunned his engine, pulling into traffic. "Get their purses. Rose will need her insurance card. And see if you can get Guy on the phone. I'll tell him what's going on."

The ambulance personnel were quick and expert. They took her vitals and eased her onto a gurney. "Is she a minor?" the lead guy asked. "Is one of you her mother?"

"I'm coming with you," Rose said to them; and then to me, "You'll take care of Finney?"

"Absolutely."

"Okay, then," the EMT said. "If you have everything, let's go."

"My phone." Rose was trying to think. "My purse."

"We have them. Let's go." He took her arm, urging her forward.

Zack handed me his phone, and as the ambulance pulled away, I spoke to Guy. "She'll be fine," I kept saying. "It was probably just a bad reaction to some medication."

"The hospital's in Southampton. I'll get there as soon as I can, or do you need me to come get Finney?"

"No, we have him. We'll get him home."

The photographer came up to me and handed me Annie's shoes. She must have kicked them off. "Tell Ms. Postlewaite I'll be here tomorrow. That's what we were supposed to do anyway . . . and I hope the girl is okay. I might have been too demanding. It was hard not to think of her as a professional."

"But she's not."

"It was frustrating for everyone." He wasn't going to take any more of the blame.

Zack picked up the empty bowl, and we started walking back to the restaurant. "She OD'd on something?" he asked.

I didn't want him to think the worst, so I explained.

"How often does that happen?" I asked. "Kids buying Ritalin and Adderall from other kids?"

"It happens in college, but honestly, at a private high school"—both Annie and Zack attended private schools—"kids who need prescriptions have them, and everyone knows that if you don't need them, they don't do much for your concentration. If you just want to stay awake, there's cheaper ways. People will grind them up and snort them to get high, but it doesn't sound like Annie was doing that."

"No, she was genuinely self-medicating, which is still stupid and dangerous . . . as this incident showed."

"Why didn't she have a prescription? Why didn't her folks make her take all those tests? You made me."

I wasn't sure how to answer that. "They did have her assessed a number of years ago, but—"

Before I could finish, one of the waiters came running out of the restaurant. "The little boy. Something's wrong with the little boy."

Thirteen

I kicked off my shoes and raced across the parking lot. Zack passed me, then paused at the door, holding it open, letting me go in. I felt my dress catch on something. I yanked it free.

The restaurant was dim. "He's in there. In there." The waiter pointed to the private room, and I heard Claudia trying to calm Finney.

The room was full of tables and chairs now. Finney was in a corner, sitting on the ground, his back to the wall. He had his hands to his face. He was hyperventilating. "Mommy," he whimpered. "Mommy."

Claudia moved aside and I knelt in front of him. "No, Finney, it's Darcy." I eased his hands from his face, unbuttoned one of his cuffs, shoved up his sleeve, and looked at his inner arm. It was covered with thick red welts.

I looked back at Claudia. "What did he have?"

"Nothing. Just water. He was so upset. I asked the hotel for some water. They gave me the bottle. It was fine. Look." She lifted an empty plastic liter. It was the same water they'd brought to Annie. It had a little bunch of cherries on the corner of the label. "It's all natural. It says so. It's all natural. It couldn't have been the water."

All natural . . . Why don't people understand that "all natural" doesn't always mean "good." This water was cherry-flavored; it would be sweetened with corn syrup—I didn't even have to look at the label. "It couldn't have been the water," Claudia said again. She thrust the bottle at me, wanting me to see. "It couldn't have been."

I waved it aside. "Read the fine print and see if you can still say that. He needs the EpiPen." I was already going over the procedure in my head . . . *Form a fist around the tube . . . ninety-degree angle* . . . as I reached for—

It wasn't there. Finney wasn't wearing his fanny

pack. I conjured up an image of him outside under the linden tree. He had been in his blue shirt and gray slacks. He hadn't had the fanny pack on. "Zack, Zack . . . did Finney take his fanny pack off in the car?"

"I don't know." Zack tried to remember. "I gave him the flowers . . . we put them in the car, he took off his blazer . . . no, no, he didn't have it on then. I'm sure of it." He thought again. "But he had it on when we got here. He was playing with the zipper."

So it was at the restaurant. "Somebody . . . everybody," I shouted, "we need to find a small black fanny pack. Try the kitchen, the main dining room. We have to have it. And call another ambulance."

The hives were getting worse. Finney was coughing, spitting up some clear phlegm. "Finney, sweetie . . . do you know where your fanny pack is?"

His eyes were darting around. He was frightened and confused. He couldn't remember. "It's okay," I murmured. "It's okay. We'll find it."

But what if we didn't?

I looked around the room, hoping to spot it. The door to the kitchen was swinging open and closed as people rushed around, looking for the little pack. Claudia was over by one of the windows, pushing aside the drapes, tilting back a chair, then pushing the drapes aside again. She knew something.

"When did he take it off?" I demanded.

She faced me. "During the pictures. The photographer said it was ruining the shot. And there was a table here, right here." She pointed to the floor in front of the window. “I put it there. It was right in plain sight.”

“Then, for God’s sake, go find out what happened to the table.”

Why hadn’t I gotten the second EpiPen from Rose? We’d gotten out of the habit because my father carried one. But Dad wasn’t here.

It was getting harder to keep Finney calm. He was poking at his throat as if he was having trouble breathing.

Zack came back through the swinging door. “It doesn’t look good, Mom,” he said bluntly. “They dropped the dirty linen on that table, and the linen service has already taken it away. Nobody remembers a fanny pack.”

We had to keep Finney breathing until the ambulance got here. The danger with anaphylaxis is that the tissues in the airway can swell, blocking the intake of oxygen. I got behind him and lifted his arms. “Listen to me, Finney. We’re going to play a game. Make your chest big. Zack is playing too. See if you can make your chest as big as he can.”

I didn’t have to prompt Zack. In an instant, he was in front of Finney and drawing deep full breaths, inhaling and exhaling loudly. A dark-haired waitress joined him. And Finney, this sweet little boy, did his best. “That’s right. That’s great. Now let’s try again.”

What if his airway closed? What would happen to the family? And Rose—how could she ever live with herself, knowing that she had forgotten to give me his EpiPen?

I felt motion at my right arm. It was one of the waiters. He had brought the restaurant first-aid kit back inside. "Dump it out," I said. "See what we have."

I was glad to see that there were gloves. I kept talking to Finney. His breaths were getting smaller, and he couldn't concentrate. He kept looking at his arms. The hives terrified him. If I hadn't been holding his arms, he would have clawed at them. He was starting to thrash, gasping and wheezing. "Call Grandpa," I told Zack. "His number is in my cell phone." But I didn't know where my cell phone was, somewhere in my purse, somewhere outside.

Zack already had his phone open. Apparently he had the number. I heard him talking to Dad. Then he put his phone on speaker and set it on the ground where we both could hear it.

The waitress was still trying to get Finney to play the breathing game.

Dad asked me a few quick questions, then said in a voice made calm by years of experience, "Let's hedge our bets and assemble things for a cricothyroidotomy."

Knowing that other people could hear him and not wanting to alarm them, Dad had spoken in technical code. A cricothyroidotomy is a tracheotomy done outside a hospital setting; you make an incision and insert a tube directly into the patient's trachea. It is a dangerous procedure, especially on a child. Their airways are small, and if you do it wrong, if you overpenetrate, you can do a lot of damage.

But, without the EpiPen or intubation equipment, it might be our only option. I would need a tube and a scalpel. Combat medics carry cricothyroidotomy kits, but there was little in the restaurant's first-aid supplies that would help.

"What do you want me to get, Grandpa?" It was Zack, talking into the phone.

"Go into the kitchen and get a knife, a small one. It needs to be sharp." Dad could have been talking about the weather, his voice was so calm. "And, Darcy, find a tube of some kind. A refillable ballpoint pen will be your best bet, the smaller the better."

A narrow gold pen appeared in my field of vision. "Take it apart," I said to whoever was holding it.

The headwaiter volunteered that he and the chef had CPR training. I nodded, but I knew that CPR would do no good if the air couldn't reach Finney's lungs. The manager of the restaurant was talking on his cell. I hoped he wasn't calling his lawyer.

He wasn't. "I called to get a read on the ambulance. Some jerk was trying to follow the first ambulance and caused an accident behind it. So traffic's backed up and our ambulance is having trouble getting through. It's going to be another ten minutes, at best."

Dad had heard that. "Keep your eye on his fingernails and lips, Darcy."

"His lips are white."

"You'll want him on a table, supine, with a rolled towel under his shoulders. You'll want to hyperextend his neck." Zack scooped Finney up and laid him on the table, stretching him out, holding him down. The waitress with dark hair had heard Dad and had rolled up a clean tablecloth. We tried to slip it under Finney's shoulders, but it was too big. The waitress unfolded it, rerolled it.

Finney was hardly struggling anymore. He was still breathing, but with a labored, croupy sound. His lips were gray. I looked down at his fingernails. "Dad, his nails are blue."

"We've got alcohol wipes, Grandpa," Zack said. "And Mom's putting gloves on."

"Good. Swab down Finney's neck. Now, Darcy, get on his right side. Someone should hold his head, but not you, Zack; I may need you. And is there anyone who can monitor his pulse?"

The manager went to the end of the table and clamped his hands on either side of Finney's head. The dark-haired waitress silently moved into place, picking up Finney's wrist.

Dad had me palpate Finney's neck. I found the thyroid cartilage. A finger's breadth below that would be the cricoid cartilage. That's where the cricothyroid membrane was.

"You're going to cut twice. The first is the skin. Put your left forefinger on the thyroid cartilage and make a transverse incision, maybe an inch, through the skin over the cricothyroid membrane. Stay in the midline as much as you can."

The little knife was warm. Someone had sterilized it with boiling water. "Darcy?" I heard Dad say.

It's just skin. It's not Finney. It's just skin. I cut. Finney flinched, but my helpers were holding him tight. Bright red blood crested over the incision. "Okay," I said.

"How's his pulse?" Dad asked.

"Steady." It was the first time I had heard the waitress speak.

"Good. This incision is transverse again, very small, just big enough for the pen. Leave the knife in."

The blood kept me from seeing anything, but in my mind was suddenly every detail of a picture from one of my old textbooks. I cut into the cricothryoid membrane. I felt a little pop. "Okay."

"Zack, are you wearing gloves?"

"Yes, Grandpa."

"Then pick up the tube and be ready to give it to your mother. When you're ready, Darcy, release the thyroid cartilage, take the tube in your left hand, and rotate the knife ninety degrees with your right, then insert the tube in the incision—it should slip right in—and pull the knife out."

Rotate with my right hand, insert with my left. I could do that.

And I did. The pop was a little louder.

Finney's chest rose sharply as his lungs pulled in air from the makeshift passage. It had worked.

I felt like sinking to my knees, in prayer, in exhaustion, but I had to keep holding the pen.

Finney wasn't reacting to the pain from the incision. The relief of being able to breath, the life-giving oxygen filling his lungs, must have overridden the pain sensors.

Dad was having Zack wrap gauze from the first-aid kit around Finney's neck and the base of the pen. I wondered when Zack had put gloves on. I hadn't told him to. I watched him as he slipped the roll of gauze under Finney's neck. His hands were steady.

A dentist would need steady hands.

The manager kept his hands clamped to Finney's head. The angioneurotic edema—the swelling—continued. Finney's eyes were getting puffier, but his chest was rising and falling. He was breathing, and he was wanting to touch his neck, to see what was hurting. We kept talking to him, telling him that he was safe now, that he was making his chest so big and was doing such a great job, but no, he couldn't move. The dark-haired waitress got a wet napkin and started dribbling cool water on the hives. Dad stayed on the phone in case something went wrong. But nothing did.

At last I heard the ambulance siren. A moment later, a strong gloved hand closed over mine, and I eased mine away. Finney was no longer my responsibility. I sagged in relief, scooting out of the way of the EMTs.

"That was amazing, Mom," Zack said. "You saved his life."

"Grandpa had as much to do with it as I did." I would not have wanted to do that without a physician's supervision. "And you, you were great."

The ambulance drivers said that I could ride to the hospital with them, but I'd have to sit in front, out of their way. That was fine. I was glad not to be in charge anymore. Zack told me that he would drive the car to the hospital. He'd get directions from someone.

The step up into the ambulance was higher than I had expected. I almost lost my balance, but I grabbed on to a handle and hoisted myself in. The other doors slammed; the siren started to blare. The ambulance swung out onto the highway, turning so quickly that I swayed against the door. I straightened, but couldn't think of any reason why I needed to sit up straight. So I leaned sideways, pressing my cheek against the cool glass window.

My dress was a mess. The place where I had gotten it caught on the door was full of snags and pulled threads. The bodice was splattered with blood and phlegm. Across the skirt front were some pinkish brown streaks. It looked as if I had wiped my hands there, but I couldn't imagine what could have caused those stains. Then I remembered. The makeup.

I touched my finger to my eye. It came back blacked with mascara. I wiped it off, leaving a black smudge along with the pink ones.

I thought about calling Guy, but I didn't have my purse. Or my shoes. I looked down at my feet. My stockings were laddered with runs, and my big toe stuck out of a hole in the left one. The edges of the hole were tight between my toes and around the side of my foot. It was uncomfortable. I reached down and pulled on the stocking until my toe was covered.

We reached Southampton and then the hospital. It

was brick, only three or four stories in its tallest wing, much smaller than what I was used to. Guy was waiting outside the emergency-room entrance, talking on his cell phone. He broke off the call and went directly to the rear of the ambulance.

I got back there as the hatch was swinging open. "How's Annie?" I asked.

"She's going to be fine . . . except that they're making her stay overnight. We're still not sure—"

He broke off. The EMTs had backed out, one pulling Finney's gurney, the other still holding the tube.

"What's going on with his neck?" Guy's voice cracked. "Is there something in his neck? What happened?"

"Didn't anyone tell you?"

"Your father . . . he said something about an emergency airway . . . but what's that in his neck?"

Guy obviously had no idea how desperate things had been. He hadn't understood what Dad had meant. He must have assumed that we had taken care of everything with an EpiPen. I put a hand on Guy's arm. "He'll be fine."

Guy hurried to follow the gurney. I moved more slowly, knowing that I wouldn't be allowed back in the treatment area. The hole in my stocking caught and pulled. The concrete was abrasive on my feet.

I got inside just as the big double doors leading into the treatment area were swinging shut. I went to the reception desk to find out where Annie was.

The receptionist eyed me and my ruined dress

uncertainly. "Ah . . . you can't go up there without shoes."

Shoes? After all I had done, they cared about my *shoes?*

My expression must have frightened her because she popped out of her chair and a moment later returned with a pair of slippers. They were one-size disposable mules, the kind given to patients to wear between the dressing room and the X-ray. If you picked up your feet, they fell off. I shuffled to the elevator. Annie's room was only on the second floor, but I wouldn't have been able to climb stairs in this footwear.

I wondered why they had admitted her. Unless she was still in tachycardia, it was probably for a psych evaluation. A teenager ingesting an unknown substance . . . the prudent course would be to hold on to her for twenty-four hours.

I got off the elevator just as Dad and Zack came out of the stairwell. Apparently they had arrived in the parking lot at the same time. Zack had my purse.

"I don't suppose you thought to look for my shoes?"

"Oops. Didn't think about it." Zack glanced down at my feet. "I suppose you don't want me to laugh."

"Honestly, I'm beyond caring."

Dad put his arm around me. "You did good work, Darcy B."

"I couldn't have done it without you. Or Zack."

"I'm sorry I wasn't there. I've never seen one of those."

"You hadn't even *seen* one?" I ran a hand over my face. "Good Lord, Dad, I'm really glad that I didn't know that."

"It didn't seem like a good time to bring it up."

We followed the signs and went past the nurses' station. At the end of the hall, Mike was talking on his phone. Jeremy was with him. I supposed there were signs somewhere about not using personal cell phones in the hospital, but most families ignored those warnings, so why shouldn't we?

"Mom!" Jeremy looked me up and down. "What happened to you?"

"She just saved Finney, that's what," Zack snapped. He hadn't liked his older brother's tone. "Mom cut his neck open with a kitchen knife and stuck a pen in his windpipe."

"You did a tracheotomy, Mom?" Jeremy turned to me. "Outside a hospital?"

My next goal in life was to keep my older son from being one of those pompous doctors who don't respect nurses. "It's called a cricothyroidotomy. Combat medics are the ones most likely to need to do them now."

"She was awesome," Zack said.

Mike finished his call. "That was Guy on the phone, calling from the emergency room. He just found out about the cricowhatever. He asked that we not tell Rose how bad things got. And, Darcy"—Mike turned to me—"he asked me to say something to you, but he didn't know what."

I flipped my hand. "All in a day's work."

There were two beds in the room, but the bed closer to the door was empty. Annie was asleep in the one by the window. Rose was in a chair next to her, and Cami was perched on the radiator. In the guise of kissing Annie, I felt her pulse. It was fine.

"We don't understand what happened with Finney," Cami said. "We heard it was a flavored water, but he would never take anything from someone he doesn't know."

"Claudia gave it to him," Zack said. He'd followed me into the room. "She saw that the water was 'all natural' and didn't read the label."

It occurred to me that I had no idea where Claudia was . . . and I didn't care.

"We've taught him to recognize the word *corn,*" Rose said. "Did he look at the label?"

"He wouldn't have thought to," I said. "He would have trusted Claudia."

Rose's lips tightened. I knew she was thinking exactly what I was. Claudia had been acting as if she were one of us, one of the moms-in-charge. But the first responsibility of such a woman is always the safety of the children. Always.

"Did you need the second dose from his EpiPen?" Rose asked. Both she and Finney carried two-dose "dual packs." "Or was one enough? I can't believe that I forgot to give you the one from my purse. I'm almost glad that we didn't hear about it until he was in the ambulance on the way here. I would have been beside myself about not leaving his EpiPen."

"You weren't holding your purse." I tried to distract her. "Zack gave it to the EMT. I'm sure if you'd had it in your hand, you would have remembered."

"Who knows? I was so sick about Annie. But you didn't answer my question about the EpiPen. Did you need—" She stopped, and I knew that she had finally noticed what a mess I was—the ruined dress, the raccoonlike makeup. She straightened. "I would like everyone to leave except Darcy."

"What?" Cami asked. "Why?"

"Just leave."

Dad organized it, touching Cami on the back, herding the men, shutting the door behind him.

"What happened?" Rose said as soon as we were alone. "That's blood on your dress. This isn't just corn exposure, is it?"

Why did I keep getting put in this spot? "Guy asked me not to say anything."

"Darcy, what is going on?"

I'm not sure I could have done what she had done outside the restaurant this afternoon. When Annie was in distress, when we had no idea what was going on, I had asked Rose to step away, and she had. She had trusted me to handle things. I would have found that harder to do than anything that had happened inside the restaurant.

I wanted to be like that: I wanted to trust people in that way.

I took a breath. "We couldn't find his EpiPen." She

gasped, but I kept on talking. "Claudia and the photographer had him take off his fanny pack for the pictures, and we think it was thrown out. So he did go into anaphylaxis. His throat was swelling. I called Dad, and we did what you would think of as an emergency tracheotomy."

"You cut into him? Into his neck?" She struggled out of her chair, knocking aside the tray table that was in her way. "Oh, my God, I have to see him."

"You can't. They won't let you. They're probably removing the tube now. He'll be sedated. And, Rose, when Annie wakes up, she'll need you here."

"Annie . . ." Rose sank back down. "It must seem that we only care about him, that she could be hanging from a bridge and we wouldn't care as long as he was all right."

"No, she cares about him too. She's more worried about you and Guy than about herself."

"Guy and me?" That made no sense to Rose, but she couldn't think about it right now. "Oh, Darcy, I can't believe what I've done. You were exactly right about her, and I refused to listen to you. I was so wrong; I couldn't have been more wrong. All I wanted from her was not to need anything, and she must have figured that out because she tried to fix everything on her own."

"Did she tell you more? Did she overhear us in California?"

Rose nodded. "Yes, and apparently she took three Ritalin tablets from your purse the next morning."

Now it was my turn to wince with guilt. I hadn't noticed they were missing.

"She took one on the airplane ride home, and she studied all the way. Then, when she got home, she said she couldn't sleep, so she kept studying. She took one before the test, and I remember . . . the teacher said that it was a good thing there were so many essays and short answers on the test because otherwise they would have thought that she'd cheated. Can a pill really make that much difference?"

"You have to need it. If a non-ADD person takes one, it doesn't do much. And the pills alone aren't enough. You've got to be motivated, you have to want to change, and clearly she did."

Rose shook her head. "Everyone was so thrilled with how she did on that test that she started getting pills from other kids. She swears she never used them as a recreational drug, and then she wrote down what she took when."

"If you have to do something stupid, dangerous, and illegal, I suppose keeping good records is the way to go."

"And the pill she took today . . . she wasn't sure what it was. That's why she hadn't taken it during school, but the photographer was yelling at her so, and it was the only one she had left." Then Rose looked at me urgently. "You know we will get her the help she needs. You know that, don't you?"

"I do."

There was a light rap on the door. It was the floor

nurse, coming to take Annie's vitals. The others trailed in. Guy was with them; Dad wasn't. He had probably gone back down to be with Finney.

Rose raised her hand to put it in Guy's. "Darcy told me what happened. Don't try to protect me, Guy. It's very sweet, but it doesn't work."

"I know that," he said. "But I probably won't ever stop trying."

"Now," Rose said firmly, "somebody needs to take care of Darcy."

"Me?" I was surprised. "I'm fine. I don't need—" Everyone was looking at me. "Okay, I am probably looking a little shopworn. I'll just go wash up a bit."

"No," Rose ordered me to stop. "Let the other people do something for you for a change. Cami, go find her something to put on. I don't want to leave Annie, so, Mike, take her into the bathroom and help her."

Cami jumped up, relieved to have something to do. Mike scooped up a towel and washcloth from the shelves near the door. He took my hand and led me across the hall and into the bathroom of an empty room. "Lord, you are a mess." But his voice was soft, even a little affectionate. He unzipped the dress and eased it off my shoulders, and it fell to the floor. I wasn't wearing a slip, just my bra and panties. I had some scratches on my arm; two were a little bloody. I hadn't noticed them before. I must have gotten them when Finney was thrashing. Mike ran the water for a moment, dampening the washcloth.

"Cold water works better on blood," I said.

"But warm has to feel better."

It did. He wiped my arms with long, firm strokes. Then he did my shoulders and neck. It was nice, the warm washcloth massaging my body. He rinsed and wrung out the cloth, then knelt down. The washcloth was warm against my legs. It wasn't sexual; it was kind. So very kind. Mike wrapped my body in the towel and then worked on my face, having to rinse and rerinse the washcloth because there was so much makeup. I had my face tilted back as if I were a child.

"You don't usually have this much stuff on your face," he said . . . and for once it didn't sound like a criticism.

"It was for those pictures of Claudia's."

"Ah . . . yes."

There was a light knock on the door. It was Cami. She handed Mike a plastic-handled shopping bag. "I found these in Dad's car. They're Annie's, but the waist is elastic. They should fit."

Mike handed me a top. It was a sleeveless shell made of unbleached cotton. I pulled it over my head. It was a little tight around the armpits, but not too bad. The skirt was also unbleached; it was long and loosely woven, falling around my calves with a soft weight. I supposed Annie would wear the clothes with a million other things, scarves and shirts and necklaces, but this was enough for me. The shoes were thick-soled black flip-flops. One strap had BERKELEY printed on it; the other one, CARROLL. That was her school in Park Slope.

I gathered up the wad of lavender that had been my dress and thanked Mike.

"No problem," he said. His back was to me. He was rinsing out the washcloth one more time.

This was wrong. I hadn't said enough.

I tried again. "I really do appreciate it. I don't think I realized how dirty I felt and how much better I would feel clean. I wouldn't have done such a good job if I had been here by myself, but I wouldn't have been comfortable with anyone but you."

There. That wasn't hard.

"You never seemed to want anything like that before." Mike was facing me, but he wasn't looking at me.

"You heard Rose. Admitting that I need something isn't my strong suit."

"You know, Darcy, I've been thinking a lot." He was looking at me. "I'm not sure I left for the reasons that I said I did, because of the mess in the house and you being late and all those things you now call ADD behaviors. I've racked my brain trying to understand why I couldn't have been more accepting, more forgiving, when there was so much at stake. But standing here, washing you, made me realize that I wanted you to need me. I knew that I was a good provider, but that never seemed to matter to you. It was always so important to you to know that you could support yourself."

I sighed. "I have trouble trusting people, even you."

"Well, as things worked out, you were right not to trust me."

"No, Mike, no. Let's not beat ourselves up about what happened."

"It's been hard not to," he said, "because I know I started us down this path. But, Darcy, one thing—I do love living alone. That's why I was so angry when you moved. I had the best of both worlds when you were still in the old house. I was living by myself, but I could go home and eat a great dinner whenever I wanted. I could have my tools and workbench, but I was still living alone. That wasn't fair to you."

"I appreciate your saying this. I really do."

"And apparently I needed to be holed up in a hospital bathroom before I could say it." And he smiled, that clear, sweet, boyish smile.

I wasn't in love with him, but I will always always always love that smile.

"We probably need to get back out there and see what's going on," I said, and he agreed.

Claudia was in the hall. She was alone, hovering outside Annie's room. She was probably afraid to go in. In her shoes, I would have been too.

"Oh, I was wondering where you were." She was relieved to see us. "Darcy, what you did was remarkable. I know that it must seem that I'm responsible for—" Then she caught sight of what I had in my hand. "That isn't your dress, is it?"

I looked down at the wad of fabric in my hand. "I'm

so sorry. I'm sure it's ruined, but here . . . maybe—" I tried to hand it to her.

"And Annie's dress?" She couldn't help herself, she just couldn't help herself, even though she had to know that caring about this was wrong. "Do you know what happened to it?"

I shook my head. "The ER would have taken it off. It'll be with her personal effects."

"Dresses?" Mike was puzzled for a minute. "Oh, right, the rehearsal dinner. We need to figure out what to do about that. I can't imagine that anyone is going to feel like a big dressy event."

Oh, Lord. I hadn't been thinking. Here it was, late in the afternoon on Thursday. We had the rehearsal dinner tomorrow, and the wedding . . . two hundred and fifty people in an English cottage garden. . .

I'd seen this before—families in the ICU struggling to figure out what to do about the wedding, the bar mitzvah, the graduation only a day away. Now it was our turn.

"You're not thinking of *canceling* the dinner, are you?" Claudia was shocked at the thought.

"No," Mike said. "People still need to eat, but in light of everything that's happened, maybe we should downsize it, make it more casual. Not have people get so dressed up."

"Not have people get dressed up?"

"Remember, the restaurant warned us that Friday nights in the summer, people wouldn't be . . ." He stopped. He saw Claudia's face. He saw how she was frantically trying to hold on to her plans. Despite all that had happened, that was what still mattered to her.

He spoke firmly. "We want to do something that's appropriate for the moment. This is a family occasion, so let's think about what's right for the families involved."

Not the dresses, the pictures, the fashion-magazine article, not Claudia's brand, but the families.

"Of course," she said. "Of course. I'll call the restaurant and see what ideas they have."

That was the right thing to say, exactly the right thing, but she had waited too long to say it.

She moved down toward the window where cell-phone reception was better. Mike watched her for a moment, then turned back to me. "I know that the wedding is the bride's family's deal, but this rehearsal dinner is ours. And it got completely out of hand. This whole thing with the dresses and coverage in a magazine, that's not us. I guess I was unconsciously assuming that you would keep us straight. Since you never tried to stop Claudia, I let myself think that it was okay."

"I couldn't get between the two of you."

"I see that now."

When Mike and I had been married, I'd been the one to get us to church on Sunday, to arrange for us to visit his mother, to plan the family vacations and to tell the boys that no, they couldn't take friends along on the trip and each would have to play with his brother, who, yes, might be a creep and a jerk, but he was still his brother.

Now Mike realized that he would have to shoulder his share of the job. With the boys nearly grown, it wouldn't be hard—not like hauling an eleven-year-old and a seven-year-old to Sunday school—but we couldn't lose sight of the fact that the job still needed doing.

"Before I got here, was anyone talking about the wedding?"

Mike shook his head. "But we had no idea what had actually happened to Finney. How long do you think he's going to be hospitalized?"

"A couple of days. They'll pump him full of antibiotics. But even if he is discharged by Saturday, he's going to be timid and clingy. I doubt that he'll want to have anything to do with a big crowd."

"Let's see what Jeremy has to say. Then we can support him." Mike opened the door to Annie's room and motioned. Both our boys came out. We explained how we were going to change the nature of the rehearsal dinner. Then Mike asked Jeremy about Saturday. "How's Cami going to feel if Finney isn't there?"

The idea made him pause. "Not good. She'll want him there."

"What do *you* want to happen?" I asked.

"I want Cami to have what she wants. I want Cami to have the wedding of her dreams."

I didn't know what to say to that. Apparently Mike didn't either. After a moment, it was, to my surprise,

Zack who spoke. "You can knock my head off for what I'm about to say, but this dream-wedding business . . . I know that everything looks great back at the house, but everyone's on edge and miserable. If this is a dream wedding, I don't want to see a nightmare."

Zack was right. Even if there had been no unidentified round pink pill or cherry-flavored "all natural" water, this wasn't the wedding of Cami's dreams.

So the four of us talked, and, like any family, we repeated ourselves a lot. We said things that didn't make any sense. We got off track and started remembering the Polar Bear regatta Jeremy's first year on the Selwyn crew, but sooner or later we understood one another and outlined what we thought should happen.

I knew one thing from watching ICU families labor with such decisions. When you are bewildered, caught between tragedy and trivia, the best thing to do is to call your clergy—your priest, pastor, minister, or rabbi—and have him or her tell you what to do. The good ones know when families need someone else to make decisions for them.

But the Zander-Browns had never joined a religious institution. They did not have a relationship with a member of the clergy.

They only had us, and yes, Mike and I were divorced, yes, we had put asunder what God had joined, but the four of us were still a family.

Fourteen

Mike and the boys followed me back into the room. Annie was awake and agitated; Rose was on the far side of the bed, stroking Annie's hair, trying to soothe her.

"This is all my fault," Annie wailed. "If I hadn't taken that pill, none of this would have happened to Finney."

"It was a whole chain; a lot of things went wrong." I touched Cami's shoulder, moving her aside so that Annie could see me. "You still aren't yourself, but the drug will wear off. You'll feel better soon."

"I don't care about that. What about Finney? And Cami's wedding? He'll be out of the hospital by Saturday, won't he?" She was begging me to reassure her.

The room was crowded—four Zander-Browns, the four Van Aikens—but everyone was suddenly listening for my response. "It's possible," I said, "but it isn't likely. The risk of infection is so great."

"Mom, what are we going to *do?*" Cami sank down into one of the visitor chairs. "How can I get married without Finney there?"

"Sweetheart, I told you"—Guy had the palms of his hands pressed together and was moving them up and down in a slight chopping motion—"we're going to do everything we can to get him there even if it's only for a few hours."

I glanced at Rose. She saw me looking at her. She

raised her eyebrows and tilted her head a bit as if she were asking me to do something. Then she gave her head a slight shake.

"That's not a good idea," I said flatly. "There's a fair amount involved—unhooking and rehooking his IVs and such. It's one thing to do that for a grandparent who would get something out of being at the ceremony, but Finney's a little boy who likes routine. He's going to be scared and confused. Honestly, Cami, I know this isn't what you want to hear, but a plan to take him out of the hospital for a few hours just pays lip service to the idea of him being there. If you're getting married on Saturday, you should accept that he won't be there."

"But I *can't* get married without Finney there."

Mike and Zack exchanged glances. They thought she was overreacting. But I understood. Finney was the glue that held the family together. If he wasn't there, Cami wouldn't feel as if her family were. Rose, Guy, and Annie could be present, but the family wouldn't. That was their weakness: all their connections went through Finney.

"What should we do?" Cami's voice was a soft wail. "I just don't know what we should do."

So Guy said it. "Do you want to cancel the wedding?"

"No, no!" Annie shrieked. "You can't cancel the wedding because of what I did. What about the flowers and the food and the chairs? Mom's gone to so much work. We can't cancel. Mom's worked so hard."

"This isn't about me," Rose said stiffly.

"But if we cancel it," Annie argued, "everything you've done will be wasted."

Rose flushed. She was mortified. Her family thought this wedding was about her.

When she spoke, her voice was light, but she wasn't making eye contact with anyone. "You're talking as if we were Marxists and believe that the value of something is determined by the amount of labor invested in it. This family is many things, but we are not Marxists."

I was standing by Mike, and he nudged me. He loved it when people remembered what they'd learned in Econ 101. "Presumably you invested so much effort," he said, "because this was important. You're a rational being; you made a rational decision."

"I wouldn't count on that," Rose put in, sounding a little more like her usual self.

As we had planned out in the hall, Jeremy now took over. "Let's go ahead and have the party. Everything's paid for, our friends are already on their way from the airport, and in fact, we do have lots to celebrate." He had started off speaking to everyone, but now he was talking just to Cami. "But let's postpone the wedding part—the actual ceremony. We'll have a great time at the party, we'll go on the honeymoon, and then we'll get married when we get home. Finney will be better, and it will be just the two of us and our families. We don't have to have a million people and a fancy cake. We can do it in a church in Park Slope."

"Go on the honeymoon before we get married?" She had twisted in her chair to look up at him. She was bewildered and overwhelmed.

"I suppose we could get separate rooms if you think that's necessary," he said, his voice softly teasing; they had, after all, been living together for a year.

"Oh, Jeremy . . ." She let him pull her out of her chair and into his arms. "I don't know why I thought I needed a wedding like this. I just want to be married. I want to be with you."

He murmured something into her hair, too low for the rest of us to hear, maybe even too low for her to hear. We all looked away, wanting to give them some privacy in this crowded hospital room.

"So is this the idea?" Guy asked. "Party, yes; wedding, no? Rose, are you sure that you're okay with that?"

"It's not about me," she said. "This seems like a good plan, but I don't even know how to start thinking about it. What will we do about the favors, the cake? The—"

"You will leave it to us," Mike interrupted smoothly. "You take care of Annie and Finney, and don't worry about anything else. Claudia's already working on the rehearsal dinner, and when we get back to the house, Darcy and I will get started on the rest."

"Darcy has done enough," Guy said.

"Try telling that to her."

Cami lifted her head from Jeremy's chest. "If there's a lot to do, my friends—the bridesmaids—are getting in soon. They'll do whatever you tell them, especially Trish and Jamie."

Guy followed Mike and me out to the hall. He handed us a card. "Call Mary Beth at the office. She has the e-mail addresses for almost all the guests."

Mike took the card, and we spent a moment thinking about cars. Rose's Mercedes needed to be fetched from the restaurant. Mike took the keys from Guy and then tossed them to Zack. "Figure it out, son."

"Sure thing."

Zack's tone had been casual, but I knew, I *knew,* what this meant to him, Mike turning a problem over to him, trusting him to solve it.

He put the keys in his pocket. "Do you need me to pick anything up for you?" he asked Guy.

"Probably . . . but I have no idea what."

I had an idea. "Guy, are there bookstores nearby? Why don't you have Zack get Rose some great big classic novel, *War and Peace* or *Crime and Punishment*?"

"*War and Peace*? Why? Don't you think she would prefer *Anna Karenina*?"

I suppose I should have been flattered that he actually thought I had an answer to that. "I have no idea. Just anything to remind her that her brain is still working."

"Fine," he said. "But she's not worried about that, is she?"

How could he not know this? Annie was right about their relationship: they needed to spend time together; they needed to be husband and wife, not only professional associates and parents of a special-needs child.

Zack set off for the bookstore, and I rode back to Mecox Road with Mike. I called Mary Beth on my cell phone while Mike called Claudia on his. Claudia reported that the owner, the manager, and the chef at the restaurant had been very accommodating. They were faxing over a menu for a more casual buffet, and Claudia had already talked to the florist about creating less formal centerpieces.

Mike told her about the plan for Saturday night, and by the time he and I got to the house, she had started thinking about that as well. "We should," she said confidently, "acknowledge that a wedding was planned. We can distribute the favors, and while the groomsmen maybe shouldn't be in black tie, the bridesmaids can wear their dresses. Cami should bustle her train and not wear her veil, but—"

"You've been a busy bee," Mike interrupted.

She blinked. She wasn't used to people interrupting her.

I spoke to Mike softly. "That wasn't kind."

He ran a hand over his face. "No, it wasn't." He could now admit to being wrong. "I'm sorry, Claudia, but you need to understand that people may not want to have much to do with you for the next few days. There may be a lot of anger."

"Anger? No." She gave her a head a little shake. "I may have erred, but everything turned out fine. We need to move forward. That's what Guy said. He left me a phone message while he was waiting for the ambulance. He said that there'd been previous corn exposures. He sounded as if it had all happened before."

"That was Guy being Guy," Mike said. "You're a guest in his home; he had to say something."

"And that was before he knew the whole story," I added.

"What do you mean, the whole story?" Mike asked.

I'd been referring to the cricothyroidotomy; while waiting for the ambulance, Guy hadn't known about that, and it was definitely not something that had happened before.

But Claudia was struggling so hard to excuse herself that she was thinking only about her own actions. "Perhaps he didn't know about the fanny-pack issue, but honestly, I didn't know how important it was. If I had, I—"

Mike interrupted her again, insisting that she explain.

"It was the photographer who suggested it, not me, and . . ."

Mike listened long enough to get the general idea. He turned to me. "If Finney had had his fanny pack, would you have had to do that tracheotomy thing?"

"No. Not as long as his EpiPen had a second dose, and Rose said that it did."

"You have to believe me, Mike," Claudia protested. "I knew that the fanny pack was important, but I didn't know it was this important. And it was the photographer's idea."

He was shaking his head. "I don't know what to say." His voice was flat. He put his hands on the arms of his chair and slowly pushed himself up. "It's going to be a long night. I'm going upstairs. I'm going to take a shower and change."

Claudia and I watched him cross through the kitchen. "He doesn't seem angry." Claudia sounded relieved.

"I think he feels responsible," I answered. He used to say that I embarrassed myself, leaving him with the need to apologize for me. But I had never, not ever, done anything this blameworthy.

"And you . . . you don't seem angry," Claudia said.

I shrugged. "I don't know. I'm drained after everything that happened at the restaurant. I don't think I feel anything."

"What about the others? Mike's wrong, isn't he? They won't be angry. They'll understand that it was the photographer's request, won't they?"

I almost laughed. "When Rose realizes you took Finney's fanny pack and didn't keep track of it, the best you can hope for is that she'll never speak to you again."

It took Claudia a moment to understand what I'd said. "Rose not speak to me? That can't be right, and you said 'realizes.' So she doesn't know?"

"She knows, but it didn't really register yet."

"So who does know? Zack must. Do you think—"

I stopped her. "I'm not getting involved in a cover-up, Claudia. Accept that you made a terrible mistake, a whole set of mistakes, because your photographs were more important to you than Finney's health. And don't forget about Annie. You let the photographer ride her so hard that she felt that she had to take that pill. The rest of us love Jeremy and Cami, and we want them to be happy. But to you, their wedding was a chance to make yourself important. It was all social-climbing to you."

I guess I was angry.

"I am not used to people speaking to me this way," she said stiffly.

"No, of course you're not," I snapped. "You aren't used to people speaking to you at all. Your whole life is on the Internet. All your 'friends' are online. You write that blog, and you're in charge, you can control everything. No one interrupts you, and if someone answers back, you can delete their comment. I don't know if those are real relationships or not, but they sure haven't given you much sense of how to be in a family."

"No, no." For once, she was looking at me directly, her light eyes sharp and intense. She wouldn't stop until I admitted that I was wrong.

And I wasn't going to do that. I held up my hand, interrupting her again. "Over the next two and a half days, my first priority is my son Jeremy, and my second is my friend Rose. Talking to you is not going to help me help them, so I'm done."

"But—"

"No, I'm done."

I went into the library to call my brother, telling him that they were welcome to come out tomorrow as planned or they could wait until we rescheduled the wedding. "But I'm sure it will be at their home in Brooklyn."

"To be perfectly honest, Darcy, that's better for us," Chuck admitted. "We kept thinking that it was such a shame to be coming all that way out and then not have time to show the girls New York City. They want to buy green foam Statue of Liberty crowns."

What a relief to speak to someone who didn't care about the Hamptons.

I left messages for the caterer and the florist, but before I heard back from them, there was a clamor in the front hall. It was Cami and her bridesmaids.

Just as Cami had said, they were a great group of girls. Educated under Title IX—the federal law requiring schools to provide girls the same athletic opportunities provided boys—these young women had played organized sports since they were age four. They knew how to be on a team. The two who Cami had specifically mentioned had been varsity athletes. Trish had been captain of the women's volleyball team, and Jamie had coxed a boat. They could lead.

They'd learned of the changed plans in the car on the way from the airport. By the time they got to the house, they'd decided on a policy, and they never wavered from it. Cami was not to worry about them.

There was no reason to apologize for the canceled ceremony. In fact, the ceremony was the least fun part for a bridesmaid. The parties were the good part, and the parties were still on. As long as they got to wear their dresses—which were, by the way, the best bridesmaids' dresses *ever*—they would be happy. Cami should look on the bright side. If something went wrong, if one of the groomsmen vomited in the swimming pool or a waiter crashed into the cake, it didn't matter, it wasn't her wedding. . . Oh, and that dark-haired guy . . . was he Jeremy's brother? Why hadn't she told them about him? Was he really only eighteen? What a shame. He was hot.

After a half hour in their company, Cami was relaxed and giggling. If this is what friends did for you, then I did need more of them.

It was late when I finally went up to my room on the third floor. I was still wearing Annie's gauzy cotton skirt and sleeveless shell. I hooked my thumbs into the arm holes, easing the pressure that the shell's tightness had caused. I sat on the bed. I was so tired. I couldn't imagine how I was going to get ready for bed. There seemed so many steps. I'd have to stand up, take off the shell, take off the skirt, put them in the hamper, find my—

There was a light knock on my door. "Darcy, can I come in?"

It was Claudia.

She had made herself scarce that evening, driving to

the restaurant in the name of checking on the new arrangements for Friday night, lingering there so that she didn't have to sit down to dinner with the rest of us.

She entered my room a little hesitantly. "I came to say goodbye. I'm leaving. There was an unfortunate family emergency."

"A family emergency?" That surprised me. She'd never mentioned any family. "I'm sorry. . . . Who is it? I'm afraid I don't know anything about your family."

"There's nothing to know. I haven't had any contact with them for years. This is an excuse. I think it would be easier for everyone if I weren't around."

That was certainly the truth. "Is Mike taking you to the airport?"

She shook her head. "He offered, but I'd rather use the car service. I wanted you to know that everything is set for the dinner. I left all the paperwork on the kitchen desk. I can't imagine that there will be any problems. Mike has my cell-phone number, but please don't let him call me. I can't be involved."

She sounded sad, and although she was facing me, she was once again not looking at me. But this time she wasn't ignoring me, she was avoiding me, dreading what I thought of her. All the air had gone out of the vinyl Bobo doll.

And I was too tired to be angry. "I know how disappointed you must be."

"No," she said softly, "I don't think you do. I don't think anyone can. Yes, I do care about the dresses and the article." Her voice grew a little firmer. "Those dresses represent weeks and weeks of unremunerated work, but that was a business decision that didn't work out. I can accept that. It's harder to accept what's happening with Mike because I don't know what I could have done differently."

"Is it over between the two of you?"

"He's too polite to say anything this weekend, but it is. Of course it is. I can't look at him again without remembering that I disappointed him, that he felt the need to apologize for me."

"He'll get over it."

"But I won't." Now she wasn't even facing me. She had turned to the window, unable even to pretend to have any direct contact. "I so badly wanted this relationship to work. It was my reward for working so hard all these years. You can't know how hard I've worked. All week long I'm at the computer or sewing machine. Then I spend all my weekends packing and unpacking sample garments, staying in the best room in the midpriced hotels that sewers choose. For years I've been making all these gorgeous clothes for myself and had no place to wear them. Then I met Mike. He took me to plays and parties. Yes, the parties were fund-raisers where I didn't know anyone, but I was there, and I had never been *there* before. Then the Zander-Browns and the house in the Hamptons—this is what I had always dreamed success would be like. I was so amazed on New Year's Day that you didn't want to go to those open-houses because you didn't know anyone and would never see any of them again. That seemed so trivial to me."

I shrugged; I didn't know what to say.

"I did hear you this afternoon," she continued, "when you said that my whole life was online. That's right. When I'm home, unless a client is coming for a fitting, I can go days and days without speaking to a person face to face. But knowing people on the chat lists and blogs is enough. It may not get me invitations to parties, but it's what I'm comfortable with . . . and maybe you're right that I need to be in control like that, but that's who I am, and I don't want to change. I don't want to compromise. If I went on learning to play golf, that would cost me as much in lost income as those dresses. It isn't worth it. I can't be you. I can't play flashlight tag."

Nobody wanted her to be me. But family life would require her to compromise, accommodate, not think of everyone as her audience silently admiring her performance. That was not going to happen. She was too afraid of what would happen if the audience didn't approve.

I stood for a moment, silent and awkward, unsure of what to say. "I hope things work out for you. Do take care of yourself."

"That I will do," she answered. Then she glanced at her watch and left the room, closing the door behind her.

As tired as I was, it took me a long time to fall asleep. Then an annoying chirp from the other side of the room woke me up. It was my cell phone, plugged into the charger. I stumbled across the room. I peered at the number. It was local to the Hamptons, but I didn't recognize it.

It was Rose, calling from the hospital. "Oh, Darcy, I know I'm waking you up." She was half whispering. "But I finally told myself that it was okay."

"Of course. Of course. You know it is. Do you want me to come to the hospital?"

"No, I just need to talk. I'm with Finney. I'm finally putting it together. You saved him. If it hadn't been for you, he would be . . ." She couldn't say it.

"I wasn't going to let him die, Rose. And it wasn't just me. Dad talked me through it and Zack was great. I was so proud of him."

"How did it happen? You said Claudia and the photographer took the fanny pack. But we were there. Why didn't we notice?"

"Because they made sure that we didn't." I reminded her how Finney had been clinging to her, blocking her "unifying diagonal." The photographer's assistant had taken him aside. "That's when it happened, and because he had that blazer on, none of us spotted it afterward."

"I suppose they thought that his fanny pack was ruining the pictures." She was having trouble keeping her voice low.

"Yes."

"And if someone had been on oxygen or wearing a MedicAlert bracelet, that would have ruined the pictures. Torturing Annie wasn't enough. Not only did Claudia give Finney the water, she took away his EpiPen. Oh, God, Darcy, maybe I'll forgive her someday, but I can't imagine how I'm going to come home tomorrow morning and face her."

"You don't have to. She's left. She had a family emergency."

Rose exhaled. "That's a relief . . . no, I don't mean that, not about her family emergency, whatever it was. What was it? I never heard her talk about any family."

"She doesn't have any, at least none that she sees. The emergency was simply an excuse."

"Well, good. I'm not going to let myself think about her. But I do need to know everything that happened with Finney. Did it hurt when you cut into him? No, no, start from the beginning. Tell me everything."

So I did. I gave her every detail that I could remember: how we had had to reroll the tablecloth; how Zack had put his phone on speaker so that we could all hear Dad; how I suddenly remembered the illustration from the textbook. She asked question after question. And then I found myself remembering more; how the chef had brought three knives from the kitchen and I had chosen the smallest; how someone had brought three bottles of vodka from the bar in case we needed to sterilize the field with Grey Goose; how the dark-haired waitress, the one who had helped the most, had whispered to me afterward that she had always dreamed of being a nurse. She was trying to save her tip money for school. I hadn't remembered that until now. Rose asked me her name—which I didn't know—and what she looked like. "Don't let me forget to tell Guy about her," Rose said.

The Zander-Browns were, I guessed, going to do one small bit toward easing the nationwide nurse shortage.

That had to be one of the best parts of having money, to be able to turn to a very deserving young woman and say to her, *Yes, if you are willing to do the work, here is your dream.*

Then Rose and I talked about Annie. "I keep asking myself why she didn't come to us," Rose said. "Ultimately, I think she was trying to protect me. She didn't want to cause me a lot of trouble. Can you imagine how guilty that makes me feel? Here she knows that I went to the ends of the earth for Finney, and I've spent a year twisting myself into knots over this wedding. So she took this enormous risk rather than bother me."

"She probably didn't think it was as risky as we would."

"No, but still . . . Did you hear her saying that we couldn't cancel the wedding because I had worked so hard? And that's what Cami and Guy were thinking about it. That Mom's little project had to be protected and patronized? How did I get here? I thought I was supposed to be able to do both—to take care of my children and work. And then Finney was born, and I couldn't. It wasn't just an issue of having the time; I didn't have room in my brain for anything else. I'd read a manuscript and not have any insight into whether it could be fixed. So I told myself not to worry, that as soon as he was settled in a school, I could go back then."

But Finney had settled into his school last year. This would have been her year. "Back at the restaurant we were talking," she continued, "and you said you were scared at the thought of not working in a hospital. That's why I've thrown myself into planning this wedding. I was scared about what I was going to do next, scared that I might not be able to do it anymore. As much as I disliked all the lists and phone calls, that was better than having to face what I was going to do with the rest of my life."

I wasn't going to tell her that I was sure her skills would come back. What did I know? But they certainly wouldn't come back if she didn't try.

"Look here," I said. "By nature you're a Mary." I reminded her of the Bible story. "You've been a Martha for eight years, and one thing about Marthas is that we don't quit. We might whine, feel sorry for ourselves, spin our wheels, and appeal to Jesus to get us more kitchen help, but we don't quit. You never quit on Finney, so don't quit on yourself."

"I was doing that, wasn't I?" She sighed. "But there may be hope. Guy got me Mrs. Gaskell, and I'm doing okay."

"Mrs. Gaskell? Is that a private nurse?"

"Oh, no," she said, laughing. "She's a Victorian novelist. He had someone pick up *Wives and Daughters*. I hadn't read her in ages. Apparently my problem all these years was that I only ever had one child in the hospital. Now I have two, and I'm able to read one of the Victorians. That must count for something."

Fifteen

The hospital discharged Annie around eleven on Friday morning. Guy brought her home, and Rose stayed with Finney, leaving the dismantling of the wedding to the rest of us. Fortunately, the caterer, the rental-company lady, and even the floral designer dropped all their la-di-da airs and proved themselves to be sensible, helpful businesswomen.

Friday evening was the nonrehearsal dinner. Mike took a carload of bridesmaids over early to check on the arrangements at the restaurant. Guy came with me. He didn't particularly like to drive at any time, and the Hamptons traffic made him crazy. I had backed my car around and was reminding myself to look for the shoes I'd left at the restaurant when Jill Allyn Stanley's beat-up BMW turned up the drive.

Guy got out of the car, in part to greet her, in part to keep her from parking us in.

"Have you checked in already?" he asked. She was staying at the nearby inn. "We're about to leave for the dinner. Do you want to hitch a ride so you don't have to drive home?"

"I would love a ride," she said as she went around to the back of her car. "But I need to shower and change first." She lifted a big suitcase. "You can wait, can't you?"

"No," he said. Her request was absurd. Couldn't she see that we were thirty seconds from leaving? "Darcy and I need to get there early. And why the suitcase? Aren't you staying at one of the inns?"

"Well, I was, but I called Mary Beth, and she said that Rose's sister's family wasn't coming, so it was okay if I stayed here."

Guy paused. And kept on pausing. I glanced over at him. I had a feeling that he had just put his poker face on.

"No," he said deliberately. "Mary Beth may have told you that Holly wasn't coming, but she wouldn't have invited you to stay here. She wouldn't have done that."

"Maybe she didn't *say* it"—Jill Allyn was disconcerted by Guy's tone—"but it would have been obvious . . . I mean, the room was empty, and you know how well I work in that room."

"I don't think that this is an ideal weekend to plan on getting a great deal of work done."

"Well, no . . . I guess not." Then Jill Allyn collected herself and went on the attack. "Rose said something to you, didn't she?"

"No. What would she have said?"

"Oh, I don't know . . . she's been on sort of a power trip ever since you got this house."

Guy blinked. "I beg your pardon? A power trip? Rose?"

She was startled by his tone. "Oh, come on, Guy, you know what I mean."

"Actually, no. I do not know what you mean."

"She's been complaining to you. I knew it. That's so petty of her. She's gotten so *small.*"

I had to think that Rose had had it worse than me. Claudia had simply wanted me not to exist. She thought she could get away with ignoring me. Jill Allyn wanted to humiliate Rose.

"She has not said one word to me about you," Guy said to Jill Allyn. His voice was firm. "She wouldn't. But I hope you haven't canceled your other reservation, because, except for the bridesmaids, we're sticking to the original plan. We're only having family at the house."

"But, Guy," she protested, "I *am* family, you know that. I'm Rose's best friend."

"Then why aren't you at the hospital with her?"

"Oh, hospitals." She shrugged. "I don't do well in hospitals, and my galleys came back on Wednesday. I have to read those. You know that."

"And no author in the history of mankind has been late with their galleys? You can't have it both ways, Jill Allyn. Either you are Rose's friend and you do what Darcy has been doing—you drop everything and move heaven and earth to help her—or you are one of our clients and all we want from you is that you do your job. Pick one—friend or client."

"But I'm both," she cried. "That's how it's always been."

"No, that's how it used to be, but it hasn't been that way in a very long time." Then with the lightning-fast, never-look-back decisiveness that had made him who he was, he made up his mind. "You know what, Jill Allyn, you're not worth it. You aren't worth it as a client, and you certainly are not worth it as a friend."

He paid no attention to her gasp. "What does your contract with us say? Thirty days' notice from either party? This is your notice from me. The Zander-Brown Agency is no longer representing you. Mary Beth will fax you a copy of that on Monday, and she'll return whatever manuscripts we have." Then he turned his back to her, moving to the car. "I believe we're ready, Darcy."

A minute later we were at the end of the driveway. "Did she call Rose *small?*" he demanded. "Did she actually call *Rose* small?"

Why was this a surprise to him? "Did you mean that, not working with her anymore?"

"I sometimes torture people, but I rarely bluff, and I certainly wasn't then." He was drumming his fingers on the console between the two seats, but after a moment he flattened his hand on the padded surface. He was forcing himself to relax. "Okay, we're done thinking about her. We're done thinking about anything. We're going to have a very good time this evening even if we feel like Pip with Miss Haversham ordering him to play."

I could, in complete honesty, assure him that I would not feel like that.

At the restaurant, I went back to see if anyone had found the shoes I'd left behind yesterday. No one had, but the staff abandoned their chores to cluster around me, eager to hear how Finney was doing, even more eager to praise me for what I'd done. Even the chef came forward to shake my hand.

I pointed out the dark-haired waitress to Guy. He drew her into a corner of the kitchen and spoke to her softly. A minute later, she had her hands over her face. She was crying. Good tears, I assumed.

Word about my willingness to stick a kitchen knife into a little boy's throat spread among the guests, and I soon found myself as much the center of attention as Cami. In the hospital, grateful families may send fruit baskets to the nurses' station or write nice letters that go in your personnel file, but you rarely see that family again. I wasn't used to the personal accolades I was getting that evening, and after a while I ran out of ways to respond. It began to get a little embarrassing.

I appealed to Guy for help. "How can I get people to shut up about this?"

"You can't," he said bluntly. "We always told our kids that they have to accept the consequences of their own actions. Now you're stuck with the consequences of yours."

"Just like the waitress—roll up a towel, monitor a pulse, and you're stuck with years more of schooling."

"Exactly," he agreed, "although I'd like to point out

that she's being much more gallant about facing her fate than you are."

"You're right. I shouldn't complain. I'm only embarrassed. She has to learn the names for all the bones in the foot."

And, let's face it, I did prefer this sort of embarrassment to the one resulting from being seated at the losers' table.

I had volunteered to spend the night in the hospital so that Rose and Guy could get a decent night's sleep. I drove myself there; Rose would take my car back to Mecox Road.

I parked, found Finney's room, and eased the door open. He was asleep, curled up on his side, one hand under his cheek. The sheets on his bed were white, and the loosely woven thermal blanket was pale blue. He looked very small. I leaned forward to kiss his forehead. He had a white bandage at the base of his neck.

Rose had been dozing in a recliner. It was a tangle of blankets and pillows. She started to straighten them, but I stopped her. "I can do that."

"And I am going to let you."

I gave her the car keys and helped her gather up her things. The bookmark between the pages of *Wives and Daughters* suggested that she had read nearly two-thirds of it, and it was probably six hundred pages long. "Do you want me to leave this here for you?" she asked. "It's really good."

"Ah . . . no, that's okay." I had finally remembered that Pip and Miss Haversham were from Charles Dickens's *Great Expectations*. I had done my duty by the Victorian novelists.

I settled into the recliner. At midnight, the nurse came in to take Finney's vitals. His temperature was normal, and he was oriented to his surroundings. He was in the hospital, and I was Darcy, not Mommy. He clearly wanted Rose, but I told him that I worked in a place like this and I liked places like this and as long as I was here, he would like it, and after a bit, he believed me.

He wasn't sleepy, so I took some things out of my purse—my phone, a tube of ChapStick, a parking stub, a credit card, a coin, about ten items in all. I laid them out on the tray table and had Finney look at them. Then I covered them with a towel and took one away. He did surprisingly well although it was harder when I rearranged the objects. Rose had said that his sense of space was one of his strongest cognitive abilities. We played for nearly twenty minutes.

At six, Guy came in, smelling like fresh soap and shaving cream. I explained the game I'd played with Finney, knowing that Finney would probably want to play it again when he woke up. Guy patted his pockets, verifying that he had enough equipment to stock the tray table.

The house was quiet when I got back to Mecox Road; everything was orderly and peaceful. I went up to my room to shower and change clothes. By the time

I came back downstairs, both nieces were in the kitchen, laying out breakfast. A line of trucks was coming up the driveway, and the day had started.

It was a relief to know that nothing could be perfect. At ten o'clock, Rose and I sat down to redo the seating chart. It was a mess. We didn't know for sure who was coming and who wasn't. There were going to be empty seats; we just didn't know which ones. So I suggested that we alert the Title IX bridesmaids, Trish the volleyball captain and Jamie the coxswain, they should get guests to switch seats if any of the tables were too empty.

"You do the best you can," Rose said, "and send flowers in the morning."

I looked up from the little escort-card envelopes that I was restuffing. "Where did you hear that?"

"Oh." She realized what she had said. "The same place you did, of course. Don't tell me that you haven't been reading Claudia's Web site. I won't believe it for a minute."

"When did you start?"

"Early enough to be tempted to buy red dishes to use at Thanksgiving. They would have looked awful with amber placemats. And I also think that you do look better with a bust pad."

I grimaced, and she laughed—we were two girls giggling in the halls of junior high.

We made mistakes. If we had thought about the cake on Thursday, we might have been able to arrange for a less elaborate one, but we hadn't. It arrived in all its architectural, camellia-coated glory. Nor had we given the music any thought. Clearly we should have called the woodwinds who were going to play during the ceremony, paid them a cancellation fee, and asked the strings to come an hour or so early. We hadn't done that either.

So the woodwinds showed up several hours before the event was to start, expecting to play during the wedding ceremony and for a respectful crowd waiting beforehand. Guy and I were outside when they arrived, and he explained what had happened. Could they just play until the strings showed up?

Oh, no. They did not play background for a cocktail party. And they weren't an opening act for a string quartet. They had accepted this engagement for the exposure. They knew who was on the guest list; they wanted to play. This event had been a career-building move for them. Apparently they too had had an agenda that had nothing to do with Jeremy and Cami.

Their proposal was that people should gather quietly and listen to them. Guy's proposal was that he would pay them and they would go away. No, they thought that they should be entitled to more than the original fee because this engagement would have led to others. Not playing would result in their occurring damages, and they should be compensated.

Guy invited them to sue him for these alleged damages. He further said that their suit would stand far more of a chance if he didn't pay them at all. In fact, if they really were planning on calling in the lawyers, it would be so much better for them if he didn't pay them. He'd actually be doing them a favor by not paying them.

They decided to take his check.

The bridesmaids had been looking forward to the hair and makeup session, so we didn't change those arrangements. This time the hair stylist brought two assistants and the makeup artist brought three. I tried to hide from them, but, like everyone else, they had heard about my little adventure as a combat medic, and one of the many assistants was sent to track me down. The makeup lady used a lot less gunk than she had on Thursday, and I actually liked the results. There was something about my eyes, and I don't know what it was . . . I just looked like a slightly better version of me.

I took another one of the mesh helmets and went up to my third-floor nanny's room to put on my amethyst Neiman Marcus, muted-print, low-contrast, mottled-leaves mother-of-the-groom dress.

This was a dark spot on my day. I wished that I loved this dress the way Jeremy had loved his first sports uniform. He'd been four years old, and his T-ball team had been issued red T-shirts and red ball caps. Jeremy's shirt had hung to his knees; the cap fit like a lampshade. But he'd loved them; they'd made him feel like a Hall of Fame athlete. He'd worn the shirt to his pre-K morning classes; he'd slept in it. In fact, the bottom sheet on his bed developed a pinkish cast in the shape of his little torso. When I would wash the shirt, he'd hover near the washer, listening to the machine thunk and vibrate.

I wanted to feel that way about my dress. I wanted to love it. I wanted to feel transformed in it. I wanted to feel that that dress was worth every penny I had spent on it. I wanted to feel that I was worth every penny I had spent on it.

But I didn't. I picked up the scissors and slowly, reluctantly, reached under my arm to cut the tags. The great big number made me sick, but I didn't have a choice. I hadn't brought any other dress with me.

I had the scissors open, the blades on either side of the tag's strings when I stopped. I dropped the scissors onto the bed and marched down the back stairs and through the second-floor hall, the tags swinging under my armpit. I knocked on Rose's door.

She was in bed, propped up against the pillows. Guy was on the other side of the massive room, buttoning his shirt. My father was spending the evening in the hospital so that they wouldn't have to worry about Finney too much.

"How nice you look," Guy said immediately. "What a pretty dress."

"Oh, shut up," I said, then turned to Rose. "I don't know much about sisters, but I do know they borrow each other's clothes. So—"

"In our family," Guy said, "they steal each other's clothes. At least Annie does."

I ignored him. "So, if you want to be all sisterly, lend me something to wear so that I can return this dress, and then I can afford to take a vacation this summer."

Rose swung her legs off the edge of the bed and went to her closet. "I've got more things in Brooklyn, but I think I've got something that would work." She disappeared into the closet.

I saw Guy looking at me. "No," I said. "No, you don't."

He threw up his hands, pretending to be innocent. "What did I do?"

"Nothing yet. But you're standing there, trying to figure out how to give me a vacation."

"It wasn't going to be a *vacation,*" he defended himself. "Just a spa weekend, you and Rose, massages, facials, wheat-germ breakfasts on trays by the pool."

Oh. That didn't sound half bad. I had never done anything like that. I needed to work on my heart-to-heart girl-talk skills; a thick white spa robe would be a great practice uniform.

If the world were truly a perfect place, Rose would have come out of the closet carrying the violet-blue dress with magenta and scarlet poppies. But the world is not perfect. She had an armful of turquoise green. Guy had already taken the cue to disappear, so I unzipped the amethyst dress and, half mindful of my hair and makeup, stuck my head through the neckline of the turquoise one.

I looked in the mirror. There was no doubt that the dress would have looked better on Rose. The low neckline needed her curves, and the looseness she needed around the hips made the dress look a bit sacky on me.

"It's too big. Maybe it would look better with a belt." Rose bunched up the fabric at the back of my waist and stared at me in the mirror. "Annie could tell us."

"No. I'm done. This is perfect." I turned and looked at the side view. Maybe I should go put on a padded bra.

Rose looked at me again. "No, it isn't perfect. It isn't bad, but it certainly isn't perfect."

"Oh, but we're done with trying to make anything perfect."

Rose nodded, agreeing. She opened her jewelry box and handed me a silver necklace and earrings. They were chunky and sort of primitive-looking, and they helped. Then, ten minutes later, Annie got her hands on me. She found a silver belt, raided everyone's jewelry boxes for more silver jewelry, and I thought I ended up looking pretty good . . . although the champagne that one of the bridesmaids was passing around probably helped my vision a bit.

Instead of making the theatrical entrance usual to a wedding, the young men and women of the wedding party were already in the garden to greet the guests as they arrived. Cami, even without her veil, looked magical; the white of her dress glowed against the weathered stone walls and walkways. The bridesmaids were everywhere; their soft green silk dresses fluttered as they moved. Instead of carrying bouquets, they had sprigs of flowers twisted in their hair; they looked like the morning fairies who come out after dawn to brush the dew off the roses.

I doubt that any of the guests truly minded not having to sit through a wedding ceremony. Instead of sitting in upright chairs, obediently silent, they seemed happy to start mingling immediately, drinking, talking, and laughing. I was surprised at how pleasant so many of them were. Of course, I said the same thing over and over . . . I was Jeremy's mom . . . yes, everything was beautiful . . . an emergency tracheotomy, that was nothing, what anyone would have done.

Again I was treated like a heroine. In fact, a few of the men glanced at my left hand and asked if I ever came to New York. I must have looked better in turquoise than I'd thought.

One of the men said he would be coming to D.C. a lot on business because his married daughter lived there and was about to have her first baby. He asked for my number, and I gave it to him.

Nothing might come of it. He might never call. I might not like him . . . although I could pretty much guarantee that I would like the baby. But if he had asked for my number a year ago, there would have been no hope. I would have judged him only by the extent to which he was or was not Mike. Now, at least I would be able to see him as . . . as whatever his name was. I had already forgotten it.

The sun was slanting, leaving golden shadows across the lawn. The catering staff drew back the curtains on the big dining tent. I went to stand on the bridge to look at the tables from there.

Each table was different. Some were round, some were square. Every tablecloth was a different color, but they were all the soft colors of a misty English garden—violet, lavender, and lilac, primrose, lemon, and buttercup, and every shade of pink. Nor did the chairs match. Some were wood, some were wicker, some wrought iron, some gilded. Everything was unstudied, informal, and inviting.

I saw Mike break free from a group and climb up the low arch of the bridge to join me.

"You look very nice," he said.

"Foil," I said.

"I beg your pardon? Did you just call me a fool?"

"No, I said 'foil' as in aluminum foil. To make dinner for one person." I started talking fast. "Put some vegetables on a piece of foil, you may have to steam them in the microwave first. Then lay a piece of fish or a deboned chicken breast on top of them, brush it with a little olive oil, maybe some soy sauce. Add some fresh herbs if you have them. Fold the foil into a little packet, but tent it so there's room for steam. Put it in the oven for fifteen or twenty minutes. Make some rice in the microwave and then you've got the kind of homecooked meal that you've been missing."

"Wait . . . wait . . ." he said. "How much olive oil?

What herbs? And what was that about microwaving the vegetables first? How do I know?"

"I'll e-mail it to you. I wrote it all out for Dad after Mom died. His dilled salmon with honeyed carrots is the talk of the retirement home."

"Would you? That would be great. The one thing I haven't figured out about living alone is a decent homecooked meal."

I could have told him how to do this a couple of years ago. "Mike, if I ask you something, will you understand that I'm not trying to get into your pants?"

He blinked. "I suppose I can stipulate to that . . . although I am eager to hear why I need to do so."

"Do you want to go on a trip together this summer? Vacations are the one thing I haven't figured out. Do you know how we always talked about going to the national parks in Utah? Let's fly out there, rent an RV, and be road bums for a couple of weeks."

"Just you and me?"

"We can invite the boys and Cami, or even see if Rose and Guy want to get an RV for themselves, but let's go even if no one else can. It would be fun to cook in one of those little kitchens."

"If you're cooking, I'm coming."

In a perfect magenta and scarlet world, I would want to trade recipes with every woman he got involved with, and he would want to golf with every beau of mine. That was probably too much to expect, but at least we had gotten to a place where we could try. I was never going to read anyone's blog again.

Rose and Guy came up to join us. Rose had her hand through his arm. I'd never seen the two of them walking so closely together. They needed to do that more often.

"Do you want to come to Utah with us this summer?" I asked. "We're going to rent an RV. I think they make them so that the bathrooms don't smell."

"An RV?" Rose drew back, surprised. "The two of you?"

"We're happy to make a caravan of it. You've got to admit that Finney would love it, a little bed over the cab of the truck or one that somehow becomes the table during the day. What eight-year-old wouldn't adore that?"

"You're serious, aren't you?"

"Why not?"

"Can I bring someone to drive ours?" Guy asked.

"No, you big wuss. You can be a regular person again."

"I suppose I can remember how to do that," he admitted, "and this isn't out of the realm of possibility, since we just got offered a phenomenal amount of money from someone who wants to rent this house for the rest of the summer, and they want to take possession in time for the Fourth of July."

That was two weeks away. "Someone comes to a party and offers to rent the house before we've even served dinner?"

"Rent with an option to buy. This is the Hamptons, baby."

"Are you going to do it?" Mike asked.

"Probably. This place isn't right for us. If we're going to unload it, now's the time. Wall Street bonuses were huge this year; those people have cash that they didn't have last year."

"But they have to take it furnished," Rose said, "and that includes the books. I just got Guy to unpack them two days ago. There's no way they're getting repacked. So we may be available for Utah, but, Darcy, in the meantime, what are you doing for the next two weeks?"

"Probably applying to graduate school."

"Good," said Rose. "I need you in Brooklyn. Your Jeremy's making noises about a church ceremony. You and I have another wedding to plan."

Acknowledgments

After I began this book, Meagan Vilsack and Jerry Ouderkirk decided to get married in the Hamptons. This book is not about their wedding, but Meagan and her mother, Donna, answered my many questions. Edwin C. Douglass, M.D., and Barbara Smith, M.D., helped me with the medical details, while Lydia Kimbrough, M.S., R.N., provided remarkable insight into intensive-care nurses.

I'm grateful to Kathleen Miller for answering questions about colleges and for suggesting a key scene. My niece, Nellie Gilles, was my source for being a teenager in Park Slope. Ann Salitsky spotted countless errors in the manuscript, while Cindy Matlack helped me with my Web site. Elizabeth Holcombe Fedorko has a more artistic eye than I do; this book is better because of her willingness to imagine what things would look like. Welmoed Sisson literally provided light; she gave me a lamp I really like. Throughout my work on this book, Pat Petinga and Julie Bowersett provided me with lots of other things to think about; then, at the last minute, the two of them stepped in and performed CPR on one of my characters. My neighbor, Mary Candace Fowler, continued to be the gracious, knowledgeable recipient of my early-morning e-mails about commas and hyphens.

I have a startling number of friends with offspring applying to medical school, a process so stressful that I am grateful to my daughters for not wanting to be doctors.